For Steve

PAYOFF

A NOVEL

JJ RENEK

Note: No portion of this novel was generated, revised, or enhanced through the use of AI.

- JJ Ranck

This is a work of fiction. Names, places, characters and incidents are either the product of the author's imagination or are used fictitiously, and any resemblance to any actual persons, living or dead, businesses, organizations, events or locales is entirely coincidental.

No part of this book may be reproduced or transmitted in any form or by any means, electronic or mechanical, including photocopying, recording, or by any information storage and retrieval system, without permission in writing from the author.

Cover Design – Jaycee DeLorenzo
Publishing Coordinator – Sharon Kizziah-Holmes

Published by

LAKEPOINT PRESS LLC

Paperback ISBN -13: 979-8-9905504-0-7
Hardback ISBN 13: 979-8-9905504-2-1
eBook ISBN 13: 979-8-9905504-1-4

O, what a tangled web we weave when first we practice to deceive.

- Sir Walter Scott, 1808

PROLOGUE

Late afternoon sun streamed through the tall, arched windows of the Kansas House of Representatives in Topeka, highlighting dancing dust motes. The recently restored chamber glowed in the soft light. All members occupied their seats, anxious to cast their votes and be done. The week had worn on.

When the duly allotted time had expired, the Speaker posed the question, "Has every member had an opportunity to record their vote?" After giving sluggish legislators additional time to comply, the Speaker announced, "The clerk will close the roll to record the vote." Another prescribed pause ensued, then, "Does any representative wish to explain his or her vote?" Hearing no answer, he continued, "Would any representative wish to change his or her vote?" Minutes passed. He then announced, "Seeing none, the number in favor is sixty-five, the number opposed sixty. House Bill 3-0-3-5 is hereby declared passed."

The Speaker slammed his large wood gavel on the podium. After calling for and receiving announcements concerning caucus meetings and other subsequent gatherings, he formally closed the day's session. Wielding his gavel, he announced, "This House stands adjourned."

Politicians stood from their desks, shook hands and chatted up fellow legislators. Some gathered papers and made for the exits. Others milled about the chamber or, in the spirit of political friendship, pursued opponents.

Representative Yates Garwood got to his feet and stuffed files in his soft leather briefcase. It had been a productive day, a productive week. Several bills finally passed, some which he'd voted for, others he'd cast votes against. This bill would be sent to the Senate for further debate and likely a vote before the end of the formal legislative session. Word was, no one expected much opposition from that chamber.

He heard a familiar voice behind him. "Garwood, how're you doin'?"

Yates turned toward the center aisle and saw Representative Dirk Benson advancing toward him. He smiled and stuck out his hand. "Fine, Benson, just fine. Well, the debate's over. The bill's passed. What do you think?"

"I think it's a damn relief. Thought we'd never get done talkin' about it. Hope those nurses are happy."

"Yeah, we'll see what happens in the Senate. Heading out?" Yates asked.

"Tomorrow afternoon."

"Well, have a good weekend if I don't see you before then."

"Yeah, you take care. Give me a ring sometime. We'll have lunch," Benson suggested, giving Garwood a slap on the shoulder.

"Will do."

Garwood finished packing papers and hurried from the House chamber, leaving Dirk Benson cornering other members. He couldn't dismiss the disappointment he felt about the bill. Dread even. The consequences of passing this piece of legislation could be momentous. Were they already teetering at the brink of the proverbial slippery slope? Maybe they should have stalled and debated longer, figured out how to throw it back to committee.

It had just never sounded like a good idea to him.

PART 1

1

March 2016
Two years later

Tuesday

The place looked like hell. Humming with activity that morning, the Capital Memorial ER was a mess.

Dr. Brock Stafford had arrived early for his twelve-hour shift, expecting the usual slow start typical of a weekday morning, but the previous night's workload had produced a far different result. Patients slumped in chairs or lay on gurneys in the hall, waiting to be triaged by the bedraggled night nurses. Depleted supply carts stood ajar, what was left of their contents spilling from half-open drawers. All the private cubicles were full, or in need of a good cleaning before the next patient could be deposited there. Monitors beeped incessantly, louder when attachments dislodged, or IV fluids ran out. Families stared at the staff from cubicle doorways or approached the desk, asking when someone would get to them. Harsh fluorescent lights cast a nasty glare over the whole scene.

Earlier, the departing physicians had given report and gladly fled. A crew of fresh nurses huddled near the main desk, hurrying along their morning report so they could get busy and handle the left-over hubbub. Stafford knew they needed to rock and roll and disposition these people. Antsy to get going, he surveyed the scene and decided to see the most seriously ill first, in particular a man named Boyd Nettley. He turned to his surgery colleague, Dr. Garrett Clancy.

"What do you think?"

"Doesn't look good," Clancy said.

"I agree. You going in?" Stafford glanced back at the cubicle where the man lay.

Without looking up, Clancy tapped computer keys, frowning as he reviewed the patient's lab and scans. "We have to. He looks septic to me. I know what his wife said, but he probably perf'd yesterday. He said his pain eased a bit last night, but it worried her that he bumped a fever during the night."

"Think I'll check him again," Brock said, walking to the cubicle and disappearing behind the curtain.

Nettley lay still as the ER doctor approached. Stafford intentionally jarred the cart and observed the patient. Eyes squeezed shut, Nettley let out a moan. His wife sprang from her hard plastic chair, shot Stafford a stern look, and grabbed her husband's hand while he lay motionless, groaning.

"Oh, he's in so much pain, Doctor...can't you do something?"

"Yes, we can. I'm Dr. Stafford, Mrs. Nettley."

"Thanks for coming in, and please, call me Karen." After a brief pause, she unleashed. "I'm sorry, I know it's busy, and we're not the only ones here, but we just want to know what's going on...it seems like nothing's happening and we just want to get him some relief, that's all. We've been here since five."

Brock rested his hand on Nettley's abdomen and gently palpated. "I know, and we're here to talk about that." As he finished his statement, Clancy materialized behind him. Brock turned, acknowledged his colleague, and added, "This is Dr. Clancy, the surgeon."

He smiled. "Yes, we've met."

Focusing on the surgeon, Karen asked, "Is my husband going to be okay? What's the next step?" After a moment, she added, "I wish our son John was here for this discussion."

Nettley cracked open his eyes, frowned, and offered his opinion. "John's busy, Karen. We can't wait on him."

"How far away is he?" Brock asked

She explained, "Oh, he lives here, but we didn't want to call him in the middle of the night. He's so busy with the Deere dealership and expansion, we know how tired he's been. But, I can call him now. I'm sure he's up, probably already at the store." She turned back and forth from her husband to Brock as she spoke.

"Why don't you do that after we go over things, then you'll have more information to give him," Clancy suggested.

Karen nodded.

Brock started, "Mrs. Nettley, your husband has an abdominal problem, as you can see. You told the doctors on nights that he started having pain three days ago, and that it's gotten progressively worse, right?"

Again, she nodded.

He continued, "And last night, he told you the pain had improved or that he felt less uncomfortable?"

"Yes, that's what he said."

Nettley groaned his own response.

"Well, the abdominal CT scan shows a bowel problem, on the right. It appears to be a perforation, or rupture, of his colon. It's been leaking, and there's fluid collected around the area of perforation, which is a serious situation. We can't tell from the films how long he's had this, or what exactly caused it in the first place, but his blood work and CT are abnormal, indicating this likely didn't just develop yesterday. It looks somewhat organized in the lower, right side of his abdomen, so it's likely been there at least several days. Maybe longer."

She cocked her head. "Organized?"

"Sort of matted together around the bowel loop," Brock explained.

"Oh, I see. I guess I should have brought him in sooner." Karen glanced at her husband. Turning back to Stafford and Clancy, she added, "I'm sorry, I just didn't know what to do. He usually doesn't complain, and he told me it was probably nothing."

Brock noticed her tired eyes and smudged eye makeup. Her cheeks held high color, and her soft brown hair was mashed on one side, the remainder haphazardly tousled. She'd likely slept only a few hours that night, if at all, fretting and fussing over Boyd.

"You didn't do anything wrong, Mrs. Nettley. Sometimes it's hard to know what's going on. We're also concerned about his blood pressure and pulse, which were a little low given his situation and his pain. That's why we have the IV fluids running at a fairly good clip, and why we started the two antibiotics. He's basically stable right now. At any rate, Dr. Clancy recommends your husband go to surgery so they can look directly in his abdomen and try to repair the perforation, clean out the fluid leakage, and fix anything else they might find. And I agree with him."

"You mean now?"

"Soon. We're concerned he'll worsen. Additional time spent waiting won't do him any good," Clancy explained.

"I'll call John."

"We'll be glad to discuss it with him," Brock added.

"I'll get him on the phone." Karen turned away and

fumbled in her bag, softly muttering to herself.

Brock stepped away from the cart and ducked around the curtain as Nettley's assigned nurse approached. Clancy stayed behind, moved to the cart, and re-examined the man. After advising the nurse they would need to prep the patient for the OR, Brock strolled to the desk and pulled up the CT and lab again. After a few minutes, Clancy joined him.

Brock glanced up. "Did she tell you the whole story?" Clancy didn't respond. "Apparently, Nettley went to a clinic in Elston for care. Has had vague symptoms for several months, but they thought he was just constipated and bloated. They treated him conservatively, tried diet changes, and gave him some simethicone. He wasn't sure if he was better or not. No blood in his stools, no weight loss. And no suggestion for a colonoscopy. He's never had one. Then, about a week ago, he started having right-sided pain, enough to make him stop and take notice. No vomiting, but not much appetite. Three days ago his pain got worse, then suddenly remitted last night. Then the fever spiked."

"Who's his doctor?"

"He doesn't have one." Clancy looked up from the chart. Brock added, "That's the point. He saw someone at a clinic in Elston staffed only by extenders. Apparently, it's too far to drive here to Topeka to see a doctor. At least it was before last night."

"Isn't there a doctor covering that clinic?"

"That's the thing…it's not required anymore."

Clancy looked at Brock, frowned, and focused on the computer. "Okay, well, it's probably a right colon lesion that blew. Let's go see what his son has to say."

Several hours later, Brock hung up the phone and spoke to the clerk. "We're transferring him. That was the colorectal surgeon at KU who'll take him."

"I know," she answered without looking up from her screen. "I've already requested the disc of his scans, and

I'm printing his chart. Transport's been called."

"Good. I know I can count on you, Nadine."

Suppressing a smile, she retorted, "You know that's right, honey."

Brock glanced at the wall clock. It was a few minutes before ten and several patients lingered, yet to be seen. Over the intervening hours Brock and an ER colleague, Dr. Anne Goodwin, had managed to see, treat, and discharge most of the backlogged patients from the previous night. The few remaining awaited study results and either admission, or referral back to their primary care provider, or to a specialist for further workup. Feeling temporarily satisfied, Brock reached for his cup of cold coffee.

"There's fresh in the back," Nadine advised.

"Thanks. Think I'll dump this stuff." He ambled toward the break room, hoping to end up in the doctors' lounge and a worn-out recliner for a few minutes, before things picked up again. Mornings weren't usually this busy and he still had nine hours ahead. As he poured a fresh cup, the intercom crackled and Nadine announced, "Transfer team's here, Dr. Stafford."

Brock took a gulp of his fresh coffee, burned his tongue, and pitched the rest. Swearing, he exited the room and headed toward Boyd Nettley's cubicle, where the number of people surrounding the patient's cart had multiplied exponentially. He paused at the door to size up the situation.

Karen and her son John hovered on either side of Nettley's head. Two EMT's stood alongside, staring at Boyd and his monitor. An ER nurse eased into the cubicle behind Brock and scanned the crowd. A narrow cart with transport equipment and a third EMT remained at the ready outside the door.

Brock stepped to the bed, greeted everyone, and began his report.

2

Karen sighed relief when the tall figure of a doctor filled the door, although she'd been staring in that direction, expecting his appearance, for the past half-hour. Her back wedged against her son's shoulder, she felt John stiffen before he stood. Sluggish, she, too, pushed up from her chair.

The trip to Kansas City seemed swift, but it had been hours since she had first called John about his father. Boyd had lain so still after his admission to Kansas University Medical Center, she felt compelled to touch or attempt to rouse him every so often to ensure he remained conscious. When she didn't, John did. It was better than just sitting and doing nothing. Karen was already exhausted, and the process was just getting underway. Obviously, Boyd was heading to surgery, and was not in a good way. She wondered if they'd done the right thing, insisting on bringing him to KU. The surgery would have probably been done by now if they had just stayed put in Topeka.

The doctor strode across the room, clad in scrub clothes

and lab coat. He had removed his OR shoe covers, but still wore his surgical hat. She noted his precise movements even before he extended his hand. She felt small as he hovered over them.

"Hi, I'm Dr. Dickerson, the colorectal surgeon. Sorry, I didn't get in here sooner. I was detained in surgery."

John spoke first. "I'm John Nettley, and this is my mother Karen Nettley."

"Good to meet you both. Let's sit down," Dickerson suggested.

Karen and John perched where they'd been seated. Dickerson sat on the end of the bed. Boyd remained still, his eyes closed. After regarding him for a few moments, Dr. Dickerson turned to them, pausing before he spoke. She hoped he was always this deliberate, that this was not a bad sign. Unaware of her own fidgeting, Karen felt John's warm, soothing hand cover hers. She took a deep breath, expelled it slowly, and tried to relax.

Pierce Dickerson began. "So, I understand my colleague has already been by to see your father."

"Yes, about an hour ago," John informed him.

The surgeon nodded. "Well, he relayed to me how this developed, and what you told him about the last several months. We've reviewed Boyd's lab, his X-ray studies, and I want to examine him. I believe you were told he has a perforation of the right side of his colon, with fluid and probably bowel contents surrounding that area in the abdominal cavity. He's had fever, his blood pressure has been low at times, and he looks infected, which doesn't surprise us."

"Infected from the bowel?" Karen asked.

"Yes, that's right," Dickerson replied. "That's what we expect in these situations." He looked at her and continued, "Has he eaten much in the last two days?"

"A little soup around noon yesterday, and some crackers, and water, but then he complained his pain was worse. He wouldn't eat any dinner last night."

"Okay." Dickerson paused and regarded the patient again. "At any rate, we need to take him to the OR and have a look this evening. We'll explore the abdomen, find the perforation and fix it, clean out the leakage, and look for other issues. I don't know how much has been explained to Boyd. Has he been asleep most of the time since he arrived at the ER in Topeka?"

"I can hear you," Boyd inserted.

The surgeon patted his leg, and Nettley flinched. "Good," remarked Dickerson. "I need to look you over. After that, I've asked anesthesia to come in and get things going." He turned to Karen and John. "Do you have any questions?"

Karen, exhausted and wondering what *other issues* meant, opened her mouth but John spoke first. "Do you think you can fix it without too much trouble?"

The doctor turned to John and explained, "Yes, I believe we can. But, without too much trouble, I can't say. It's possible he may end up with a colostomy or ileostomy. If so, either situation might be temporary, which we would hope to take down or reverse after a few months, if he does well. That is, if we don't get in there and encounter more extensive problems than we expect. The op permit contains information about those procedures." He paused, then added, "And, of course, the issue of infection may affect how he does."

Karen then asked the surgeon to explain what exactly a colostomy was and how that differed from an ileostomy. The surgeon obliged and both listened intently, asked a few clarifying questions—forgetting about *other issues*—and exchanged worried looks.

"Will you let us know if you have to do that?" John asked.

"Yes, I can come out at that point and discuss the situation with you."

Karen shot him a questioning look.

Dickerson clarified, "I'll have a team of surgeons with me on this case. I can come out briefly to speak with you if it's necessary to proceed with that."

She barely whispered her thanks and acknowledged with a nod.

Boyd cracked an eye and said, "I'd appreciate that, Doctor, if you would tell them before going ahead."

Dr. Dickerson nodded. "Sure."

With that, Dr. Dickerson stood and moved to the left side of the bed. He bent over and auscultated the patient while John and Karen looked on. Boyd, obviously awake now, scrutinized the surgeon's face as the examination proceeded. Out of the corner of her eye, Karen noticed John motioning her to join him in the hall. They eased toward the door.

"Don't go too far," Boyd instructed them.

"We'll be right out here, Dad."

In the hall, they moved away from the door. Periodically, they heard low moans from Boyd and a few words from the surgeon, as Dickerson finished his examination.

"Oh, John, I'm so worried."

"I know, Mom, but they have to go ahead."

Karen searched her son's face for the confidence and reassurance she lacked.

"This is only going to get worse if they wait. He's in good hands here. I'm sure it'll be fine."

"I should have taken him to the hospital sooner," she lamented. "I just didn't think he was this bad. And the pain got better last night."

"It's all right. You did the right thing. You didn't cause this to happen."

Karen leaned in and rested her forehead on her son's shoulder, thankful she wasn't alone.

He wrapped one arm around her shoulder. "We'll go

down and get something to eat when they take him. I could use some coffee. And I need to call Beth and let her know what's going on."

Karen, trembling, nodded into his shoulder.

John added, "There's a hotel across the street where we can stay. I'll call and get us rooms."

They parted when Pierce Dickerson emerged from Boyd's room and approached, wearing a concerned expression. Karen's skin prickled. An unwelcome cold sensation crawled through her feet and rose slowly, finally gripping her core. Though she fought it, a single dark thought intruded. *Cancer...is this cancer?*

"Doctor, one question...what did you mean by *other issues?*"

3

Friday

Karen poured another cup of fresh coffee, then reclaimed the waiting room chair. She glanced at the wall clock: 7:30 a.m. The room smelled stale. Too many people in and out over the course of a day and night, some of whom obviously afforded themselves frequent smoking breaks. And the cleaning staff hadn't begun their daily chores yet. She glanced around at other visitors lounging on couches and chairs, wondering what they were waiting to hear. A pit gnawed her stomach, which food didn't soothe for long. It was Friday. So much had changed in less than a week.

Boyd had been extubated successfully Thursday morning. The ICU nurses had explained they were decreasing his pain medication, so he should wake up more often. By Thursday evening, he had seemed more alert and conversant for a brief while. They hoped he could transfer out of the unit by the weekend.

Just an hour before, she and John had rolled out,

prepared quickly, and she'd hurried across the street to the hospital, hoping Boyd's day would go well. John, confident his father was stable, had left for Topeka. Karen knew he would return later with his wife, once he'd made sure things would be okay at the dealership. Beth had held down the fort over the past three days, but he wanted to check on the business and her, and make arrangements for weekend coverage.

Karen thought of John, how proud they were of their only son, who had taken on significant responsibility buying the dealership just six months before, preferring not to ranch as his father and grandfather had done. He had assured them, though, he was committed to keeping the ranch in the family, and seeing to its continued success when Boyd and Karen could no longer manage. That was, at least, reassuring to them both. Now, with the diagnosis of colon cancer haunting them, Karen realized those days were likely upon them.

She swallowed the bitter taste that welled in her throat, and took another sip of coffee. The conversation during and after surgery with Dr. Dickerson had shocked and depressed her. Things were a mess when they got in and freed up the bowel, the surgeon told them. They worked for a long time to clean it out and make repairs. Boyd ended up with an ileostomy. He would hate that. The pathology report showed a poorly differentiated carcinoma, whatever that meant, which had gotten larger presumably because it was on the right side rather than the left. And, they explained, usually signs and symptoms develop later in that situation. She had rehashed those explanations and conversations too many times to count since Tuesday night. Boyd was only fifty-nine years old. How could this have happened to such a vigorous man?

Bottom line, one persistent thought pestered her. Was this thing there that long, and was it missed? Why didn't she insist he see a doctor in Topeka three months ago when he first went to that clinic in Elston? He was stubborn, but she could have done something or asked John to take him. But he had come home singing the praises of the clinic and how nice the girls were there. He didn't want to spend any more time in some doctor's office just to be told the same thing. Tired of analyzing, Karen stood and made her way to the waiting room bathroom before returning to the ICU. Maybe she could catch the medical team before too long when they made rounds.

In the distance she heard a loud, indistinct announcement from the PA system. Not two minutes later, she opened the restroom door and noticed the other bedraggled-looking visitors, now alert, staring toward the ICU doors. Suddenly, someone in blue scrubs sprinted past the waiting room door. Then the announcement was repeated, "Code Blue, second floor, surgery ICU." Everyone in the waiting room looked at each other. A few visitors stood up. The room felt hot and close.

Karen moved through the room, at once convinced she should check on Boyd. She stepped into the hall. Cold air hit her face, her head felt full, her heart pounded. Her vision blurring, she instinctively lowered her head and grabbed a handrail. After a few moments, she took a deep breath, forced herself to straighten, and walked toward the ICU double doors. They loomed larger as she neared. She pressed the automatic door pad and as the door eased open, she slipped through.

Once inside the unit, she immediately noticed more noise than usual, and rounding the corner of the nurses' desk, saw a crowd filling Boyd's small room. She stopped abruptly and stared. Equipment spilled through the door. Pulling herself together, she approached slowly, her legs like heavy weights, and maneuvered close enough to see around the crowd. A tube again protruded from Boyd's mouth. The cardiac monitor displayed what looked to her like undulating lines. Shocked, she felt utterly useless, watching a team of people work on her husband, a drama in which she had no role and couldn't control. One young doctor, perched over Boyd, vigorously compressed his chest. She watched in horror when they delivered a shock and Boyd's body jerked. How could this be happening?

She felt a presence, then a touch on her arm. She turned to find an unknown woman standing at her side. Karen wasn't sure why, but she'd expected it might be John, returned. The woman looked at her kindly, likely not understanding Karen's surprised expression.

"Mrs. Nettley?"

"Yes?"

"I'm Susan, the ICU Coordinator. I'll stay here with you. Would you like a chair?"

"What?" Karen managed, then said, "No." Barely able to hear through her pulse pounding her ears, she stared into Boyd's small room, mesmerized by the orderly process underway, unable to assimilate the murmured remarks of the code team concerning her husband's condition.

He was at Boyd's door before Karen realized Dr. Dickerson had arrived. She turned, took tentative steps toward him, but noticed he stood stiff, hands on his hips, totally focused on his patient in the bed. How long would it take? How long to get Boyd awake again? She stopped when Susan touched her arm. The others ignored Dickerson and continued to work on Boyd. After a few minutes, which seemed like hours, a younger doctor stepped away from the bedside and joined the staff surgeon at the door.

Karen heard only Dr. Pierce Dickerson mutter, "Jesus. What happened?"

4

Monday

"Good morning, Comprehensive Care Clinic. How may I help you?"

"I'd like to speak with the nurse who saw my husband."

"And who is your husband, ma'am?"

"His name is, was, Boyd Nettley. He died last Friday, March fourth. I'm Karen Nettley."

There was a pause on the other end, then the receptionist said, "Just a moment, Mrs. Nettley, let me put you on hold, and I'll check on that."

Karen sat down at her kitchen table, pulled her coffee cup closer, and arranged papers in front of her. It was Monday morning, just three days after Boyd's death, and she was determined to get some answers. Canned music played continuously, which she found irritating, but it was better than silence. Out of tears for the moment, and running on nervous energy, she braced for the mountain of details and funeral plans begging for her attention. But, this call had possessed her thoughts since Friday. She finished her cooling coffee before the woman came back on the line.

"Are you still there, Mrs. Nettley?"

"Yes, I am."

"Okay, your husband saw Lindy Burnett—Rosalind Burnett—one of our providers, but she's on vacation right now. I can leave a message for her, or I can put you through to her voice mail, if you'd like."

"I'd like to speak with whoever *is* there today, if you wouldn't mind."

"They're all with patients right now. I can take a message and ask one of them to call you back. Maybe you should speak with our director."

"Yes, that sounds good. And who is that?"

"That would be Erica Simons, ma'am."

"Fine. I'd like her to call me as soon as she can. I'll be home all day." Karen gave the receptionist her contact information and hung up. She tried to get up from the table, but lethargy weighed her down. Glued in place, and considering what to do next, she doubted this Simons woman would call her back any time soon.

~ ~ ~

Erica studied the message left by the receptionist while she was in a room. The scribbled editorial comment— *husband died, sounds upset*—caught her eye. She didn't recognize the name Nettley, so she suspected she hadn't seen him. Still, she closed out the patient chart she had open and typed in the name Boyd Nettley. There was one man by that name registered with the clinic; she didn't require his birth date for further identification.

There were two clinic visits for Mr. Nettley, the first four months prior, and a quick follow-up visit not a month and a half ago. Rosalind Burnett, a younger nurse practitioner, had seen him both times and the visit notes were brief: abdominal bloating, constipation, partial relief with conservative measures, no other co-morbidities. No mention of a personal physician since his doctor in Elston retired three years ago. No history of colonoscopy, and Lindy hadn't charted she suggested referral for one. Erica scanned through the remainder of the chart and closed out the window. Uneasy, she looked at the message again, and stuck it in her pocket. She'd think about when to call Mrs. Nettley, though admittedly, she dreaded the prospect of that conversation. Glancing at her morning schedule, she rose, picked up her tablet and left her office.

"Good afternoon, Creative Business Solutions."

"Mr. Scanlon, please. This is Erica Simons."

"Hold please, Ms. Simons."

Erica sat at her desk at the end of the long day. All the patients had been seen, and the staff were departing. She'd made sure the other practitioners were gone before she placed this call. She hoped Mr. Witter Scanlon would make himself available. Not only was he the principal of his own business enterprise, but he was also chief financial officer of an organization—Citizens for Economic Freedom—with which she was very familiar. After what seemed a long wait, Witt picked up on the other end.

"Well, hi, Ms. Simons. What a pleasant surprise. We haven't spoken in some time. How're things with you?"

"Fine, thanks. Look, it's getting late, Witt, and I'll get right to the point."

Scanlon cleared his throat. "Please do."

"I've got a little issue here at the clinic. I need to run it past someone, and I finally decided you might be just the person who could help."

"Oh? I hope things are going well there, Erica." He paused, but she supplied no reply. "What kind of issue?"

"One of my associates saw a patient several months ago, a man who came in for nonspecific symptoms. I received a phone call today from his wife about his visits. In the meantime, my nurse looked up his information and found out he died just last Friday at KU. The obit was posted today. I'm still trying to get more details about the case, but before I call her back I wanted to check with you and CEF."

"How is it you believe we might be of help?"

"Well...I recall you pledged continued support for independent clinics even after the legislation passed. I wondered what you specifically meant by that, and just how far your support might extend."

Witt Scanlon fell silent. *Was he studying his cell phone or the bookshelves lining his well-appointed office?* Erica could only imagine.

Clearing his throat again, he said, "Yes, well, as you know we support the independent function of such advanced practice clinics as yours, as part of our position on economic freedom. We're obviously not in a position to comment on clinical care issues—of course, we don't want to get involved in that—but we can take a look at your concerns as it pertains to your business practices. Perhaps our lawyer Kemp Anderson should speak with you."

Erica, impatient with his tone, replied smoothly, "Yes, perhaps that would be best. How can I reach him?"

5

Brock watched as Dr. Garrett Clancy threw back the curtain and approached the ER desk. Clancy wasn't wearing a smile. He had asked the surgeon for a consultation on a fourteen-year-old boy with acute appendicitis and, keeping the surgeon busy, now needed another opinion.

"What else do you have, Brock?"

"The lady in nine has had right upper quadrant pain since last night. The scans show stones and gallbladder wall thickening. I need you to see her. Her labs don't look too bad, but her white count is 11,500 and her liver functions are a little elevated. Bili's normal."

"Okay. She'll be next. I'm taking the kid in five to the OR after I finish my next case. Have the staff get him ready to roll." Clancy turned to the computer on the desk, while Brock signaled a nurse to join them. He turned back to Clancy.

"Remember that case we had last week, the man with the right colon we sent to KU?"

"Yeah, how'd that turn out?"

"Not good, I hear."

Garrett Clancy looked at Brock over the computer. "How so?"

"Well, we got him transferred, they took him in and resected the colon, cleaned out the mess, had to do an ileostomy. But, three days later, on Friday, he coded and died in the unit. The staff surgeon, Pierce Dickerson called today with the news. They had him extubated and almost ready to transfer out of the unit when it happened. Everyone was pretty shocked and upset."

"I bet. Did he throw a clot?"

"Don't know yet. They're doing the post."

"I don't recall he had other problems. He wasn't on anything in particular, was he?"

"No. I looked back at his chart. It was a fairly straight-forward case in a middle-aged man who didn't go to the doctor much, and denied other conditions."

Clancy focused again on the computer. "Let me know what you find out."

"I will." Brock turned briefly and conversed with the nurse attending the fourteen-year-old, then turned back to Garrett. "I'm thinking of going to his funeral. It's Thursday."

At that remark, the surgeon glanced up. "You have the time for that?"

"Think I'll make time."

Not answering, Clancy resumed his charting.

"I just wonder what happened."

"I'm sure you'll hear after they finish the post."

"Yeah, probably. But, I mean, what happened when he went to that clinic in Elston? Did they not suggest a referral or any further workup, or did he just not go back?"

Clancy didn't look up. Stafford continued, "That could be an issue in the case. Do you know how many of those independent clinics there are around the state?"

"I have no idea. Didn't they pass that bill several years ago?"

"Yeah, I think so." Brock paused. "Might be worth checking on, see how many have sprung up since then."

"Good luck with your research. I need to get back to the OR. You're keeping me busy."

"Could be interesting to see how many cases have come in here from those clinics. Maybe medical records can help with that."

"No doubt with the new EMR they can give you all the data you want."

"If they'll share it."

Clancy pounded a few more keys, then stood.

"Maybe we should watch for similar cases," Brock added.

"You do that, man. Let me know what you find out. Check you later."

Clancy turned and walked briskly away from the desk, leaving Brock staring into near space.

6

Thursday

Brock slipped silently into a back pew just before two. He glanced around and shifted in his seat. A woman in front of him turned and stared, but meeting his eyes, she looked away and tidied her skirt.

Solemn music from the huge pipe organ wafted through the sanctuary of the old stone Lutheran church in Elston, its lofty ceiling augmenting the acoustics. Shafts of sunlight streamed through the large stained-glass windows, highlighting floating dust particles, and tinting guests with a rainbow of hues. It was the appropriate thing to do, coming here to pay his respects, though, he couldn't remember when he'd attended services for any other ER patient.

Brock straightened his tie and opened the bulletin in his lap. It took a mere five minutes to read about Boyd—his birthdate and place, his departed parents' names, where he attended school, how he spent his days ranching, serving his church and community, scripture passages he or his family favored—and now, where and when he had died. It struck him how briefly we can encapsulate a person's lifetime. Turning his gaze to the front of the church, he studied the portrait of the deceased in his earlier and healthier days, numerous huge floral arrangements, and listened to the strains the organist pulled from the gigantic pipe organ. He expected he would have an opportunity to speak with the Nettleys after the service, probably before he could seek them out.

Brock heard shuffling and murmured comments coming from the narthex to his right. Briefly glancing in that direction, he noted pall bearers, a funeral director, and a minister gathering. He caught a glimpse of Karen and others, likely family. He let out a long sigh and tried to relax. Funerals were not his favorite pastime.

A pause developed, then louder music interrupted his thoughts as the organist cued the crowd that things were about to begin. Last minute stragglers quickly descended the sloping side aisles and found seats. Slow, methodical music began. The congregation rose. Brock took his cue from the others surrounding him and stood, as well. Down the center aisle came Boyd Nettley's casket, six large men bearing it up, with Karen, John, and a pregnant Elizabeth Nettley following. A black-robed minister brought up the rear. The family peeled off into the front pew and greeted other relatives already seated, who extended pats and hugs. The pall bearers delivered the casket to the waiting bier then took front row seats opposite the family. The minister moved to stand behind the casket. John appeared stoic. Brock wasn't so sure Karen, wedged between John and Elizabeth, would make it through. Wan was the fitting word to describe her demeanor.

After everyone appeared settled, the minister's deep resonant voice began, "Dearly beloved, we are gathered here today…"

Forty-five minutes later, Brock stood with the other mourners as the family recessed from the sanctuary. At the ushers' cues, each succeeding pew slowly emptied as the crowd moved out.

The shortened message, a sermonette, had reminded all there of the brevity and uncertainty of life, the foolishness of wasting one's time on earth, and of God's grace. Several longtime friends had eulogized Boyd, injecting humor with stories few others there knew. A nephew barely made it through his accounts of shared outings with his favorite uncle and the encourager he'd been. Many mourners barely made it through his stories as well. It struck Brock again how little he knew about his patients and their families as they scooted through the ER.

The crowd wasted no time proceeding to fellowship hall for an abundant potluck meal provided by the church women. Brock mingled briefly in the narthex, but only caught glimpses of several people who looked vaguely familiar. Former patients from the ER? He hoped not. Along with others, he drifted toward the large room, hoping he could express his condolences to the Nettleys sooner rather than later. He didn't intend to end up at the cemetery afterwards.

As luck would have it, Karen spotted him shortly after he entered the room. Holding up better than he'd expected, she was obviously trying to detach herself from an older woman who stood square on, patting her arm. Brock went to the beverage line, picked up the requisite punch, and scanned the room. Several people regarded him, but no one initiated conversation as he took a position where Karen could clearly see him. She disengaged herself and crossed the room. When she was within ten feet, she mustered a faint smile.

"I'm so glad you came," she said. "Thank you."

"Oh, you're certainly welcome, Mrs. Nettley. I wanted

to pay my respects. I was shocked to hear what had happened."

She studied his face for several moments. "Yes, I appreciate that. And it's Karen, please."

Brock nodded.

She paused and looked around. Seeing an elderly couple making a bee line toward her, she turned and faced Brock, moved closer, and said in a low tone, "I want to thank you for what you did for my husband. I can't imagine what would have happened if I had not brought him in. Well, you know, we'd probably still be *here*, but..." Brock touched her arm. "Anyway, I've thought maybe we should have just stayed in Topeka for the surgery. I hope you don't think transferring him caused more problems with the delay, or meant we didn't trust you, but John insisted he go to KU to see the specialist, and I guess I just wasn't thinking straight, right then..."

"No need to explain and please don't second guess yourself now. He was very ill, Mrs. Nettley, Karen, and I know Dr. Dickerson and his team did a superb job with the surgery and care afterwards. He called me this past Monday. These situations are always a shock."

The couple hung back, politely not interrupting, murmured to themselves, and cast an occasional glance at Brock.

Karen bowed her head momentarily, then stood erect, and looked directly at Brock. "We want you to know...we don't hold you, Dr. Clancy, or the hospital responsible for what happened. And we don't fault Dr. Dickerson or KU. If we have a problem with anything, it's the clinic he went to before that. We, at least I, want some answers, and am not getting them."

Brock couldn't conceal his surprised expression.

"I called the clinic on Monday and got the run around. Had to leave a message for their director, but I haven't heard back yet. It figures." With more gusto, she added,

"I'm just sorry now I didn't go with Boyd when he saw those people. They don't know me from Adam, and I doubt they'll be calling back any time soon." She glanced away, saw the couple lingering and let out a long sigh. "I want John to have a chance to speak with you, too. Can you stay a while?"

Brock glanced at his watch. "I'm due back in Topeka before too long. But, I can stay for a bit and speak with him."

"Good. You go on over and get something to eat, and I'll fetch him. So many people have him and Beth tied up right now, anyway." She patted his arm and headed off across the room, the elderly couple trailing behind, not making it to her son before being waylaid by another small group of mourners.

Brock stood and watched for a moment, then spotted John and his wife in a far corner pinned in by other acquaintances. It might be a while before they had a chance to speak. Mulling over what Karen had just told him, he turned his attention to the tables spread before him laden with rich, home-cooked food, and decided a good meal— perhaps his last for the day—was not a bad idea. He'd phone Meredith and let her know he'd already eaten. Relieve her of having to cook, if she didn't want to.

Now where to begin? He couldn't go wrong with anything he saw within reach, food good for the soul. The only thing missing—a bar. But, why would he expect the Lutherans to provide such as that at events such as this?

7

Monday

Erica assembled the papers on her desk, and glanced at her patient list for the remainder of the morning. Rosalind Burnett was back from vacation, and things were underway that busy Monday. She was anxious to discuss the Nettley case with Lindy, but debated when to broach the subject. Noon might work, but later in the afternoon would be better. Still better, she considered, would be Tuesday or Wednesday when she would take an administrative day and focus only on clinic management issues. She really didn't want the other two practitioners, nor the staff, to be privy to the situation or their conversation. Her thoughts churning, she picked up her laptop and headed toward an exam room and her next patient. She would figure out the right time after she finished her morning clinic.

"I don't recall seeing him, but I'll look at his record and

see if I can place him. You say he first came in four months ago?"

"Yes, that's right. And then he had another visit with you a month and a half ago. I checked the chart last week when his wife called. In fact, she called just last Monday."

"Then, you've spoken with her?" Lindy asked.

"No, not yet. I deferred calling her back until I had a chance to discuss the case with you. I do know he died the Friday before last at KU." Erica paused. She watched Lindy frown as she shifted in her chair and crossed her legs. Erica pulled two stapled sheets of paper from the top of a pile and passed them across her desk to the young nurse practitioner.

Lindy leaned forward for the slim record.

"Your notes were fairly brief, and didn't give any indication you picked up on any red flags," Erica said, then remained quiet as she watched Lindy scan her notes.

The nurse looked up and met Erica's gaze. "I remember him now. A rancher who had really vague symptoms. A man of few words. He downplayed everything. I couldn't get much history out of him. He said he didn't go to the doctor often, didn't really like going to doctors 'cause they always try to find something wrong.' He used to see Dr. Bates before he retired." She paused and looked at the printed notes again. "I got the feeling his wife wanted him to see someone, but he didn't make a big deal of her not coming with him. Anyway, he said he thought he was better when I saw him the second time, with the few things we tried."

"Did he refuse to come back again, or did you not suggest a follow-up visit?"

"I don't remember."

"I see. But you do seem to remember quite a bit from two such brief encounters." Lindy shrugged, and Erica asked, "Do you remember suggesting he might need a colonoscopy, or to see a specialist?"

Lindy looked away. Erica hoped she was mentally sorting for honest recollections and would produce something which could diminish their culpability.

Lindy finally spoke. "I honestly don't recall."

"And I don't recall that you presented him for discussion at our recent clinical care conferences, either."

"No, ma'am, I didn't."

"You didn't think his was an interesting case?"

"I guess not."

"Or, you didn't have any questions about managing him as you went along?"

The nurse glanced again at the papers in front of her.

"Lindy, that's why we have those monthly meetings. To discuss cases, give input to each other, offer ideas. No one should feel inadequate bringing up a case which seems rather typical. You never know what another associate might contribute. Plus, it spreads responsibility. We have to keep that in mind as we go."

Lindy nodded, but said nothing.

"Right." Erica glanced at her computer screen, then continued, "I want you to take those notes, look them over again, and go into the record. Maybe if you read through the demographics and initial history, your memory will improve. Either way, I want to speak with you again Wednesday when I take an administrative day. Check your schedule, and let's carve out about thirty minutes to discuss this."

"Sure." Lindy stood and started for the door.

Erica added, "And don't change a single thing in the record."

Lindy stopped, and glanced over her shoulder, as Erica added, "Have a good evening."

"Of course." Lindy passed through the doorway, not looking back.

Erica glanced at her watch—3:45 p.m. Her last patient was due at four. She picked up the phone and dialed the number on the wrinkled, pink message slip from the previous Monday.

It was four forty-five when she finally dropped into her chair, worn out from the strain of the day. There was still time to place the call, better to get it done than put it off again.

"Foster, James and Levy. How may I direct your call?"

"I'd like to speak with Mr. Kemp Anderson, please."

"Just one moment. I'll ring his secretary."

Classical music emitted from the receiver Erica propped on her shoulder as she stared at Boyd Nettley's chart. The call an hour earlier with Karen Nettley had not gone well. The family was upset. This was a bad situation, and she wanted to share the burden with someone else. She recalled her conversation the previous week with Witt Scanlon but, until now, hadn't called the CEF lawyer Kemp Anderson. Nor had he called her. It was time to take the bull by the horns. The music paused.

"This is Barbara, Mr. Anderson's assistant. May I help you?"

"Yes, this is Erica Simons from Comprehensive Care Clinic in Elston. I'd like to speak with Mr. Anderson."

"Is this in reference to a particular case?"

"Not yet."

"Oh. Well, he's out of the office for the rest of the day. I can take your name and number, if you'd like, and he'll return your call tomorrow afternoon or Wednesday. He'll be in conference all of tomorrow morning."

"I see. Well, I'd appreciate you giving him my information. And I'll look forward to hearing back from him." Erica finished by relaying her contact information. She tried to suppress her frustration and irritation. Of all people, she didn't want to put off this woman.

8

Tuesday

"He was doing what?"

Brock looked up from the leg wound he was exploring to explain. "He was stealing some frozen cookie dough."

"Eating some," the patient clarified.

"Someone shot him in the leg over cookie dough?" Clancy asked.

The injured man raised his head. "Yeah, man. That old lady just hauled off and shot me."

Clancy and Brock exchanged deadpan expressions. Clancy piped up, "They're the most dangerous type, pal."

"No shit. Hey, ain't you gonna give me somethin' for pain? You're hurtin' me, man. Ain't you almost done, doc?"

"You just lay back there. I'll give you a rest. Be back."

The two doctors left the cubicle. Brock spoke to a nearby nurse, who disappeared behind the curtain to attend to the man's IV and narcotic needs. An officer of the law stood sentry outside the cubicle, seemingly bored with the whole process.

Garrett Clancy spoke as they ambled toward the desk. "I thought you were going to keep it quiet down here tonight."

"I do my best."

When they reached the central desk, Brock continued, "So, he broke into this house sometime after three. Apparently, the woman of the house came out of her bedroom, she said around three-thirty, and found this guy in her kitchen eating cookie dough from her freezer. Armed with a hunting rifle, she didn't wait for much explanation. She took one shot and hit him in the leg. Told police she was really aiming for other parts."

Clancy erupted in laughter. Brock drolly continued, "He yelled at her, dropped the dough, and fell on the floor. She threw him a kitchen towel, held him at gunpoint, and called the police. He told the officer he thought it was his aunt's house and he was hungry. Said he entered through an unlocked back door."

Enjoying the moment, Clancy sputtered, "Like that makes it okay. With her gun skills, I guess she doesn't need locked doors." He dropped into a chair at the nearest, vacant computer and signed on.

Brock smiled. "I'll clean him up, but I need you to take a look."

"Sure. Might just take him up tonight and get it out. They'll want the slug for evidence."

"Say, while you're here I wanted to tell you what I'd found out about those nursing clinics around the state. You know that case we had two weeks ago with the bowel perforation."

"Yeah? What's up?"

"Did a little research and found at least ten clinics scattered around the state, which are manned solely by nurse practitioners. Another couple are owned by PAs, and staffed by other PAs and nurse practitioners. None of them list a physician covering them, which is what we understood was the case."

"Oh, really? Where'd you get that information?"

"On the internet. It took some drilling down, but I finally came up with it. I'm still waiting for medical records to bring me information on the cases we've seen from any of those clinics over the past year or two."

"Interesting. You're really going after this thing," Clancy said, looking up from the computer. "What are you doing with the information?"

Brock looked at Clancy. "Don't know yet."

"What difference do you think you can make even if you find more patients who were overlooked at those clinics?"

"Not sure I can make any difference...on my own. But if it's a number of cases, it might need some attention from other quarters. I'm working on a letter I plan to send to the state board. See what they think."

Clancy nodded and resumed his computer charting. "I'll see that guy when you're done in there with his leg. Obviously, he's not from one of *those* clinics." Brock smiled. "I want to go ahead and get it done if I'm taking him to the OR tonight."

"Sure," Brock answered, turning toward the now quiet cubicle to finish his work.

~ ~ ~

"I'm sure he's just tied up, Erica. Did you say you left the message yesterday?"

"Yes, that's right, Witt. Naturally, I'm anxious to touch base with Mr. Anderson after you suggested I might do so."

"I take it you're still worried about that situation with the patient one of your gals saw."

"Whom one of our advanced practitioners saw, yes." Erica enjoyed correcting him with such formality. "But I wouldn't say I'm really worried. Just wanting to prevent any problems if I can."

She grated at Witter Scanlon's tone and the patronizing manner with which he referred to her associates. She'd met and dealt with him on a number of occasions since CEF and groups of advanced practice nurses had joined forces four years earlier to push for the practice freedom legislation. A non-lawyer MBA, she had concluded Witt thought highly of himself and his ability to cultivate important connections around the state. He'd been CFO of Citizens for Economic Freedom for seven years now, since its inception, and it was obvious he intended to keep his position. He was an excellent lobbyist, keeping members, business owners, and large donors happy. "I wondered if you might be able to reach him and encourage him to return my call sooner rather than later."

Witt paused on the other end. "Well, it's just Tuesday, and I suspect he'll call you before too long, but I'll get in touch with him and see if I can stir things up."

"I'd appreciate that Witt, I really would. I'll be in all day tomorrow, taking care of administrative tasks. You can shoot me a message when you reach him. You have my email?"

"Yes, I'm sure I do, but give it to me again." He paused, then added, "I expect he'll call you soon. And don't worry. There are some things we can do for situations like this."

"Oh? And by *some things,* what do you mean?"

"In due time, Erica. In due time."

9

Friday

"Yes, this is Karen Nettley."

"Mrs. Nettley, this is Kemp Anderson with Foster, James and Levy." Karen sat silent. *Who is this?* Kemp continued, "I'm a lawyer representing the organization Citizens for Economic Freedom. I'm calling you today—"

She interrupted, "Mr. Anderson, I don't take solicitation calls, and I don't need any legal help. I have that covered."

"Excuse me, Mrs. Nettley, I'm not calling in the usual sense to solicit your business at this time. And I would like to extend our condolences to you regarding your husband's recent death. If I might have a few minutes of your time to discuss an issue which may be of some interest to you about that situation."

Shocked he knew of Boyd's death, she finally answered, "I can spare a few minutes."

"We understand your husband was seen at a clinic in

Elston, a clinic called Comprehensive Care."

"Yes."

"The Citizens for Economic Freedom group asks our firm to assist them, from time to time, with the legal aspects of certain healthcare legislation. They support the development of clinics such as Comprehensive Care, and believe strongly in the exercise of economic freedom those clinics represent. Several years ago, during the process of getting the bill passed and ensuring freedom for the clinics and practitioners involved, we provided legal advice and counseling." He paused, but Karen said nothing. "Have I lost you yet?"

"No. Go on."

"As a result, when a situation arises which involves the operation of such clinics, they often turn to us for advice. So, I am calling you today to make you aware of our firm, and ask if there is anything you need, or some aspect of your situation we can help with."

"That sounds a little vague, Mr. Anderson. What exactly does your firm do in situations like this?"

"There are ways we can help with details, plans, or even unexpected expenses. We can also help families move in the right direction as they make decisions after an episode such as this. Occasionally, families find themselves getting calls from other attorneys about their loved one, you know, such as that."

"Mr. Anderson, I'm not sure I'm hearing you clearly or understand what you're proposing, but I have to leave for an appointment and need to get off the phone. I'd like to think about what you've said, and discuss this with my family."

"Of course, Mrs. Nettley. May I call you back at this same number next week?"

"I guess so. Give me a few days before we talk again."

"That's fine. I look forward to speaking with you again. Have a good day."

"Thank you."

Karen cradled the receiver and stared at the phone. Though confused by the lawyer's vague verbiage, she couldn't deny her gut feeling that she understood clear enough what he implied. What exactly *was* he offering? Probably money. He hadn't said he was a malpractice lawyer, but maybe that was his roundabout way of introducing himself and his ambulance-chasing firm. And what on earth is the Citizens for Economic Freedom? She'd have to tell John about the call. Thank God, she wasn't left entirely alone.

Glancing at her watch, she pulled herself from her chair, and grabbed her bag off the kitchen counter. It was time to keep her Friday appointment at the store. The refrigerator was still full of leftovers from neighbors and church members, well-intentioned friends who had delivered food nonstop for two weeks. Too much food she couldn't possibly eat, and more than she could pass off to John and Elizabeth. Everything had aged out or was stale. The time had come to clean out and start over. She climbed into her Ford Explorer and backed out of the garage.

As Karen reached the end of their long, gravel drive, she turned east onto the highway toward Topeka and the closest Walmart. Brisk March winds bent the tops of roadside trees, still devoid of spring leaves. Grey clouds hung low, further depressing her mood. A cold front had barreled through the night before. If any rain came it might turn to ice. Heaven forbid, it was time for spring to arrive. In the meantime, her barn coat, gloves, and boots deflected some of the chill.

Passing familiar farms and ranches, she saw no one near the road to greet or return a wave. But, she hadn't really expected that either. Her neighbors were absorbed in their own busy lives. Although they had visited regularly and expressed shock at Boyd's passing, they couldn't sit and hold her hand for long.

Her thoughts cascaded as she absentmindedly steered the vehicle along the highway. How will she deal with the ranch? Can she even keep the ranch? Admittedly uneasy there alone, she had said nothing to John. It wasn't time yet to make any big decisions. John hadn't broached that subject either, and she had purposely avoided bringing it up. She didn't want to be a burden to him and Elizabeth, especially with their first child on the way. A first grandchild Boyd would never see. An ache gripped her heart. The past eighteen days—though it seemed like months—had flown by in a blur, and now on the quiet road utter loneliness overwhelmed her. Had she become a stranger, traversing an unfamiliar route for the first time? She forced herself to focus on the road, straddling the yellow line marking the middle, and felt anxious to get to town, to see other people, possibly greet the few cashiers she knew. There must be other errands she could drum up as well.

Suddenly out of nowhere, Karen heard her own voice, "Damn it, Boyd, why didn't you tell me? How could I help when you didn't tell me?"

In answer, only a deep, guttural moan issued forth as tears paved rivulets down her face and dropped silently onto her lap.

10

Sunday

S tanding on the front porch, she knocked before letting herself in. "Hello…I'm here," she called out. A happy golden retriever skidded down the hall to greet her as she closed the front door.

"Hi, Mom," John yelled from the kitchen. "Come on back." Karen balanced her dish in one hand, petted Gracie with the other, and navigated the hallway toward the back of the house.

Beth smiled, relieved her of the casserole, and gave her a quick hug. "Get down, Gracie," she warned the Golden, who dutifully removed her front paws from the counter after surveying the food laid out for Sunday dinner.

"Glad you could come by, Mom. How's your weekend been?" John asked without turning from the table where he rearranged chairs.

"Okay, I guess. I finally dumped all the leftovers and went to the store Friday. It felt good to get out."

"Hmm, I bet. You can come by the dealership any time, you know."

"I know. But, I don't want to take up your time. What with all you've got going on. I've just been going through things and trying to get organized."

John stopped and watched his mother as she fussed over dishes on the counter. "It's no bother."

"I'll pour some water," she offered.

"Well, let's get dinner on," Beth suggested, carrying a platter of chicken and a bowl of mashed potatoes across the kitchen. Karen conveyed other side dishes to the table. Certainly more food than the three of them could finish off. Gracie plopped down and stretched out on the floor, hoping for fallout. Joining hands, the Nettleys said grace.

John frowned. "I wish you would've called me after you heard from them, Mom."

Karen squinted at her son over her coffee cup, her neglected dessert pushed aside. She shrugged. "I knew I'd talk with you about it today, and I wanted some time to mull over what he said."

"So, now you've mulled. This Mr. Anderson...you said he's a lawyer with some firm here in Topeka? And that firm works with this bunch at CEF?"

Karen saucered her cup, and looked up at John. She felt Beth's steady gaze as well. "Yes, a Mr. Kemp Anderson. I wrote all that down right after we hung up. His firm is Foster, James, and Levy. Have you heard of them?"

"No, can't say that I have. I'll check with Mason. He may know something."

"Sure. I hadn't thought about asking him. We haven't spoken since the funeral, but I know he's busy working on the estate right now."

"Actually, he called me this past Thursday and asked if we could meet with him this week. There are some things we need to go over about the ranch. I'll ring him tomorrow and set up a time."

"Any time's good for me; I'm flexible."

John glanced at his wife, then turned back to his mother. "We can ask him then about this Kemp Anderson and his firm. Meanwhile, if you get any more calls from either group—CEF or Anderson's firm—I want you to tell them they need to speak with both of us, at the same time. Do not field those calls alone."

"I'm not a child, John…"

"I know, Mom."

"…and you don't have to lecture me. I brought it up because I want your opinion and help with whatever they're up to." She paused and took another sip of coffee. "Speaking of the ranch…how do you think things are?"

"I've been through some of the books, but not all yet. And I've spoken with Colt about the herd. We're in good shape this spring. Hopefully, we'll have a decent calving season again next year. The hunting leases on the other land are still good for a while. Other than that, I haven't had time to do any planning. We'll talk more when we see Mason. I think Dad left things in good shape." An uncomfortable silence settled over the room.

Finally, Karen said, "You know I called the head nurse last Monday at that clinic Boyd went to. Her name's Erica something-or-other. I've got it written down at home. Anyway, she seemed friendly enough at first, but when I started telling her about your father, she got real quiet. Didn't say much after that, then she got a little snippy. I told her we were unhappy with what had happened, and that we didn't know why his condition wasn't discovered before he wound up in the ER that night."

"Did you mention we might sue?"

"No, not in so many words, but I did say we might talk with someone about our concerns and our options."

"Nice way to put it, Mom," Beth interjected, patting Karen's hand.

"Anyway, she didn't say much after that, but she did offer her condolences, and said she'd continue to look into his visits there."

John pushed his plate away and leaned back on the chair legs. "That shouldn't take her too long. He only went there twice, right?"

Karen nodded. "Now John, you know your father didn't like to doctor. He felt abandoned after old Dr. Bates retired. Never cared to find another after that. He wouldn't let me go with him to the new clinic, told me I fretted too much."

John exchanged glances with Beth. "Okay, let's just table this for now and talk with Bob Mason when we see him this week. He'll help us sort this out. I'm still not ready to just let it go, though."

"Nor am I."

11

Tuesday

"Glad you're here. It was a busy night."

"How so?" Brock asked.

"Oh, just a lot of small stuff slowing things down. And a couple of big cases thrown in to keep it interesting."

Brock stood at the central desk as the shifts changed that Tuesday, and prepared to receive morning report from his colleague. He'd worked the previous weekend and was looking forward to his day off come Thursday. "Tell me what you've got."

His colleague gave him the rundown. "Okay, everyone's stable now. Cardiology is seeing the man in three with acute coronary syndrome. His symptoms are controlled, and he's going to cath shortly, so that's covered. The lady in five is getting prepped for the OR for her gallbladder. Surgery's already been down to see her. And the kid in nine has huge boggy tonsils and is infected again. ENT should be here soon to take a look at him. He's stable. The other three are ready for discharge. The nurses are taking care of them."

"Sounds like you've cleaned house."

"Well, you just missed another situation we had." Brock looked up from his computer and listened. "A sixty-four-year-old man came in about midnight with hemoptysis. He wasn't erupting, but it looked scary to him and his wife. He has COPD, and his X-ray shows a mass in the left upper lobe. Anyway, pulmonary admitted him, so he's up in the unit getting worked up."

"Who sent him in?" Brock asked.

"Brought himself in," the other doctor clarified.

"Where's he from?"

"Northridge, I think."

"Does he have a doctor there?"

"I'm not sure from what they said. He apparently was seen by a nurse practitioner about six months ago, was diagnosed with pneumonia, and given a round of antibiotics. He didn't go back or follow up wasn't scheduled. That was a little unclear from what his wife said. Of course, they were pretty upset when he first got here, and I saw him."

"That's the second one this month," Brock said.

His colleague shot him a quizzical look, "Second one, what?"

"A patient who's gone to an advanced practice clinic for care and has shown up here with a bad problem. A clinic staffed only by extenders, no physician coverage."

"That doesn't sound good."

"No, it doesn't."

"Well, take it easy," his partner said as he closed down his computer and rose to leave.

"Yeah, thanks for getting things in order," Brock answered, not looking up. He scanned the list from the night before and found the name: Lamar Spencer, sixty-four years old, hemoptysis and lung mass, room 625. He turned away from the desk to make rounds on the patients remaining in the ER. He'd try to find time to go up and see Mr. Spencer during his shift, if it remained quiet.

It did not.

Shortly before two p.m. the ER doors flew open and the paramedics sped in with a young woman on their cart, an oxygen mask strapped across her face. Two nurses scurried toward them and with the paramedics pulled the cart into the cubicle. Brock stopped what he was doing, stood from his desk chair, and strode to the bedside.

His first impression: a pale, rather thin young woman, awake, alert, with a mass of blonde hair splayed on the pillow. Lying still, breathing rapidly, she gripped the sheet covering her to her neck. Definitely looked afraid, but not writhing in pain.

The nurses immediately attached various monitors, pried one arm loose and applied a blood pressure cuff, and transferred her oxygen mask tubing to the wall oxygen outlet. They pulled out a tourniquet, various tubes for blood, and surveyed the IV fluids already hung.

One EMT gave report in an efficient, abbreviated manner.

"Twenty-two-year-old pregnant female—twenty-four weeks—passed out at home. First pregnancy, no drugs, no history of other medical problems. Her husband came home to pick up something during lunch. She complained she felt out of breath. He advised her to call her doctor. When he came up from the basement, he found her 'out' on the kitchen floor. He thought she still had a pulse when he checked it. He called 911 and her parents. Kept trying to wake her up. When we arrived, she responded quickly to supplemental oxygen at 100%. Denied chest pain or contractions. Tracing showed sinus tach, O_2 sat around 90%."

"Make sure the O_2 is at 100%," Brock instructed a nurse, who made a quick adjustment of the oxygen setting.

The young woman said nothing, the oxygen mask covering half her face. She stared wild-eyed at Brock who had already begun his exam. He listened to her heart and lungs, then pulled back the sheet, palpated her gravid abdomen, and glanced between her legs. "Any bleeding?"

"None so far," the paramedic answered.

Brock looked down at the young woman. "Any contractions? Any pain?"

She shook her head. He patted her arm.

"Blood pressure 90 over 58, pulse 116," called out a nurse. "Sat 92%."

"Heart tones?"

"Doppler—132."

"Okay, let's get some labs and a blood gas...and a twelve lead," Brock ordered, "and get another line in. Set her up for an exam, and have Nadine call the OBs."

"Will do," one of the nurses confirmed and hurried to the main desk.

The EMTs eased away as Brock said, "Thanks," and advised, "You guys take it easy."

"You bet. Hope it goes well here."

"It'll go."

Brock stepped out of the small, crowded cubicle to go in search of the young husband.

12

Thursday

The huge roll-top desk laid claim to a good bit of space in Brock's home study. His grandfather had given him the old oak giant when he'd graduated from medical school. The story of how his grandad had acquired it was changeable and sketchy, but he'd had it in his front room for years and knew Brock admired it. His grandmother had hidden a Norman Rockwell china figurine—*The Doctor and the Doll*—in one of the cubbies when they'd delivered it to him. His little daughter Fayth loved that figurine and insisted her daddy keep it where she could see it whenever she came into the study, sometimes with her own dolls, ready for another examination. He glanced at it now. Things had certainly been simpler in the past.

Meredith, his wife, had left to put in a few hours of volunteer time at a local food bank that Thursday, and to run errands before picking up Fayth from kindergarten. The house was quiet, and he was glad for time alone. He knew Meredith sensed his preoccupation, but he wasn't ready to share his concerns with her. A nurse herself, he wasn't sure how she would react to the situation, and didn't want to raise her ire before he had a better handle on whatever the situation was. This issue called for attention, and he intended to pursue it to whatever conclusion. At least that's what he had determined over the past forty-eight hours.

Settled in at the desk, he picked up his letter—already sent—and re-read what he'd written. It was concise; it covered his concerns without rambling. He'd closed with the phrase, *"You see what you know,"* an oft-quoted saying in medical education circles. How true it is, he concluded, as he picked up the phone.

"State Board of Medical Arts. How may I direct your call?"

"I'd like to speak with Mr. Hughes, please."

"Mr. Hughes is in a meeting. Who's calling, please?"

"This is Dr. Brock Stafford from Memorial here in Topeka."

"One moment. I'll check to see if he's available. Please hold." Canned music played as Brock straightened in his chair and reviewed his letter. Soon he heard a man's voice.

"Dr. Stafford, good to hear from you. I know you're busy there at the hospital. How can I be of assistance?"

"Thanks for taking my call, Mr. Hughes. Actually, I'm off today, so I took the opportunity to get hold of you."

"Call me Prescott."

"Sure. Say, I'm wondering if you've received and reviewed my letter of last week." There was a pause on the other end of the line. Likely Hughes was frantically searching his desk for the letter, lost under piles of other paper. Or, worse it had landed in the circular file already.

"Well, I'm sure I have, but refresh me again about your concern."

Brock heard scratchy noises and muffled voices.

Dispatching his secretary to find it? He resumed. "I wrote concerning several situations we've had over the past month at Capital Memorial. The situations I referred to involve the independent practice of medicine in the advanced practice clinics around the state." He paused.

Then followed more muffled comments and indistinct noises on the other end. Likely Prescott Hughes' secretary had just hurried back into his office and whipped the letter in front of him.

Hughes said, "Yes, I see here what you're referring to. I admit I reviewed your letter just recently, but haven't studied it closely. Which clinics in particular are you referring to?"

"Specifically, I know of three cases so far, two from Elston and one from Northridge. All three were admitted with advanced problems, which had gone undiagnosed when the patients were seen at those clinics. I know three cases don't make an overall trend, but they may indicate a larger problem."

"I see."

"And I think the state board should be aware of these situations, which may be more widespread than we realize. Perhaps the board could look into this."

"Well, you know it's been two years since the legislation passed. I'm wondering why this hasn't come up before now."

"Maybe it has. It's possible there are unidentified cases elsewhere. I work in the ER. We see patients when they first arrive at the hospital. The cases I'm aware of involved difficult clinical scenarios. One man, in fact, has just died from what appears to be a delay in diagnosis. Perhaps it's taken this long for the situation to surface."

Hughes cleared his throat. "If the patients' families are unhappy with their outcomes, perhaps they should contact a malpractice lawyer. Have they done that yet?"

"I'm not privy to that information, Mr. Hughes, and I

don't typically suggest legal recourse to patients or their families. It seems appropriate to me that the board would look into these clinics' setup and consider the wisdom regarding lack of physician oversight."

"I'll take your suggestion under advisement, Dr. Stafford, and will share your letter with the board at our meeting early next month. It might be helpful for you to also contact your state representative, since many of them voted to pass the legislation. I recall there was a certain pushback from the medical communities around the state, particularly in the larger cities, but eventually, as you know, the bill passed. This might be of interest to them, since they may be hearing from some of their constituents."

"Sure. I may do that."

"What else can I do for you today, Doctor?"

"Nothing more today, Mr. Hughes. But I'd like to hear back from you after the next meeting with the response to my letter."

"I'll get back to you as soon as I can."

"I look forward to the board's response."

"As soon as I can."

Brock hung up and leaned back in his chair. He had expected a lukewarm response or the runaround, but was surprised at how frustrated he felt at the bureaucrat's remarks. He scanned the list of members on the state board's website. Maybe he would contact another member, one of the doctors, and copy them in on his letter. He closed the window after printing off various members' names and contact information, opened up his state representative's website, and found the number.

13

Friday

Karen dropped the bank record on the counter when the phone rang. She considered whether to let it go straight to voicemail. The phone call solicitations had become tiresome and vexing since Boyd's death. She wondered when they would stop, but decided to answer, anyway.

"Hello?"

"Hello, Mrs. Nettley, this is Kemp Anderson again. How are you today?"

"As best as can be expected."

"Well, good. I'm calling back as we agreed last Friday to see how you're doing, and to ask if you have any other questions regarding our conversation last week."

"No, I really don't, and I'm rather busy now."

"I see. If you can spare a moment I'd like to mention again what our firm can do for families such as yours."

"Mr. Anderson, I've discussed this with my family, and

my son John would like to be here if we speak again. Naturally, I want him to hear more about your firm and what exactly you have in mind. Would you please call when he's here again?"

"I'm rather busy, but of course. And when might that be, Mrs. Nettley?"

"Matter of fact, he's coming by the ranch this afternoon. Would you call then?"

"I'd hoped you and I could just come to an agreement, but all right then. I have meetings this afternoon, but I can try to work in a call, I'm sure."

"Why don't you call after three? Otherwise, I don't believe we have much to say to each other. Good day."

Karen hung up. Her heart pounded. She let out a long sigh as dizziness washed over her. Grasping the counter's edge, she slid onto a barstool. *What is going on?* She glanced at her watch—half past eleven. She hoped John would hurry, and that he'd have some information from their family lawyer Bob Mason after their conference the previous day. Probably too soon to expect much of an opinion, but Bob would know what they should do. Taking a few deep breaths, she turned back to the unfinished bank statement, certainly a tedious distractor.

"Hey, Mom, where are you?" John called out as he came through the back door.

"I'm here." Karen rose from her desk and met him in the kitchen. Thankfully, her anxiety attack had abated an hour ago. They exchanged a brief hug. "Glad you're here."

John put down his tool bucket and shrugged off his flannel shirt. "Got any soda?"

"In the fridge." Karen took a stool at her counter. "Had any lunch, yet?"

"Yeah, grabbed something on my way out."

"By the way, that Mr. Anderson from the law firm in Topeka called again this morning. He was a little annoyed,

I think, when I wouldn't discuss things with him right then. I finally told him he'd have to call back when you were here, or I didn't have anything else to say to him."

"Good," John managed to say around a swig of Dr. Pepper.

"He upsets me, John. There's something about his tone of voice and the way he phrases his comments that makes me nervous. When I got off the phone, I felt dizzy...my heart was pounding. I don't usually react that way, and I'm worried. Maybe all this is taking a toll."

"No doubt. Look, Mom, you did the right thing. Is he calling back?"

"He said he'd try. I suggested after three." They both glanced at the wall clock—one-thirty. "How long do you think you'll be here?" she asked.

"At least 'til dinner." He smiled at his mother. "You and I have a lot of little things to do, right?"

"Right, and my list has gotten longer," Karen added, sliding off her bar stool.

"Let's get at it, then."

The ringing phone disturbed the peace as they came through the back door. John motioned with a nod for his mother to pick up.

Karen hurried to the kitchen desk and paused before answering. "Hello?"

"Hello there again, Mrs. Nettley, this is Kemp Anderson. I trust this is still a good time?"

"It's okay."

"Is your son there, yet?"

"Oh, yes, he's here. Wait while I put him on speaker." Karen glanced at John, who approached from across the room. He propped himself against the desk, crossed his arms, and nodded. "We're both on now, Mr. Anderson."

"Good. Mr. Nettley...John, correct?"

"Speaking."

"Kemp Anderson. As your mother may have told you, I'm from Foster, James, and Levy. Our firm does legal work for CEF. Are you familiar with that organization?"

"Can't say that I am, Mr. Anderson."

"Well, it's the Citizens for Economic Freedom group, which formed about seven years ago. It supports economic opportunity within Kansas. Many businesspeople around the state are members and work with us toward those ends. You own the John Deere dealership here, I understand. I'm surprised you haven't heard of CEF."

"Perhaps I should get more information on that group," John inserted, shooting his mother a smirk.

"Yes, well, that sounds good. Anyway, as I explained to Mrs. Nettley, we are aware that your father recently passed. I am truly sorry to hear of your loss. I understand he was seen at a clinic—Comprehensive Care in Elston—several months ago. CEF strongly supported the development of such independent practice clinics around the state before the advanced practice legislation passed. And they've been pleased with those clinics' growth since then. The organization believes in the exercise of economic freedom those clinics represent. As to my involvement, our firm gave them legal advice and did advance work on their business issues. CEF asked us to contact you after Mr. Nettley's unfortunate death and see if there was anything we might assist you with at this time."

"I'm not sure how you can assist, Mr. Anderson. Could you be more specific?"

"Yes. In situations such as yours, families are often faced with details, plans, or unexpected expenses, such as that. Sometimes other individuals or groups contact you and offer representation. There are ways the group may help with those issues."

"You mean your firm or CEF?"

"CEF, but our firm can help coordinate those efforts."

"I see." John winked at his mother, who stood straight,

her arms wrapped around her waist. He motioned for her to sit down. "Can you explain how you propose to coordinate efforts?"

Kemp Anderson paused on the other end, and John felt tempted to hang up, but admittedly was enjoying the back and forth.

Anderson cleared his throat and began. "CEF has authorized my firm to offer and facilitate a benefit for your mother Mrs. Nettley to compensate her for the untimely death of your father three weeks ago. It is a generous gesture, which is designed to make her transition easier at this difficult time." He paused, then added, "I'm sure when you look at it, you'll agree it is most ample, and quite unexpected for an organization like CEF to bring such an offer."

"Unexpected, yes. And if my mother were to accept such an offer, what expectations or limitations would you place on her after that?"

"That's an astute question, John. The main thing the CEF agreement stipulates is no further legal action would be required. There would be a few other minor details, which we could discuss further if she's interested."

"I'm sure. Look, Mr. Anderson, it's very early and we're still digesting this whole situation about what exactly happened to my father. We're looking for some answers, and it doesn't sound like you're providing any. So, we're keeping all our options on the table for now." John paused and looked at his mother, whose face reflected her stunned reaction. He added, "Your offer sounds a little unusual. In fact, it sort of sounds like a payoff to me."

No immediate comment came from the other end.

"Good day, Mr. Anderson."

John dropped the receiver into the phone cradle and turned to Karen. "Jerk." Seeing her stricken expression, he reached out, pulled her from her chair and wrapped her in his arms. He felt her quiet sobs begin.

"Why don't you come stay with us this weekend, maybe for a while?"

Trembling, she nodded into his chest, and mumbled, "Yes, maybe that would be best."

He rested his chin on her head, restrained his own emotion, and stared across the room at his father's empty leather recliner.

14

Monday

The ER was slow that morning. Brock leaned on the main desk, sipping coffee and checking news on the hospital website. A few patients waited for X-ray results, others anxious for their discharge papers to be completed. He knew it would pick up after a bit.

Nadine cleared her throat. He wasn't aware of another person standing behind him, but caught the clerk's nod as he looked up.

"Dr. Stafford?"

He turned and saw a short, stout woman holding a sheaf of papers which she thrust toward him. He smiled. "Yes?"

"I have the admission notes and discharge summaries you requested."

He looked at her for several moments. "Summaries?"

"The patients referred in?"

It dawned on him what she meant. "Oh, yes. Hey, thanks for your extra work, and for bringing these by."

"No problem. If you need anything else, just let me know." She smiled, turned, and beat a hasty retreat from the ER.

Brock glanced down at the small collection of papers, took another sip of coffee, and addressed Nadine without looking up. "I'll be in the lounge if you need me."

"Sure, hon. Interesting stuff?"

"Maybe."

Clancy stuck his head in the door. "Keeping it quiet down here today?"

"Trying to. You pulling extra shifts?"

"Yeah, I traded with Holt. He had something with his kids at school tonight." Brock nodded. "You busy right now? Want some lunch?" Garrett asked.

"Yeah, I could use something to eat." Brock thumped the papers in his lap. "This morning, I got those charts I requested from medical records. You know, the cases from the independent clinics."

"Oh, really? How many?"

"Four from the clinic in Elston where Nettley went, and one from another clinic. I don't know if you heard about that case last week…a guy came in with hemoptysis late Monday night, got admitted, and stabilized. Big lung mass."

"Thoracic would have seen him if you all wanted a surgical opinion."

"Yeah, well, pulmonary and oncology took him. He'd been seen at a clinic in Northridge, X-rayed and given antibiotics, but not worked up before he presented here."

"So, what're you going to do with it?"

"Not sure, yet. But, these cases may be only the tip of the iceberg."

Clancy sank into a nearby chair and propped his feet on the small, well-worn coffee table.

Brock continued, "You know Bennett came by and I

mentioned it to him. He listened, but is not enthused about getting involved. Says he doesn't want the ER to be seen as criticizing clinics which send patients to us. And he doesn't want the doctors crusading around about issues that are already settled. That legislation, he means." After a pause, Brock added, "He pretty much told me to cease and desist."

Clancy weighed in. "He's a good guy, Brock. Made a lot of needed changes around here, and he probably just doesn't want it messed up. You and several of the other docs he's brought on board are a product of his efforts. He picks his battles and generally avoids controversies. I know that much about him."

Brock looked at his colleague and put down his coffee. "Okay, I know. But that doesn't mean I can't pursue this on my own. I don't need his vote to continue digging."

"You don't want to screw up your position, right?"

Brock stared at Clancy. "Well, he didn't threaten me with that...yet." He continued, "There's something that doesn't feel right about these cases, and it looks like patients have been harmed, at least the ones we're aware of. They didn't get the care they needed."

"You may be right." Clancy pushed up from his chair. "Why don't I run to the bistro and get us a couple of sandwiches?"

"Sure...turkey on wheat, the usual."

"Be back in a few." The surgeon exited.

Brock remained in the recliner and turned his attention to Boyd Nettley's discharge summary again.

The intercom speaker hummed on. "Dr. Stafford, your X-ray's back," Nadine announced.

It remained an unusually uneventful day, and Brock was glad for that. It had given him time to reflect on his approach to the uncomfortable issue bugging him. But by midafternoon, he was tired of the day dragging, tired of scanning the internet news and sports stories, and worried that if he sat in the lounge any longer he'd succumb to a nap. He forced himself to get up and leave the room. As he made his way across the ER toward Nadine's desk, she motioned him to the phone, announcing, "line four." Turning on his heel, he reached the satellite desk toward the back of the quiet ER and picked up the extension.

"Dr. Stafford here."

"Dr. Stafford, glad to reach you. This is Yates Garwood, calling from the state house. I don't believe we've met. You called late last week?"

"Yes...yes, I did." Surprised he'd even received a call back, Brock hastily recovered. He remembered that he'd given Garwood's office only his cell and home numbers, not that of the ER.

"Well, how may I help?"

Brock lowered his voice. "Mr. Garwood, I called your office because of a situation I've unearthed over the past month. I've practiced ER medicine at Memorial here in Topeka for nearly eight years. Recently, it has come to my attention that a number of patients we've treated in our ER have been seen at several advanced practice clinics in the area. Unfortunately, these individuals have presented to us with conditions previously overlooked at those clinics, to the patients' detriment. In fact, one man I was directly involved with died after being transferred to KU for further care."

"I'm sorry to hear that. What kind of numbers are we talking about?"

"Five total cases that I'm aware of, four from one clinic, and one case last week from another clinic nearby."

"Okay, but that seems a small number, considering how many patients I gather you all see in a year, or even a month, right?"

"Yes, but I suspect there are more out there we're not aware of."

"I'm not sure how I, or my office, can assist you with this."

"I'm interested, Representative Garwood, in understanding more about the legislation passed two years ago, giving those clinics the right to practice independently, without any physician oversight. How the legislation developed and who backed it."

Garwood cleared his throat. "Sure. If you'll recall, the first efforts began about five years ago. Several groups lobbied for this, long before a bill was introduced. There was intense debate, both in the house and the senate, for some time. We tossed it back and forth during three sessions, if I remember correctly, before it came up for a final vote. It was covered well, I believe. I'm sure you were aware of the push for it." He paused, but Brock did not affirm or deny his earlier knowledge of the legislative efforts. Garwood went on, "We heard from many doctors, as well as the advanced practice nurses and their supporters. The doctors were rather evenly split about the change. Particularly from the urban areas."

"I'm sure. Can you give me more information, though, on who specifically supported the nurses' initiative?"

"Let's see...of course, several of the nursing organizations advocated for the change including educators in the programs in Wichita and Kansas City. As I said, doctors and their groups were split. There were some other groups, though, who supported the nurses—"

"Yes?"

"The Citizens for Economic Freedom, I believe, sent a spokesman here to brief us. You know, to bring us up to speed on the need for better health care coverage across the state. So many doctors have retired or left the rural areas. It's a shame." He paused. "Their basic position was, it was a restriction of economic freedom to prevent the nurses from practicing independently, especially in areas of need. They had all sorts of statistics from other states about the benefit to people in sparsely populated counties."

"I'm sure they did."

"In fact, at one of my town halls, many voters voiced frustration at having to drive so far to see a doctor or go to a hospital. I don't recall exactly, but maybe thirty percent of the people in the district voiced favor for such clinics coming to their towns."

"I see. Well, I'm sorry I was working and missed those town halls." Brock immediately regretted his sarcastic tone. "What else can you tell me, Mr. Garwood?"

"Well, I'm not sure, but I can have one of my aides get back to you with additional details. Anything else I can help you with today?"

"Yes, there is." Brock paused for effect. "I have one last question, Representative Garwood. How did *you* vote?"

15

Wednesday

Morning light poured through the slanted shutters in his study, and broke across the rug in evenly-spaced lines. Wolf, his border collie, content to lay in the fractured sunlight, soaked in the warmth. The house was quiet. Fayth was at school, Meredith at the gym. Coffee steam wafted from his monogrammed Northwestern mug.

Brock sat at his desk with the summaries organized in front of him. He had locked them in a drawer Monday night after arriving home from the ER. Tuesday, he'd tried to ignore what he had read the day before and concentrate on patient care. It was Wednesday. Now, he hoped to analyze them with fresh eyes. Other than his brief chat with Garrett Clancy on Monday, he'd mentioned it to no one else. Well, other than Representative Garwood, but that was it.

He sipped coffee and picked up the first set of records.

One of Dr. Clancy's surgery partners had dictated: *This*

72 y/o white female presents with upper abdominal pain x 72 hours. She c/o nausea, denies vomiting. No documented fevers; (+) chills. No melena, nor hematochezia. She denies inflammatory bowel disease, 'colitis,' or irritable bowel history. She is s/p TAH, BS&O, 15 yrs. ago. No other abdominal surgeries. No HRT. No chest pain, SOB, cough, no recent infections. She was seen at Comprehensive Care in Elston 1 month ago with same symptoms. Given MiraLAX and Prilosec with occasional relief. Abd Sono at that time revealed stones and mild gallbladder wall thickening. O/w no further workup suggested. Doesn't recall follow up app't scheduled. Husband accompanies patient.

Brock read through the remainder of the history and physical, and reviewed the abdominal CT findings, which reported a hydrops gallbladder. The lab revealed the patient was obviously infected upon presentation. She was taken to surgery shortly after being admitted. It was a challenging procedure as described in the op report. The patient ended up in the ICU for five days post-op, on the ventilator managed by pulmonary, on two antibiotics, and followed for mild renal failure by nephrology. The discharge summary continued. She recovered well enough to be transferred to the floor, where she remained for another seven days, before being discharged to a skilled nursing unit to continue recovering. The plan included a possible need for rehab after that, if she regained enough strength to manage aggressive daily physical therapy. This all in a nonsmoker, apparently healthy older woman, with no past history of diabetes, cardiac, gastrointestinal, or pulmonary disorders. Thank God, she hadn't presented with a host of other problems to start with.

Brock dropped the reports and took another swig of coffee. A neighbor dog barked, and Wolf joined in, racing to the front door. Interrupted by the racket, Brock made his way to the front hall, released his dog into the front yard, where Wolf, obviously annoyed, was barely restrained by their invisible fence. Brock stood in the door for a few moments and observed a UPS truck parked at the curb across the street. He watched as the driver leapt from his seat and ran to the neighbor's door. Satisfied Wolf wasn't about to bolt the fence, Brock returned to the study. He readjusted the louvers and shuffled papers again, finding the next patient's summary. He heard the UPS truck pull away and the dogs' barking immediately ceased. They had performed their duty.

This fourteen-year-old male presents with worsening asthma over the past 3 months. He reports daily symptoms, using his LABA twice daily, with use of Albuterol at least 4x/day for acute relief. The hospitalist's dictation went on: *He admits to sporadically using an inhaled steroid when given a sample. No regular script. He denies smoking, use of recreational drugs. (+) seasonal allergies—little relief with Claritin, or occasional Benadryl or Zyrtec tried at bedtime. He denies recent infections, but reports he had a mild cold or bad allergies a month ago. No fevers, chills, N/V, rashes. He has trouble with sports—track/runner, often has to stop practice due to dyspnea. His mother reports he isn't sleeping well, and she has to give him a breathing treatment during the night ~ 3x/week. He presents with his parents.*

The young teen was admitted to telemetry, then transferred to the adolescent unit, where he remained for two additional days.

Brock finished reading the discharge note. The kid was stabilized on an inhaler regimen, the long-acting beta agonist (LABA) inhaler was stopped, and a steroid inhaler started. He received one dose of steroids in the ER. Two more doses on the ward. Pneumonia and acute or chronic sinusitis were ruled out, and an allergy regimen was fashioned. He was admonished to continue that without interruption, whether he thought he needed it or not. Saline nasal washes and nasal steroids were also implemented. He received renewed asthma management education including appropriate use of the short-acting albuterol. His family participated. He was discharged home, with a follow up appointment scheduled with pulmonary.

One good outcome, at least.

Brock set aside that summary, leaned back in his chair, and picked up the most recent case from the ER. The young pregnant woman he'd dealt with only a week ago. Turned out, her workup was underway for several serious cardiopulmonary conditions, including primary pulmonary hypertension. Bad deal any time, but add in a pregnancy—not a good situation. Admittedly, it was not real common, but not unheard of either. Something you had to know about, or suspect, in patients with unexplained shortness of breath. Particularly young women; particularly young pregnant women.

Because it was closer to home, she had gone to the Elston clinic twice during her pregnancy, complaining of feeling breathless, which apparently had been ascribed to usual pregnancy symptoms. They had asked her about an asthma history which she'd denied. They'd asked her whether she was sleeping well. She was not. They'd then checked routine bloodwork which turned out normal—no anemia.

Apparently, they were not aware of other possibilities including such things as pulmonary embolism or pulmonary hypertension, or congenital heart disease. Clinical situations pregnancy could predispose to such as pulmonary embolism or worsen, as in the case of pulmonary hypertension or congenital cardiac abnormalities. The last visit there was at about eighteen weeks gestation. She was told to see Ob-Gyn, and someone there assisted her to secure an appointment, but not for another four weeks. Her symptoms persisted. She missed that Ob appointment due to car problems. Then the sudden episode at home a week ago.

Brock continued reading, though he knew what she faced. Obstetrics responded and took over her care. They quickly consulted cardiology. The first echocardiogram was not encouraging, and it was determined that day to arrange immediate transfer to KU's high-risk pregnancy unit. The young woman would require advanced evaluation and treatment if she and her baby had any chance of survival. Curious and concerned, Brock had called her obstetric team at KU the previous Friday for an update. After additional studies were obtained, the pulmonary hypertension team jumped into the case. Last he'd heard, she was heading to Cesarian section delivery and then faced more invasive procedures to complete her diagnostic workup. And her baby faced a very long haul in the neonatal ICU. Frustrated and saddened, he tossed the papers aside.

He stood, picked up his mug of cold coffee and left his study. He let Wolf in, and walked back to the kitchen, his neck stiff as a board. Rubbing it, he rolled his head, poured more coffee, and made his way back to the study. Wolf trotted along and dropped down at his feet under the desk.

He then turned his attention to the summaries and radiology reports on Lamar Spencer. Quickly reviewing the documents again, he thought back on his visit to Lamar's room after his admission, the same day the young pregnant woman had presented.

The man had looked awful—pale and cachectic. On oxygen, he labored to breathe, coughing jags erupting periodically. Brock had greeted Spencer, but spoke primarily with his wife, who'd been worried and eager to tell their story. She described being upset about his condition for the past six months and didn't believe the antibiotics given to him 'helped at all.' She had accompanied him to the clinic in Northridge and saw the X-ray herself, remembered the hazy place in the lungs they'd pointed out to her. Remembered they'd told her it was probably pneumonia. Since the visit, she reported her husband had lost weight, become more short of breath, had coughed up a little blood-tinged gunk, but didn't return to the clinic for follow-up. When asked, she denied he had fevers or chills, but said his appetite was 'way off.' Then he had coughed up more blood the night before admission, looked like volumes of blood to her. Brock had spoken with the patient for a few moments and read the progress notes. He remembered thinking the man was in good hands. So, he had bid them well, and asked them to keep in touch about Mr. Spencer's progress, handing her his card with the ER number.

Setting aside the reports, Brock stood and stretched his back. Ambling to the kitchen, he poured out the coffee he'd hardly touched—done for the day. His stomach reminded him he'd had too much, anyway. Lost in thought, he rinsed his cup, more times than needed.

What struck him about the four cases from the Elston clinic was the range of ages and various patient conditions. He couldn't say one specific type of patient or clinical scenario was probably mishandled compared to others. For the most part, pretty standard cases which he saw all the time in the ER: abdominal pain and its myriad causes, hematochezia—blood in the stool—asthma exacerbations, abnormal chest X-rays, and hemoptysis, or less alarming, blood-tinged sputum. Nothing exotic. All clinicians saw patients with these conditions, except for the young pregnant woman with an unusual disorder. He'd give them that one. But why had these patients, and likely others, gone without workups or referrals, especially if their symptoms didn't improve or resolve? And some should have been referred right away.

Shoving his ruminations aside, he stared out the kitchen window, silently arguing with himself. Was he going to continue with this? Would it yield any results or just frustrate him, or worse? Was he willing to pound around on his own, colleagues expressing concern, but walking away to the next case? Should he call Prescott Hughes again, update him on the numbers?

He placed the well-washed mug on the counter as uncomfortable thoughts intruded. What had *he* overlooked or missed in a patient? What had *he* passed off as something minor? Everyone has at some time or another, right? What had they entrusted to their own ER extenders, without making their own assessments?

He saw Meredith's car pull around to the garage, then heard the door go up. Moving quickly to the study, he stuck the patient papers in a bottom file drawer of the desk and turned the lock. He heard the kitchen door close. "Hi, hon," he called to his wife. "Good workout?"

They met in the hall. "Yeah." She gave him a peck on the cheek as she passed by. "Done in the study? I need to check some emails."

"I'm at a stopping point. What do we have for lunch?"

"I brought some deli meat from the store and a few other things. There're leftovers in the fridge. I'm running upstairs. Help yourself."

Brock walked over and pilfered the refrigerator, then went into the pantry to survey the stock there. He felt distracted and couldn't concentrate on what he wanted to eat. Nothing appealed. Maybe if he went for a run, he'd clear his head, and get a grip.

~ ~ ~

Back in his study later that afternoon, Brock startled when the desk phone rang. Caller ID displayed an unfamiliar string of names. Curious, he put down his medical journal, and answered.

"Hello?"

"Is this Dr. Brock Stafford?"

"Yes, this is Dr. Stafford. Who's calling?"

"Dr. Stafford, my name is Claire Randolph. I'm an attorney with Lewis, Bates, and Dunning in Kansas City." The husky voice went on, "I'm representing the family of Mr. Boyd Nettley in a legal matter. I believe you are familiar with the gentleman."

Brock recovered from his surprise at the sound of her voice, and the imagined appearance of the woman on the other end. "Yes, I'm familiar with Mr. Nettley."

"The family, that is, his wife Karen Nettley and her son John, have retained our firm to look into the matter of Mr. Nettley's unfortunate death a month ago. You are aware he passed?"

"Yes, I am."

"So, I'm in the division of malpractice litigation with our firm, and I would like to discuss this with you."

Brock remained silent, sorting his options, but not really surprised to receive such a call.

"I assure you the family finds no fault with your care. They have sung your praises, and are favorable about Dr. Clancy, as well. Nor are they concerned about any of the care Boyd Nettley received while at your hospital or at KU Medical Center."

"Okay."

"However, they are interested in what may or may not have happened at the clinic he attended in Elston, the Comprehensive Care Clinic. Are you familiar with that facility?"

"Not specifically, no."

"I see. So, I would like to set up an appointment with you to review the case, and to generally discuss the issues involved. Would you be willing to sit down with me sometime next week? Be reassured, you are only considered a witness."

Brock hesitated, then answered, "Yes, I can arrange that. In fact, I have next Monday off. I work the weekend." He regretted blabbering so much information to this woman he'd not yet met. But her voice was so disarming.

"I have an opening at two p.m. Monday. Will that work?"

"That sounds fine. And your office is...where?"

"I'm at one of our branch offices on the west side of Kansas City, in Johnson County, near the Doubletree in Corporate Woods. Do you know the area?"

"Fairly well. The address?" He grabbed a scrap of paper and scribbled down what she told him.

"Very good, then. I look forward to meeting you next Monday."

"Yes, I'll be there."

Brock remained at his desk after hanging up the phone. How had this attorney found out his home number? He could hear the TV in the background, and Meredith and little Fayth chatting in the kitchen over dinner preparations. Someone let Wolf in the back door, and soon he heard the dog's clicking toenails on the hardwood floor coming his way.

"Dinner's ready," Meredith announced.

Wolf bounded in and sat dutifully at his feet, staring up at him. Brock absentmindedly patted the dog's head. He knew he should let the Chief of Emergency Medicine know what was going on, and they—Dr. Bennett and administration—might want to contact their malpractice carrier. But he wasn't sure he wanted all of them involved right then. He found himself looking forward to the prospect of meeting and speaking with this Claire Randolph, but should he tell anyone about the appointment, yet? Maybe it was better to wait until he had met the lawyer and knew more.

"Daddy, come to dinner." Fayth's voice, closer then, drew Brock back to his surroundings.

He turned and gazed at his daughter's cherubic face. "Oh, sure, sweetie."

Getting to his feet, he took her hand and together they ambled to the kitchen, Wolf tagging along. Trying to appear relaxed, he hoisted Fayth into her chair.

"Smells good. What do we have?"

16

April 2016

Friday

It was Friday morning in Topeka, and the House of Representatives hummed with activity. Here and there small clusters of legislators chatted, anxious to leave for the weekend. It had been a busy week, and their staff still labored under mountains of paper. Bills languished in committees, while others had escaped and were due for a vote within weeks. Yates Garwood spotted Dirk Benson, from District Sixty-eight, just off the rotunda and gestured to him. They met in the corridor under the huge John Steuart Curry mural of the larger-than-life figure of John Brown—raging between union and confederate soldiers, backed by prairie fires and a menacing tornado—and shook hands.

"How the hell are ya', Garwood?" Benson asked.

"Doin' fine, doin' fine."

"Family's all well?"

"Family's fine, Dirk. Kids are growin' like weeds. How're Cindy and the boys?"

"Good, good."

"Still have a son at K-State?"

"Yeah, graduates this May. Matt, our other one's been out two years. Still in Manhattan, though." The pleasantries dispensed with, Benson changed subjects. "Say, what do you think of the farm bill we finally cobbled together?"

"Not sure yet. Has some weak spots, but overall I think it's good. Probably the best we're going to get this go round, if we don't run counter to what D.C.'s doing. Most of the people I've heard from are for it."

"Yeah, that's the sentiment in my district, too, but I hear from more voters about the tax bill. I think we may finally get some movement on that, too."

"We just might." Garwood looked around and asked, "Say, are you in a hurry, or do you have a minute?"

Dirk Benson glanced at his watch. "Have a few minutes." He smiled. "Shoot."

Yates stepped closer to the wall, and Benson followed. "I got an interesting call from one of my constituents Monday, a doctor here in Topeka. Seems he's concerned about a few medical cases he's seen of late at the Memorial ER."

Benson gave him a curious look, then joked, "Since when did you become a medical expert?"

Yates chuckled. "Not aware I was, either." After a pause, he said, "He brought up the issue of some independent nursing clinics in the area. He's concerned mainly about a few patients who didn't do so well."

"How so?"

"One man died at KU after he was seen at Memorial. The others spent some time in the hospital here getting straightened out. I didn't make much of it, but he obviously thinks those clinics are causing a problem. At least, that's what he implied. Have you heard from anybody about this?"

"No, can't say that I have. Have any others in your district contacted you with concerns?"

"No, not yet, just him."

Representative Benson smiled. "What'd you say his name was again?"

"Believe he said Stafford."

"Well, it's probably not as big a problem as this Dr. Stafford thinks. Matter of fact, I recall getting a lot of letters and calls from doctors before we passed that bill. Nurses, too. But that was over two years ago. Went through quite a process, if I remember correctly. Thought we'd never get done talkin' about it. Not really much activity since then."

"Yeah, I recall we spoke after that vote. This is the first I've heard of it since that session."

Benson patted Garwood on the arm and summarized, "Well, I wouldn't worry about it too much. Those folks, once they've said their peace, usually drop it." He looked thoughtful, then added, "You know, Citizens for Economic Freedom was a strong advocate for that measure, and they're a solid group. Usually do their homework before backing something. They provided my office with a pile of information about the nurses' initiative. It sure helped my staff understand the issues so they could brief me. That CEF bunch, well, they've always been loyal supporters."

"I've heard."

"Matter of fact, as I recall, they contributed more support to a number of campaigns that cycle than the doctors did." Benson chuckled, apparently amused at his own comment.

"Yeah, you may be right. Well, I just wondered if you'd heard from anyone."

Benson shook his head and glanced again at his watch.

Not finished, though, Garwood said, "You know, at the time, I wondered if we should have stalled longer, figured out how to throw it back to committee. Basically, it just never sounded like a good idea to me."

Benson looked impatient but said nothing.

Garwood wasn't deterred. "One last thing…do you know how many such clinics are in your district?"

"Hell no, don't have any idea. Do you?"

"Yeah, actually I had one of my aides look into it. There's one in my district. This doctor is complaining about two others, one in Fifty-one and another in District Sixty-one. And he asked me how I voted on the bill."

"Sure glad he's one of yours. Look, I bet he's got nothing, probably just snooping around, seeing if he can raise the issue. Don't get too worried. And don't let him badger you. I've been around here for more than ten years. Most of the time people like him tire and go away. You can ignore a lot of that."

Garwood stood silent.

"Well, I've got to head out. Have a good weekend, and I'll catch up with you next week. Take it easy." Benson turned and started across the rotunda. He'd only managed to cover about ten feet when Representative Garwood stopped him with a question.

"Matter of fact, Dirk, how *did* you vote?"

17

Karen glanced out the kitchen window as John descended the ladder he had propped against the house. She was glad he was in such good shape and didn't mind climbing onto the roof. He'd come by again that Friday afternoon to finish several little projects not completed the week before. She watched him walk toward the barn. No doubt going out there to see if their loyal ranch hand Colt needed any help. Karen knew John wanted them to keep the place. She just didn't know if she could live there alone much longer. The previous weekend's visit to John's had only lasted through Monday. She'd felt anxious to get back home, but had to admit she didn't like the isolation. Especially now considering the calls she'd received.

She turned away from the window and crossed the room, startling when the phone rang. Her stomach lurched when she saw the caller ID—Foster, James, & Levy. No doubt Kemp Anderson again. She stared at the phone, and by the fifth ring decided to let it go to voicemail. John needed to be there for any conversation she'd have with that lawyer. She returned to the window, but didn't see her son in the yard or in front of the barn. Fretting, she left the house and walked across the yard. As she approached the barn door, she saw the backlit figures of her son and Colt. They stood opposite, silhouetted in the gaping opening, gazing at a pasture and the hills beyond.

Both men now, they could handle anything the ranch could dish out. But this other...

"John?"

"Hey, Mom."

At her voice, Colt turned. "How's it going, Mrs. Nettley?"

"Oh, as well as can be expected, Colter. Say, I hope I'm not interrupting anything?"

"Oh, no, ma'am," Colt reassured her. "Just bendin' John's ear 'bout the herd. We can finish up later."

"Thanks. I need you, John, for something in the house. Shouldn't take long. Could you come in for a few minutes?"

John approached his mother and put his arm around her shoulders. He turned and let Colt know, "Catch up with you later."

The ranch hand nodded. "Sure." He touched his hat brim. "Ma'am."

Karen and John departed the barn and headed to the house. When they were out of earshot, John asked, "What do you need in the house?"

Karen met his gaze. "After you came down off the roof, the phone rang. It was that Kemp Anderson again. At least, the caller ID gave his firm's name. I let it go to the machine."

"Did you listen to his message?"

"No, not yet. All I could think of was getting you. He bothers me, John."

"I know, Mom. Let's see what he had to say."

Just as they crossed the threshold, the phone rang again. Karen and John exchanged glances as they hurried toward the kitchen desk. The caller ID revealed a call from Foster, James, and Levy. John motioned to the phone, but Karen shook her head. After the fourth ring, John answered on speaker phone. "Hello?"

"Hello. Is Mrs. Nettley there?"

"This is John Nettley."

"Kemp Anderson, from Foster, James and Levy. Is Mrs. Nettley available?"

"Yes, I'm here, Mr. Anderson," Karen informed him. "We're on speaker."

"Great. I hope you all are enjoying your afternoon and the fine weather we're having."

"Yes, we *are* grateful for fine weather, but we're busy with things around here. Tell us why you're calling this afternoon," John said.

"Of course." Anderson paused briefly, then continued, "I've been authorized by Citizens for Economic Freedom to contact you again. See if you've made progress with your decision concerning the offer we discussed last Friday."

"It hasn't left our mind, Mr. Anderson," John answered, looking at his mother.

"And have you come to a conclusion yet?"

John's face darkened. "Yes, we've come to some conclusions."

After an extended silence, Anderson asked, "And would you care to share those conclusions with me?"

John and Karen did not immediately respond.

Anderson added, "I should inform you there is a time limit on the offer I mentioned. It's not going to remain on the table indefinitely. That, in part, is why I called this afternoon."

John looked at his mother. Karen shook her head. John informed Kemp, "Mr. Anderson, whatever your deadline is does not change our position. We've retained an attorney, so you may discuss your deadlines with her regarding my father's untimely death a month ago."

"Mrs. Nettley, is that your conclusion, as well?"

"Yes, it is, Mr. Anderson. And please don't call here again. If you need to contact us, please speak to our attorney."

Surprised by her own determined tone, Karen felt John's gaze rest on her as he squeezed her shoulder.

"And who is your attorney?"

"Claire Randolph, Mr. Anderson, with Lewis, Bates, and Dunning in Kansas City."

"Thank you, Mrs. Nettley. I know the firm."

PART 2

18

Monday

Brock sat in the large, well-appointed waiting room. He had arrived ten minutes early, wanting to relax a bit before meeting this attorney. The leather club chair was too comfortable, a little low for his tall frame, and he feared he might doze off if they kept him waiting long. He'd donned his navy sport coat and khaki slacks for the occasion, but had refused to fuss with a tie. His standard button-down collar blue shirt was dressy enough for this initial meeting. One other client, a man, sat across the room, looking calm, reading a book. Brock wondered what his legal situation entailed.

He picked up a slick brochure from the side table and scanned the firm's particulars and their group picture, set against a wood paneled wall, the whole lot decked out in dark suits. There were three women pictured, about a quarter of the group. He wondered which one was Claire Randolph and pocketed the handy brochure. Why hadn't he checked out the firm's website? Other than busyness, he couldn't answer that question. Glancing around, he took in the expensive-looking framed artwork, a few strategically placed sculptures, and a large framed version of the same portrait as in the brochure. Sunlight streamed through the window blinds, angled downward to enhance the subdued environment and to throw filtered light on one large Ficus tree. Obviously, someone maintained this setting regularly.

"Would you like a coffee or water, Dr. Stafford?" the smartly dressed, middle-aged receptionist asked. The other client looked over his reading glasses at Brock.

"Oh, no, thank you. I'm fine."

She smiled and returned to her computer.

He searched the side table for other reading material and settled on a recent issue of Ingram's, a popular Kansas City business publication. Thumbing through the glossy magazine, he didn't notice the woman as she crossed the waiting room.

"Dr. Stafford?"

Brock looked up, surprised to see a tall, striking woman approaching. He stood. She stopped three feet from him and extended her hand. He made eye contact and took her offered hand.

"Yes. Ms. Randolph?" he inquired and waited an extra beat before releasing her hand. As the awkward moment passed, he reached down for his file folder.

"Yes, I'm Claire Randolph. Shall we?" She gestured to a door across the room. He followed her into the back hall of the office suite, which exuded a hushed calm. This counterpoint to the sounds and frenetic activity of the ER struck him, considering both their professions were too often involved in human misery and misdeeds. Chatting about the weather, they navigated their way through a maze of hallways, flanked by clusters of cubicles, finally reaching her corner office. She waited by the door and closed it after him, then motioned him into a chair in front of her desk. "Please, make yourself comfortable."

Brock sat and arranged the file on his lap, propped one foot on his other knee, and tried to relax. Not easily accomplished for a doctor in a malpractice attorney's office. She smiled, asking again if he wanted something to drink. He declined, but glanced around to see if she had the requisite office bar. She did, but it remained closed. It occurred to him that a shot of whiskey might help his nerves and smooth the meeting's progress that afternoon.

She began. "I'm glad you were able to meet today. I'll start with how I became involved in the Nettley matter, and where things are at this time. I hope you'll be able to clarify a few points for me. Hopefully, we can continue to work together on this case." She concluded with a smile.

His observational mode not diminished since entering her office, he fought to compartmentalize his assessments of her. She wore a well-fitting, beige skirted suit and heels, though not stilts. Her dark hair was pulled back in a bun, accentuating her facial structure and straight nose. Large green eyes sparkled beneath well-shaped brows. He was struck with how little makeup she apparently wore, or perhaps he was deceived by the expert application of cosmetics to achieve the natural look. He noted a rather large diamond wedding set, a watch, conservative earrings, and no other jewelry. As that tract ran, he realized he needed to rein in his imagination and attend to the business at hand. He hadn't come there to look at a beautiful woman all afternoon.

"Yes, I'll try to be of help."

"The Nettleys, the widow Karen and her son John, contacted me a week and a half ago. Their family lawyer Robert Mason referred them. I've met with them once. They described Boyd's condition when Karen took him to the ER, their interaction with you and Dr. Clancy, and what transpired at KU Medical Center. Karen also told me what she knew about her late husband's two visits to the

Comprehensive Care Clinic in Elston and admitted she had not accompanied him there. She also described her frustration when she didn't hear back from the clinic very soon after calling them. Since then, I've requested his medical records. We've received a portion of those." Claire paused, then added, "So, I'll take a few notes as we go. If, after this meeting, we agree you'll be a witness, we'll then discuss further documentation of your observations and your probable testimony. Fair enough?"

"Yes. That's fine."

"First, did you bring your resume today?"

"No, I did not. Do you need that?"

"Yes, but you can email that to me later this week."

He nodded.

"Why don't we start with you giving me the basics of your education and then we can look at the documents you brought?"

"Sure. I'm from around Salina. I went to K-State for undergrad, then medical school at KU, graduated in 2004. I did my residency in emergency medicine at Northwestern in Chicago, finished in June 2008. I like this area and decided to return to Topeka to practice."

"Are you board-certified in emergency medicine?"

"Yes, I am."

"Did you accomplish that the first time you sat for boards?"

"Yes, in the fall of 2008." Claire scribbled a few notes on her legal pad, then looked up and smiled. "Are you married, have children?"

Brock shifted in his seat and straightened. "Yes. I met my wife, who's a nurse, during training. We've been married ten years now and have one daughter. She's five." Brock noticed she made no note of those facts.

She turned again to the matter at hand. "Okay. Why don't you tell me how you came to know Mr. Nettley and the facts about his presentation to your ER, and what happened up until you transferred him to KU?"

"All right." Brock drew out his small stack of reports and found Boyd Nettley's on top. He referred to the ER record and summarized. "Mr. Nettley presented to our ER around five, the morning of March first. His wife brought him in. He exhibited abdominal pain and rectal bleeding. He was febrile."

"Had a fever?"

"Yes. At first, he seemed out of it, not answering questions, and obviously in distress. His blood pressure and pulse were low, he—"

"How low?"

"Let's see...ninety over sixty, and pulse sixty-four. I would expect the blood pressure to be down with the blood loss, but his pulse was concerning. It should have been higher for his condition."

"Due to blood loss?"

"That, and his pain, and fever. His wife said he hadn't eaten well for a while, so he was volume contracted perhaps even before he bled. He looked septic."

"Septic? Infected?"

"Yes, and the secondary consequences of that."

"Okay." She scribbled and he continued.

"Not long after he presented, they got a CT. It showed he had a perforated right colon with an adjacent fluid collection in the abdomen."

"To clarify, an abdominal CT, right?"

"Yes."

"And *they* would be the doctors on the night shift?"

"That's correct. When I came on at seven and looked at the scan, I consulted Dr. Garrett Clancy, a surgeon, thinking he would need to take Mr. Nettley to the OR. We also obtained a chest X-ray, which showed a small left pleural effusion."

"Pleural effusion?"

"A fluid collection between the lung and the inside of

the chest wall."

Brock watched as Claire continued to make notes. "Go on."

"So, Dr. Clancy saw him, looked at the lab and studies, and planned to operate. We'd stabilized him in the meantime with fluids and antibiotics, and his blood pressure and pulse had improved. His urinary output was still low. When we went in to speak with Mrs. Nettley, she wanted us to talk with their son John, who hadn't yet made it to the ER."

"About what time was that?"

"Let's see. Around eight. Anyway, when we spoke with John he brought up the idea of transferring his dad to KU to see a specialist."

"And so you did that?"

"Yes, John arrived about eight-thirty. After I brought him up to speed on his father's condition, and he spoke with Dr. Clancy, he insisted we transfer him to Kansas City. He wasn't upset about our care, he was just stressed and wanted to go that route. He and Mrs. Nettley made it clear they trusted us. He just wanted to do that for his dad."

"So, he was transferred. About what time?"

Brock consulted his summaries again. "Around ten the transport team arrived to pick him up."

Claire fell quiet, reviewing her notes, then asked, "So, that's the extent of your contact with the Nettleys?"

"At the hospital, yes."

"What other contact have you had with them?"

"I attended his funeral Thursday, a week later."

Claire looked at him for a moment, then glanced at her desk calendar. "So, that would have been March tenth?"

"Yes, he died at KU the Friday after he presented to us, on the fourth. Pierce Dickerson, the colorectal surgeon called me the next Monday with the news."

"And he told you of the cancer diagnosis?"

"Yes. The pathology report had returned before Mr.

Nettley died."

"I see. Okay. So, you went to the funeral...did you speak with the Nettleys there?"

"Yes, Karen, Mrs. Nettley, seemed intent on talking with me, and John also came over and we spoke."

"Did they just chat, or did they share any concerns with you?"

"They didn't chat. They got right down to business and told me they wanted answers. That they weren't upset with any of us at Memorial or KU. Karen and John let me know they were angry with the nurse at the clinic for not finding the problem earlier. She told me then they weren't getting any answers. Apparently, she'd called the clinic the Monday after Boyd died, and by Thursday, the day of the funeral, no one had returned her call. That didn't sit well with them."

"Did they know which nurse saw Mr. Nettley?"

"Mrs. Nettley hadn't accompanied her husband to the clinic. The clinic receptionist mentioned a name to her during her first call to them, but she couldn't recall it at the funeral. She'd left a message for the clinic's director, who hadn't returned her call by that Thursday."

Claire put down her pen, leaned back in her desk chair, and made eye contact with Brock. "What do you think happened here?"

"I think they missed it."

"The colon cancer?"

"Yes."

Claire remained quiet. She rocked back and forth, killing a few minutes.

Brock added, "You know, there's a saying in medicine. *You see what you know.* I think that's applicable here."

She gazed at him. "It may be. Have you spoken with them since the funeral?"

"No."

Claire sat forward, and asked, "So, what are the other

papers you have there?"

"Four other cases which have presented to the ER, three from the same clinic as Nettley's and one other from a clinic in Northridge."

Claire frowned. "So, you've spent some time gathering information. What made you suspect there were other cases?"

Brock unfolded his legs and sat forward in his chair. He looked directly at her. "After Karen Nettley told me where her husband had been seen, I was uncomfortable with the situation. I also recalled the legislation passed about two years ago, which gave advanced practice nurses the right to practice independent of physician oversight. In the meantime, two other cases arrived in the ER which I was directly involved in, or made aware of, both with serious, previously undiagnosed conditions. I wondered how many other cases we might have seen from similar clinics and decided to find out. Our medical records department helped with the search and brought me the five case summaries."

"Similar clinical conditions?"

"No. The patients' disorders were varied. And their ages spanned the spectrum. We had one older woman with a gallbladder problem and a fourteen-year-old boy with poorly controlled asthma. Then, two weeks ago a young pregnant patient presented with syncope—"

"Passing out?"

"Basically, yes, from pulmonary hypertension, which had gone undiagnosed, despite persistent symptoms and repeat visits to the clinic. All four of them were also seen at the Elston clinic."

"Would you mind briefly going through those?"

"Not at all."

Brock shuffled his papers and began.

Without any interruptions, his review took all of ten minutes. He placed the summaries in his lap and looked at Claire.

"So, that's all you have on the other cases?" she asked.

"Yes."

"Of course, my firm is not involved with any of those other situations, but I understand your concern about what happened with them. It's an interesting issue. I can't say that I've heard of any other cases which involve the advance practice clinics, yet. Is there anything else you've found out about this issue?"

Brock set aside his paperwork. "Yes, there is."

She smiled. "I'm listening."

He shifted, placing his hands on his knees. "In the process of looking into this, I've contacted the state medical board and my representative, Yates Garwood."

Claire's eyebrows rose. "Who did you speak with at the board?"

"The board president, Prescott Hughes. I first wrote him a letter, then followed up with a call."

"Oh, yes? I've met Mr. Hughes."

"Yes, well, we had a brief conversation on March 24. He was polite, but a bit evasive. He suggested I speak with my state representative, and also suggested any concerned families might wish to consult a malpractice lawyer. He did agree to share my letter with the entire board at their next meeting. I asked him to get back to me after that."

"Has he done so?"

"Not yet. They'll meet this week, I think."

"And you called your rep, Garwood?"

"As a matter of fact, I did. He returned my call last Monday, a week ago, after I left a message."

"Was he receptive to your concerns?"

"Maybe."

"What exactly did you hope to find out from him?"

"Additional information about the legislation. But he just reminded me the legislation passed two years ago and the opinions from doctors before the vote had been mixed. I pressed him a little on who supported the legislation, who rallied for the nurses. He recalled the nurse practitioner programs in the state had promoted it, and finally told me that CEF strongly backed the nurses' initiative. I wasn't familiar with that group before he mentioned them."

"I know a little about CEF."

"I've looked at their website since then. That same day, I received the summaries for the other patients who'd gone to such clinics. I sat down and reviewed those last Wednesday, and that's when you called."

"Your interest in patient outcomes is admirable. It's not typical of ER doctors to follow up, is it? At least, most of the ER doctors I've worked with."

He didn't refrain from frowning. *What kind of comment is that?*

Claire explained, "I don't mean that in a pejorative way. It's just that you're not usually in a position to check on what happens to patients you see, admit, or transfer. I'm under the impression you disposition people, then move on to the next case. And your shifts don't allow you to run around the hospital seeing how patients are doing, right?"

Calmer then, he said, "Basically, that's right. Our medicine and surgery colleagues sometimes let us know how a patient did or what they eventually found. In general, though, you're right. We don't often know how it all sorts out."

"So, after telling me all this, do you have any other thoughts? What do you plan to do to pursue your angle?"

"I'm not sure at this point if I'm going to do anything. I'll wait to hear back from Hughes. Perhaps Garwood, or his office, will contact me."

"Well, I hope they do get back to you. What I would like you to do in Mr. Nettley's case is agree to be a witness. You're well-informed about his case, and your testimony will be very helpful as we look into this further. I hope you're not reluctant to assist in this matter."

"No, I'm not, but I work an irregular schedule."

"That shouldn't be a problem. It will give us some flexibility." She smiled.

"All right." Brock gathered his papers and stood. "I'll wait to hear back from you, then."

Claire got to her feet. "Good. Thank you." Before he could turn toward the door, she asked, "Is there any other reason for your interest in those clinics and their independent practice?"

He stood in place, gripping his file folder and paused before answering. The moment had come. Looking her square in the eye, he said, "My younger brother died when he was thirteen because a diagnosis was missed. I was sixteen at the time. I guess you could say it made a big impression on me."

19

Friday

Erica scanned the horizon, her loose, dark curls ruffling in the wind. "I'm always glad when I come here. It's so beautiful, especially this time of year. That sudden velvet green, after the range burns...spectacular! I'm sorry I missed it this year."

"Yeah, too bad you couldn't come then. Went well. Not so many windy days this year when we couldn't burn." Langston Carlisle smiled, then grew serious. "What you're lookin' at is most of Morris County. Tallgrass prairie. And it's not just a place. It's part of me." He took a swig of whiskey, gazing into the distance from the protection of his wide wrap-around porch. "Sometimes, I think I could just sit out here all day, but can't say that'll ever happen."

It was a treat, his expression of feelings, which he rarely offered. She knew he'd suffered setbacks, losses, and not a small measure of grief over the years. But he rarely spoke of such things; there was mystery about the man. Erica lowered her sunglasses and looked at him. His tall, trim physique, his graying hair and hazel eyes, his tanned skin—all of it drew her. And now his confidential tone. He wore his fifty-five years well, for a man who embraced the outdoors and shunned anything close to sunscreen. She smiled at the thought of him ever fussing over his skin.

"You'll never slow down or stop, not you. They'll have to carry you out of here in a box."

Langston chuckled. "You're probably right about that." Silence extended between them, both relaxing in the tall rocking chairs, lost in thought. The sun in the southwest sky beamed in under the deep porch roof and warmed their legs. Winter finally over, it felt good to be outside.

"So, why'd you come down today? Anything wrong?" he asked.

"Oh, you know, just felt like I needed a break from the clinic. It's been busy the last several weeks."

"I thought you planned to come next Friday."

"I did. Anything wrong if I come both times?"

"Not at all. Just didn't expect you. I've got to take care of some fencin' tomorrow out on the far north end. Shouldn't take more than a while."

"I don't mind just puttering around here while you do that." Erica looked away and brushed back her hair. "Or, I could ride along."

"We'll see." He took another sip, asked, "The clinic's been busy, huh? I thought you'd said it'd been slow the past several months."

"Well, it's picked up." She rested her head on the back of the rocker, adding, "And some things came up last month."

"Oh? What kind of things?" Langston swirled the contents of his whiskey glass.

"Our volume's picked up, which is good. But we had a case several months back, and a problem developed."

"Problem?"

"Yeah, one of the nurses saw a man about four months ago. Then again for a second visit. He wound up in the ER early last month with a big problem, got transferred to KU, and died there. The family's pretty upset."

"I'll bet. An ol' boy?"

"No, only fifty-nine." Langston silently stared into the distance. Erica went on, "So…when I finally talked with his wife, she read me the riot act about his condition being missed. Hinted they might sue. Take us to the cleaners. Shut us down. I've been a little preoccupied since then."

"Why didn't you mention this sooner?"

"I knew you had calving, and I didn't want to bother you. Plus, there's not much you can do about it."

"Don't know why you'd say that. I've got an interest in that clinic, and I don't like to see you so upset. That's not good for us, now, is it?" Langston shot her a lazy smile.

"You're right, but I guess I wanted to see what transpired before I involved you."

"I'm already involved. We're involved. You shouldn't keep something like that from me, darlin'. I'm a big boy. I can handle it." He squinted at the distant hills. "Look at all this. How could I have grown this place with Dad, and now by myself, if I didn't know how to handle tough situations?"

"I know." She paused, then asked, "How long's your father been gone?"

"Coming up five years." He took another sip and stretched out his long legs. "Seems like yesterday. You know, Grandad came into this piece of land right after the first war. Took a big chance, bein' so young. And it paid off. He and Dad weathered the dust bowl years together and didn't lose it. That…was a big deal. Dad was tough; his instincts never steered us wrong." He sipped and swallowed hard. His voice rough, he added, "I was sure blessed to have such a father. Hope I can carry on just as well."

"Seems you have." Erica paused then asked, "So, isn't one of the girls planning to come back?"

Langston smiled. "Yeah, Katie says so. She's a sophomore at K-State. She's a good little gal, loves the ranch. Just like her mother did. But, I'd hate to see her out here all by herself. It's a hard life."

"Maybe she'll find someone who'll love it as much as she does."

Langston glanced at Erica. "Maybe. I always thought Jim would take over, but he's got that farm supply business in Emporia. Maybe he's the smarter one, after all."

"What's Christine doing now?"

"Chrissie? She's up in KC, won't ever come back to stay. Likes the city too much. But visits when she can. Loves to ride." Langston took the last gulp of whiskey and set his glass on the porch floor. "So, back to your deal...what're you gonna do?"

"I'm not sure yet. I've contacted our malpractice carrier, just so they'd be informed. And...I spoke with Witt Scanlon."

"Really? I haven't talked with 'ol Witt in a while. What'd he have to say?"

"Basically, he sounded sympathetic, but said they, meaning CEF, wouldn't get involved with a clinical issue. He suggested I speak with their attorney Kemp Anderson."

"And did you?"

She nodded. "When he finally called me back. Said he'd look into it, tried to reassure me, and informed me he couldn't do a lot until they made a move. If the family made a move, like if they decide to sue."

"You think that's where it's headed?"

"It's certainly possible." Langston frowned as Erica added, "God, I don't want anything to happen to the clinic. I've worked too long and hard to watch it come apart."

"Yes, you have. We have. Let me see what I can do. Might rattle some cages." He stood, stretched, and reached over, pulling Erica out of her rocking chair. "You know, darlin', I'll do anything to support you. And that clinic." She felt his strong arm encircle her waist, as he planted a firm kiss on her mouth. Smiling, he steered her toward the door.

"Now, let's head on inside. It's gettin' pretty chilly out here."

20

Tuesday

"That's about it. Any questions?" Brock asked.

"No, thanks. Have a good evening. See you Thursday."

Brock turned to leave the ER, his shift completed, when his colleague commented, "It's pouring out there."

"Thanks."

Once he cleared the clinic's back entrance, Brock sprinted across the parking lot, glad his key fob worked as he jumped in the driver's seat and started the Jeep. His hair was matted from the rain, his scrubs spattered with water. Frequent flashes of lightning lit the darkening sky. Almost continuous thunder and the pounding rain made it impossible to hear the radio. Forgoing any weather reports, he turned his wipers on high and backed out.

Strong spring storms in Kansas usually drove people indoors, at least temporarily, and the ER had been less busy the last hour or so as a result. He wasn't aware of any severe storm warnings or tornado watches issued while he had been cloistered there the past twelve plus hours. Nor had their cell phones or the police radios sounded any alarms.

Traffic was light as he turned west onto Sixth Street. Relieved it wasn't hailing, he was anxious to get home, see Meredith and Fayth, and relax. He texted his wife a quick message letting her know he was on his way. Turning right on Gage, his usual route north toward I-70, he saw only green lights ahead. He kept a steady speed despite the weather, glad for no stop-and-go traffic. As he drove, his thoughts drifted to the previous weekend.

He and Meredith had taken their daughter Easter shopping. Brock was amazed at the volume of dresses and other outfits little Fayth found enchanting. And the shoes. How did little girls ever expect to wear so many shoes? He'd stopped paying attention to his wife's shoe collection long ago. In Brock's mind more than several pairs of shoes, and a pair or two of good boots, seemed a waste. As he'd lounged against the nearest clothing rack, he'd smiled and nodded approvingly as Meredith skillfully reined in Fayth's shopping pursuits. Maybe someday they would have a son, and he'd teach him the right way to judge clothes—only buy what you need. Eventually, they left the store with fewer bags than he initially feared.

Meredith had secured a babysitter for Saturday evening, who looked to Brock not much older than Fayth, and he and Meredith set off on a date night. It had been a while, and he and Meredith needed some time alone. They'd enjoyed dinner at a newer upscale restaurant in Topeka and caught a recently released movie. Later, they relaxed at home, ending up in bed sooner than expected.

On I-70, and lost in very pleasant recollections, he took a curve faster than the weather and road conditions dictated. Jarred, Brock glanced at his speedometer—70 mph. He mashed the brakes. Nothing grabbed. The brake pedal depressed like mush. Now at full attention, he stamped on the brakes, vigorously pumping several times. Nothing. The windshield wipers beat furiously, barely clearing the rain between swipes. Oncoming headlights appeared as blurred bright orbs, glaring the pavement ahead. As he steered his car toward the side of the road before the Danbury exit, he caught sight of a hill in front of him and bee-lined for the embankment. One other car passed on his left and laid on their horn as Brock careened off the shoulder and up the slope. After bouncing and running another ten yards, his SUV finally slowed and, mired in the mud and weeds, shuddered to a stop.

He sat inert, breathing hard, his heart pounding. His arms ached. He dropped his limp hands to his thighs, aware then of how hard he'd gripped the steering wheel. The wipers slapped the windshield; periodic thunder interrupted the steady rain. He reduced the wiper speed and didn't move, hoping the Jeep would stay put. But what kind of stupid thought was that? It was stuck, clearly not going anywhere.

Moments later, he became aware of another noise, finally realizing someone was knocking on his side window. Through the wet glass he saw a distorted face and lowered the window.

"Hey, man, you okay?" the stranger asked. "I saw you run off the road back there."

Brock stared at the man clad in a windbreaker, his hair plastered to his head. He finally answered, "Yeah, don't know what happened. I'm fine. I think I'm fine."

"I called the highway patrol from my truck when I saw you take the hill. Should be here any time. Want me to call an ambulance?"

"No, no, I'm a doctor…I'll be fine."

"You're a doctor? Where?"

"Memorial…ER. I'm fine."

"An ER doc? Jesus. Look, I'll stay until they come."

"Okay…hey, thanks. You want to climb in out of the rain?"

"No, I'm on the shoulder back there," the stranger said with a head jerk. "I'll just stay in my truck 'til they show up, if you think you're okay."

"Yeah, I'm okay. Shocked, but okay."

"So, you're not sayin' you're in shock—"

"No, not shock, just surprised."

"All right. Take it easy, Doc. Just stay put. This thing ain't gonna fall over. Looks stuck down pretty good."

"Okay, thanks."

The man gave Brock a salute, before he moved away through the wet weeds. Brock watched his rearview mirror as the stranger disappeared down the incline and out of sight. He could see the truck's red flashers on the shoulder. He quit monitoring the mirror and stared out his windshield. He'd better call Meredith and explain what just happened. What had just happened? He dialed her cell, but no answer. Where was she? Certainly not outside with Fayth in this storm.

He heard wailing sirens in the distance, then closer. They suddenly ceased, but flashing red and blue lights pierced the damp darkness. Brock could easily see the colorful display in his rear-view and side mirrors.

Soon, a bright beam in his side view mirror caught his attention. A flashlight advanced up the slope behind him, accompanied by muffled voices. He lowered his window. The rain had let up. Only distant thunder rumbled now and then. A moment later a highway patrolman shone a light in Brock's face and quickly scanned the interior of the Jeep. Another officer stood nearby at the vehicle's rear door.

"You all right? Man down the hill says you're a doctor."

"Yes, I'm all right. Dr. Brock Stafford. I work the Memorial ER."

"Got some ID, registration and insurance cards, Doc?"

"Sure." Brock pulled his wallet from his hip pocket and

handed his license through the window. He leaned across the front seat, found his registration and insurance cards in the glove compartment, and stuck them out. The patrolman quickly scanned the documents with his flashlight and handed them back.

Brock offered an opinion before the officer began his questioning. "I don't know what happened, but my brakes failed. Had to run up this hill to stop."

The officer stared at him. "Okay. We'll take your statement in a minute." He further advised Brock, "We already called a tow when we pulled up. No way you're gonna drive this thing off this hill. Is someone comin' to pick you up?"

"I haven't reached my wife yet."

"You want to go see your friends in the ER, just to check things out?"

"No, I'll be fine. If I develop a problem, I'll go back in. My wife's a nurse."

The highway patrolman said, "So, she'll keep an eye on you."

"I'm sure she will."

"Why don't you come on down to the patrol car, and we'll do the report. Then me or Chad here'll give you a lift home."

"Sure." Brock closed his window, grabbed his stethoscope and glanced around for anything else he needed to remove. He opened the door and slid out, standing for a moment in the tall, wet grass and mud making sure his legs worked.

"You okay?" the officer asked.

"Yeah, guess so."

"Watch these wet weeds here."

They descended the short hill, slipping on the wet vegetation, and arrived quickly at the patrolman's Blazer. Brock climbed into the back seat and listened to the dispatch radio as the stout patrolman pulled out his tablet and started pecking keys. He wondered if he should try Meredith again. But then, maybe he'd wait until he got home to tell her what happened. She'd be alarmed, and no need for her to drag little Fayth out this time of night in this weather. A tow truck pulled up, and Brock watched as it maneuvered the exit ramp and tricky incline toward his SUV. Finally satisfied they knew what they were doing, he occupied his time contacting the on-call person at his chosen repair shop, who finally agreed to meet the tow truck at the garage and secure Brock's car in his pen.

Fifteen minutes later, the officer handed his tablet over the back seat, Brock signed his Etch-a-Sketch signature on the proper line, and the officer hit send and signed off. They were ready to go. The tow truck had just finished securing his vehicle, and after confirming the shop Brock preferred to use, pulled away. The highway patrolman put his vehicle in gear, instructed Brock to 'buckle up back there,' and departed the scene. They said little to each other until they reached his house, a mere two miles away. Brock said his thanks and, as he prepared to get out, the patrolman shared a thought.

"Do you think anyone could have messed with your car?"

"Oh, I doubt it. Don't know why anyone would."

The officer didn't voice any more ideas and merely added, "We may have more questions for you in a few days."

"You know how to reach me. Thanks for the ride."

"Sure thing. G'night, Doc. You take care, now."

21

Brock punched in the garage code and prepared to greet his worried wife. He entered through the laundry room door, and hearing no voices, moved through the kitchen into the main hall where he abruptly met Meredith. She stood fastened in place.

"What happened to you?" Her face registered alarm, as she eyed him thoroughly. He'd removed his wet shoes and socks by the back door, but his hair was a mess, and his scrubs wet, and mud splattered.

"There was an incident."

"Incident...or accident?" She moved toward him and removed a twig sprouting from his pants' leg. "Are you hurt? Come in the kitchen." He followed her without protest and took a seat at the counter. "I'll make some coffee," she added, inserting a K-cup into the coffee maker. "Okay, what happened?"

Brock ran his hand through his hair, wiped the dampness on his scrub pants, and looked at his wife. "I ran off the road coming home."

"Ran off the road?" Meredith exclaimed, turning to face him.

"Well, I drove up the embankment on I-70 when I went around the curve over here near the Danbury exit." He rubbed his hair again. "Look, I want to get out of these crummy scrubs. I'll be back." He stood from the barstool, walked to the laundry room, and stripped down to his shorts. He set off for their bedroom, pausing at the kitchen door to say, "I'll be fine," and disappeared down the hall.

Meredith stared after him for a moment, then turned back to the coffee cups and searched the pantry closet for something to eat.

Brock returned in sweatpants and a clean t-shirt, his hair towel dried, sticking out in all directions. He sat at the counter again. Meredith joined him at the bar, gave him a kiss on the forehead. "So, go on. Tell me what happened."

He sipped coffee and bit into a cookie. "Fayth's already down?"

"Yes, she went to bed about an hour ago. She wondered why you weren't here."

Brock attempted a smile. "So, how far did I get?"

"Went around the curve on I-70, ran up an embankment."

"Yeah, it was raining real hard, but I could see. Well, mostly. Lightning everywhere. I was probably going sixty or so when I came to that curve. *More like, 'or so'.* When I hit the brakes, nothing happened."

He didn't miss Meredith's dubious expression before she asked, "What do you mean nothing?"

"Nothing. Nada. Mush. I tried to brake and control the car, but I kept going. Before I knew it, I was up the hill on the right side of the road. Drove up about ten yards. It wasn't too steep, but it felt steep as I was climbing. Came to a stop in the taller weeds. Some guy saw me, stopped, and came up to see if I was okay. He called the highway patrol."

"Why didn't you call?"

"I did, but you didn't answer."

"I got your earlier text that you were on your way. But the thunder was really loud for a while, and I was helping Fayth with her bath. I guess I didn't hear my phone."

Brock looked at her and nodded. "I was stunned and just sat there. The car was so stuck in the mud it wasn't going anywhere. After the highway patrol showed up, and we finished the report, I didn't want to bother you to come get me."

"So, where's the car?"

"I had it towed to the garage."

"Who brought you home?"

"They did."

"The highway patrol?" Meredith eyed her husband.

"Yeah."

"What do you think happened?"

"I don't know. I guess the brakes failed."

"How could that be? We just had routine service three weeks ago. Everything checked out okay, including the brakes."

"Well, something changed." Brock finished eating his first cookie and reached for a second.

"Honey, you look awful. Are you sure you're okay? Did you hit your head?"

"No, don't think so." He felt his forehead. "No headache. The seat belt grabbed, apparently the only thing that grabbed. I ache a little across here," he added, touching his chest.

"Do you want me to take you in? Maybe you should let them look you over."

He covered her hand with his. "No, I'll be okay. If I start acting weird tonight, you can drag me in."

Meredith managed a small smile. "Weird is pretty nonspecific. You're not an easy one to manhandle. I'd have to call the neighbor for help. Do you want some more coffee?"

"No, I don't." Brock slid off the stool, braced both hands on the counter, and lowered his head.

"Hon, what's wrong?"

"Nothing. I'm okay. Just feel a little off kilter." He looked up at Meredith.

Obviously worried, she stared back at him. "Something's wrong...other than you running off the road."

"Maybe."

She cleared away their cups, put cookies back into the Tupperware box, and waited for Brock to continue.

"I don't know. Something the patrolman said when I got out..."

Meredith prompted, "Yes?"

"He asked me if anyone could have messed with the car."

She stopped moving and turned to him. "Oh, my God. Who would have done something like that?"

"Exactly. Who?"

"Brock, does the highway patrol really think someone disabled your brakes? I can't believe that."

"I know. And, no, I don't know if they suspect that. They'll probably do some sort of investigation. May question me again."

Meredith moved to his side and placed her arm around his waist. "Well, we probably won't hear any more tonight. Let's try to table that thought and go on to bed."

He slung an arm over her shoulder and pulled her into a hug. "Ouch, that does hurt." He winced, touching his chest wall.

She eased from their embrace. "Brock, let me take you in."

"No."

Without asking, Meredith raised his tee shirt and examined his muscular chest wall. No obvious signs of trauma, no faint bruising.

"Okay, but no doubt you could at least use a couple ibuprofen, and maybe a cool pack." She clasped his arm and turned off the lights as they left the kitchen.

As they slowly made their way down the hall, he informed her, "Tomorrow, I've got to call the garage where they took the car. I'll need a ride to the ER in the morning."

"Are you sure you feel like working in less than twelve hours?"

"Don't have a choice. There's no one to fill in."

"There has to be someone. What happens if you're really hurt?"

He shrugged, then winced.

"And you know you'll feel worse in the morning, and the next day."

"I'm sure looking forward to that."

22

Thursday

"You're sure?" Brock asked.

"Yeah, Doc, we're sure. Took us longer than we thought, but it was obvious after we looked at 'em again. Got 'em fixed up."

"Have you notified the highway patrol?"

"Did that."

"When will you know about any other damage?"

"Already do. There's nothin' else, 'cept a few bumps and scrapes. Nothin' a little body work won't take care of."

"That's good. When can I come get it?"

"You better check with them 'bout that."

"Okay, sure. Thanks." Brock hung up and stared into near space. The intercom in the physicians' lounge interrupted his thoughts.

Nadine announced, "Dr. Stafford, your CT's done."

Brock turned and left the cramped room.

Things quieted down again by midafternoon, and Brock finally made it to the lounge for a late lunch. Cold chicken, cold potatoes, cold green beans. But, it was better than going without. He ate quickly and swigged water between bites. His chest wall still hurt—hurt a lot—whenever he moved his torso, but he ignored it, trusting any relief he might achieve to twice-a-day Naprosyn and occasional Tylenol. He thought back to what the garage owner had told him, and wondered when the highway patrol would contact him. If it stayed quiet he'd start making some calls.

Not ten minutes later, he got up, winced when his shoulder grabbed, closed the door, and picked up the phone. It rang five times before the other party picked up.

"Hi, Mrs. Spencer, how're you today?"

After a pause, she said, "Pretty good."

Brock clarified, "This is Dr. Stafford from Memorial Hospital in Topeka. I came up to your husband's room when he was in the hospital. We spoke briefly about his lung problem. How's he doing?"

"All right. I remember you now. You came up from the emergency room one day."

"Yes, that's right. About three weeks ago."

"Yes, well, Lamar's doing okay, I guess. No more coughing up blood."

"That's good. Has he seen the lung doctor again since he was discharged?"

Bonnie Spencer paused. Brock waited and wondered if they'd been disconnected. "Mrs. Spencer?"

"Yes, I'm here. Sorry. Well, see, he's getting some real good care."

"I'm glad to hear that. With the pulmonologist, the lung doctor?"

"No, we've not been back to him. Lamar's going to this other clinic."

"Would you mind telling me which clinic that is?"

"I guess not, seeing that you're asking and seem to care." Brock said nothing and waited for Bonnie to explain. "The lung doctor in Topeka wanted him to go to the Cancer Center in Kansas City, at KU, but we went to the Center for Diagnosis & Treatment instead. The one in Des Moines that deals with cancer. I took him there about ten days ago. They're real nice, you know, and seem to know what they're doing.

Brock grabbed a handy scrap of paper and scribbled down the name. "Okay. What did they tell you about his disease?"

"You mean the cancer?"

"Yes."

"Well, they said it had been there a while, and that Lamar was lucky to get to your hospital before he bled real bad. That blood he coughed out was awful, real scary."

"Yes, ma'am, it is."

"Anyway, they did some more tests and said some of the limp nodes inside his chest showed cancer, too. That was real hard for us to take, you know, bein' here by ourselves and all."

"Where did you say your children live?"

"Well, our son Robert is in St. Louis, and Catherine, well, she's got herself way down in Texas."

"That's right, I recall you telling me about them."

"They've both been here, but can't stay, you know. They might get back home around Easter, though."

"I hope they can. Say, how did you get plugged into that cancer clinic?"

Bonnie Spencer cleared her throat and excused herself momentarily. Brock heard her yell in the background, "Just hold on. I'll be there in a minute. Doctor's on the phone." She came back on. "I'm sorry, Lamar's calling me from his room. I'll need to get off in a minute."

"Sure, Mrs. Spencer."

"You asked about us getting into that cancer clinic?"

"Yes, ma'am."

"Well, you see, after he got discharged from the hospital, we got a call from the clinic in Northridge where Lamar first went. They were real concerned. Offered us some assistance to get into the best place for Lamar's treatment. And, they suggested that clinic."

"Assistance?"

"Well, you know, some money to help with the treatment expenses. It can run so high."

"That's true. Have you received any of that, yet?"

"Treatments?"

"Treatments or money?"

"Matter of fact, first check came just this week. Said they'd help until the treatments are done, or…"

"Or?"

"Or, until Lamar passes."

Brock cleared his throat. "I see. So, this money is coming directly from the clinic in Northridge where Lamar went? Where he saw the nurse and was diagnosed with pneumonia?"

"Yes, that's right. We don't fault them, you know. He'd been a smoker, and there's that risk, you know. They're paying for me to stay there in Des Moines, too. They've just been real nice."

In the background Brock heard Lamar Spencer call out to his wife again. Brock's stomach churned from his lunch and, he suspected, Bonnie's story.

"Sounds like that's all set up for you. Listen I'll let you go. I know you're busy. You and Mr. Spencer take care. I hope his treatment goes well and he feels better."

"Thank you, Dr. Stafford. You're real kind to call."

"You're welcome. Goodbye, Mrs. Spencer."

"Bye, Doctor."

Brock hung up and sat in the worn recliner. This referral process sounded rather strange. The patient ending up somewhere else, not all that uncommon, but this situation just didn't make sense. With KU being a NIH-designated center, there was no reason not to go there, plus it was obviously closer to Topeka. And something about Bonnie Spencer's tone of voice, and her hesitancy, didn't ring true. Something wasn't right. The advanced practice clinic in Northridge is now paying for Lamar Spencer's care, instead of Medicare and insurance? How would they have that kind of money just sloshing around ready for such situations? Did they offer to help all their patients with bad diagnoses? Brock doubted that. He considered calling Claire Randolph and letting her know about this development. But what would she care about the Spencers' plight? She wasn't involved in their case. Neither was he, actually. Other than casting a wide net and gathering case reports. And why had he become such a crusader? He knew why, and wished he could just let it go.

The door opened and a nurse stuck her head in. "The kid in fourteen finished his second treatment. Do you want to see him before they leave?"

"Yeah," he answered, pulling himself out of his chair and his thoughts. Setting aside Bonnie Spencer's tale, he put the scrap of paper with his scribbled notes in his scrub pants pocket. He'd add it to Lamar's file when he got home.

"Dr. Stafford, you have a call on line three." Nadine watched him approach the desk from one of the patient cubicles, then veer off toward the doctor's lounge.

"Okay, I'll take in it the lounge. Line three?"

"Yes, three."

Once in the room, he closed the door and picked up the extension. "Stafford here," he said, anxious to hear from the highway patrol.

"Doctor Stafford? I hoped I'd catch you there." Brock was surprised to hear a familiar woman's voice instead.

"This is Claire Randolph, from Lewis, Bates, & Dunning. I trust this is a good time to talk?"

Recovered then, Brock stood in place, his feet planted apart. Firm and steady. "Yeah, this is okay. Interesting. I was just thinking earlier about contacting you."

"Oh? About the case?"

"That, and another development."

"Go ahead."

"No, you called. Why don't you tell me what you want to discuss."

"All right." She paused, then relayed updated information regarding her review of Boyd Nettley's medical records from KU Medical Center, including his autopsy report, and the complete records from Memorial Hospital in Topeka. She informed him, "I'm still waiting on the records from Comprehensive Care in Elston. And I received a call from the lawyer who does work with CEF. Interesting conversation."

"Oh?"

"Yes. He's fishing. Wanted information on the Nettleys, you, and the surgeon at your hospital. Also, tried to get me to reveal our specific complaint against the clinic in Elston."

"How much did you tell him?"

"Nothing. We volleyed back and forth until he finally gave up."

"Do you think he'll go away?"

"I don't know. We'll see. I've checked around a bit. He graduated KU Law about fourteen years ago. Admitted to the Kansas and Missouri Bars. His firm does corporate work, and he's aggressive in his defense of CEF positions, I'm told." She paused, then asked, "So, when can you review these records?"

"Well, I can't tomorrow, and I'm on this weekend. Maybe sometime next week. I'll have to look at my schedule."

"Okay. You can let me know. Now, what did you have on your mind?"

Brock paused, then began. "Do you recall the case I told you about last week, the man who came in from a different clinic coughing up blood?"

"Yes, vaguely."

"I just spoke with his wife this afternoon. It may not be anything, but she told me the Northridge clinic is now paying for his cancer care. Said it's an ongoing thing until the treatment is completed or he dies."

"Where's he going? KU?"

"No, Northridge referred him to a clinic called Center for Diagnosis & Treatment in Des Moines. They've been there once and are scheduled to go back. He'll probably stay for a while when he returns there in a week. She said the clinic will pick up all her travel expenses, too."

"The clinic in Northridge?"

"Yes."

"That does sound a little strange. Is that how it struck you?"

"Definitely. I've never heard of a clinic having some sort of slush fund to pay for patients' treatments elsewhere."

"What do you know about the Des Moines clinic?"

"Nothing yet. I plan to look them up but haven't had a chance."

"Let me know what you find out. And they're not suing the Northridge clinic?"

"No, not from what she said. I've been mulling it over since I talked with her and wondered if you thought it might be pertinent."

"Well, that's an interesting thought. You mean pertinent to our case?"

"That, and these clinics' situation."

"Could be something for us to keep in mind. Was that it?"

"There's something else." Brock sat down in the recliner and pulled the phone closer. "Two nights ago, when I left the ER and it was raining, I ran off the road." Claire remained quiet on the other end. He continued, "I was going too fast for the weather, but I didn't skid due to the wet pavement. My brakes failed."

"Good grief! I'm sorry to hear that. Were you hurt?"

"No. The thing is, our Jeep had just been serviced and the brakes were fine. Someone tampered with my brakes, Claire. The garage called today with the good news."

"My God, Brock, you're sure?"

"They're sure."

"Do the authorities know?"

"Yes. That's who I thought was calling when they rang you through."

"I see. Well, that *is* a troubling development, and—"

"Scary."

"To say the least. Do you have any idea who might do something like that?"

"No, not at all. It's just peculiar that six weeks ago I saw a patient with a misdiagnosed problem, then two more showed up in our ER three weeks later. Then I started snooping around for other cases, talked with the state board president, my state rep, and then you. I agreed to be a witness for Nettley's case. Eight days later, I drove off a road and nearly wrecked my car, and me, because someone messed with my brakes. I'm looking for a link here, Claire."

She waited, then said, "I hear you, Brock. I'm not sure there's anything I can say or do to specifically help. When you speak with the highway patrol or the investigators on the brake issue, I'd mention all that to them. They'll probably have interest in what you just told me. And let me know what they say."

"I may just do that. Look, I've got to go. I'll look at my schedule and see when I can review those records. I'll let you know."

"Okay, Brock. You've got my email. Just shoot me several times that are good for you, and we'll work it out. Take care, and stay safe."

"Yeah, thanks, Claire." He hung up before formal goodbyes could be exchanged. Brock stared at the phone for a minute before he stood.

~ ~ ~

Claire gazed across her desk at the opposite wall, where large, framed photos hung of her and her husband taken during past vacations. What had just transpired? Now, we're on a first name basis? They'd only met a week ago.

She looked away from the photos and down at the neat pile of medical records in front of her. She felt uneasy, and wished she could attribute it to hunger. She glanced at her watch…maybe she still had time to reach him at his office, if he wasn't out on a case. It had been a long time since they'd spoken, but she felt confident he would take her call. Pulling her rolodex closer, she flipped through the plastic-coated pages to the K's. She found his name and dialed the number.

23

Friday

Brock glanced at his cell when it chimed. He let it go to voicemail as he sped through the yellow light. Rounding a corner, he spotted the garage ahead sandwiched between several small warehouses. He got out of his wife's car and noted a few other vehicles in the lot.

The garage owner looked up from his desk when the door buzzed, announcing Brock's entry. "Can I help you?"

Brock noted his name emblazoned across his shirt pocket. The man who had called. "Hi Pete, I'm Dr. Stafford. I came to see my Jeep with the brake problem."

"Oh, yeah, Doc. Let me get Jimmy for you." The portly garage owner spoke to his intercom, asking the mechanic in the shop to come fetch the doctor. He pulled himself up out of his chair and extended his hand over the counter. "Don't believe we've met. I'm Pete."

The two men shook. "Brock Stafford."

With a huff, Pete sank onto his chair. "How's your day

goin'?" he asked.

"Fair, I'd say." Brock leaned on the countertop.

"Must be off today?"

"Yeah, I'm on this weekend."

"So, they say you drove off the road at that curve up on 70? That's a bad one. Had several jump off there before. Rainin' real hard, was it?"

"Yes, it was. Did you say you had already fixed my brakes when you called?"

"Yeah. The patrol said to go ahead. Had us take some pictures and write up a real long report. One of them's already come to see it."

"Okay. I'd like a copy of that if you could."

"Sure, Doc. I'll make you that right now."

Jimmy appeared through a back door, interrupting their chat, and stopped short of the front counter. His labeled work shirt hung half out of his black pants, the color of which might disguise any adherent grease. Dark hair, in need of a good haircut, stuck out here and there from beneath a billed cap. In Brock's estimation, Jimmy looked like he could use a good spruce-up in general, which he hoped the young man would undertake before embarking on any evening plans. He also hoped Jimmy's appearance indicated he spent a lot of time under vehicles and knew what he was doing.

"This here's Dr. Stafford. He's got that black Jeep back there with the messed-up brakes. Can you show him what we did?"

The younger mechanic stared at Brock. "Sure." He hitched his head toward the swinging door leading to the back.

Brock thanked the garage owner and set off through the door with Jimmy. Fifteen minutes later, he re-emerged into the front office alone. Pete looked up again.

"How's it look to ya', Doc?"

"A little banged up, but otherwise good. I appreciate you

getting that done so soon."

"Hey, no problem. Here's that report and pictures. You gonna take it now?"

Brock accepted the stapled packet from the garage owner. "No. I've got my wife's car. We'll come back later. When do you close?"

"Oh, around six, but someone's usually here 'til later. If you get here before eight we'll pull it out for you. Were told to keep it inside 'til you came for it."

"The highway patrol?"

"Yeah."

"Sounds good, thanks. Have a good day." Brock turned to leave.

"Thanks, Doc. Hey, you take it easy," Pete advised, turning to other paperwork.

Back in Meredith's car, Brock checked for messages before getting on the road, and noted a missed call. No voice mail waited, but the 913-area code likely indicated a call from Claire Randolph. But it wasn't the same office number as before. Calling again today? They'd just talked yesterday afternoon. At this rate, she might merit joining his frequent contacts list.

He had to admit he looked forward to speaking with her, and probably even seeing her again, but was irritated with himself for having such thoughts. He wasn't sure that agreeing to be a witness for Boyd Nettley's case had been such a good idea. Especially if he had to spend more time alone with Claire Randolph. He wanted to help the Nettleys if he could, but he'd have to figure out some way to handle the distraction. He remained in the parking lot and redialed the number.

A few moments later, a receptionist answered the phone, announcing, "Lewis, Bates, & Dunning." His hunch had been right.

"Claire Randolph, please. Dr. Stafford returning her call."

"One moment, please." The canned classical music played. Brock waited, suddenly warm inside the closed vehicle.

"Hi, Brock, glad you called back," Claire greeted him.

He replied stiffly, "Yes, hello. I received your call earlier."

Claire paused, then asked, "How's your day going?"

Is everyone really that concerned about my day? "Oh, fine, I guess. I'm here at the garage, checking out my car."

"Is it drivable?"

"Yeah."

"That's good."

Brock remained quiet and waited.

"I called because of that issue. It bothered me yesterday when you told me about the brake failure, and I recalled the other cases you'd mentioned. It may not be so far-fetched to see a connection there. So, I ran it by a friend of mine who's an investigator. He agreed it's concerning."

"Who's your friend?"

"Someone I've known for many years."

"A private investigator?"

"No."

"Claire, tell me who you discussed my incident with, and whatever else you told them about me," Brock demanded.

"All right. It's Fletcher Steele at the KBI office." Stunned, Brock sat silent. "Brock, are you still there?"

"Yeah, I'm here. I don't get why you thought you needed to speak with some FBI agent."

"Kansas Bureau of Investigation."

"Whatever."

"So, I'm concerned the brake failure might have been an act of intimidation, and I wanted to get his opinion. He listened, asked a few questions, and basically told me you need to keep an eye out for activities around you which may seem suspicious or out of order."

"Activities which may seem suspicious. Seriously?"

"After sleeping on it, I felt very uneasy. So, I decided to let you know."

"Claire, you didn't answer my question. Did you tell him I'm poking around where I'm not wanted, investigating various clinics in the area? That I've contacted the state medical board and my state representative?"

"I mentioned those things, yes."

"He probably thinks I'm some kind of nut."

"No, I doubt that. I suspect he thinks you've struck a nerve somewhere and you're making some important people uncomfortable." Her words silenced Brock. "In fact, he's concerned enough to suggest that you watch your back, and that you send your wife and daughter to stay with family or friends elsewhere for a while. And he suggests you go to a hotel or let the KBI take you to a safe house."

"No! My God, Claire, what *is* happening?" His neck tightened, and every still-sore muscle complained, as he stared through the windshield at bland warehouses across the street. Pressure gripped his chest wall where the seat belt had grabbed three days before. Pickups came and went as his world turned upside down.

"We're not sure yet, but those were his suggestions. He's looking into a few things and will get back to me the first of the week."

"Look, I've got to work this weekend, and it'll be busy. I want to think about this, talk with my wife, and see how we feel by Monday. This sounds like things are getting out of hand."

"I hope we're overreacting, Brock."

"Me, too." Furious, he added, "So, I'm off again Tuesday. Maybe I can look at those other records then, if I'm not vaporized in the meantime."

"Don't even think it."

Brock adjusted his shades and started the car. "I don't

know what to think now…about anything, counselor." He disconnected and put his car in gear.

~ ~ ~

The phone rang once. No caller ID. "I told you not to call me."

"It was time I did."

"So, what? What happened the other night?"

"Be more specific."

"With the doctor."

"We took care of it."

"Well, apparently not enough."

"What are you gettin' at?"

"He's still walking, isn't he? Free to roam around and cause more trouble."

"Thought you just wanted us to scare him."

"Scare, and put him out of commission for a while. I thought we understood each other."

"I only know what I was told."

"Are you saying this was a *failure to communicate?*"

"Maybe."

"Look, I want these interventions to have the desired effect. Can you come through?"

"Oh, we can come through, don't you worry. And then I'll be comin' through to get my remuneration, as you say."

"I don't like worrying. See that you take care of things efficiently."

The line went dead.

24

Reaching the top of a knoll, they reined in the horses and stopped. The thick limbs of a massive oak tree sprouting early spring leaves hung over them. Vast pastures lay beyond, soft velvety green covering the rolling hills. A herd of cattle grazed in the distance, and a nearby pond sparkled in the sun.

"It's wonderful to be out like this. Glad I got here early enough to ride."

Langston smiled and glanced at Erica. "Glad you came. Like to ride when I can. Give the horses a workout. And there're places out here best reached on an animal." From under his hat brim, he squinted at the horizon. "So, how were things this week?"

"A few developments. We received a request for medical records from an attorney for that man who died at KU." Langston quit scanning the horizon and looked at Erica. "And, I heard from Kemp Anderson, CEF's lawyer. That didn't help my worry," she added.

"Let's go," he said, directing his horse down the small

slope. "We'll talk while we ride."

Erica followed along, slowly maneuvering her mount down the incline.

When Langston reached a creek winding through the shallow valley, he slowed and allowed Erica to come alongside. "So, tell me what Anderson had to say."

"You know Kemp?"

"Not well. Met him a couple of times." They walked their horses along the creek, moving over a beaten down path in and out of low brush and weeds. The sun warmed their jacketed shoulders and jeans-clad thighs.

"Well, I've only spoken with him on the phone twice. What do you think of him?" she asked.

"He's maybe in his late thirties, early forties," Langston answered. "Believe he went to law school at KU. The times I was around him, he seemed ambitious, sure of himself. Witt Scanlon told me he's an aggressive defender of corporate positions."

"How long has his firm been doing CEF's legal work?"

"Don't know. Witt hasn't ever mentioned any other lawyer except Anderson and his firm."

Erica said, "I'm surprised I didn't meet him when they lobbied for our legislation. We went to so many meetings and hearings. It all became a blur, I guess."

"I'm sure he was there. So, what did Kemp have to say?" Langston asked.

"In a nutshell, the family won't accept their offer."

Langston gave her a steady look.

"The offer CEF made, and Anderson's firm is coordinating," she clarified. "He said the son is not friendly, seems to be bolstering his widowed mother. She's no retiring little woman, either. I could tell that from the first conversation I had with her about a month ago. Anyway, her son John even used the term payoff when Kemp spoke with them."

Though he remained quiet, a frown etched Langston's

face.

Erica continued, "And when he called them a week later, they both told him to buzz off, in so many words, and to speak with their attorney."

"Did he say who their attorney is?"

"Yes, some woman malpractice lawyer in Kansas City."

"Name?"

"Randolph...Clara, Clarice, something like that. It was hard to read her signature on the record request." She paused, then said, "I brought it with me; it's back at the house. Anderson has spoken with her. He described her as experienced, a no-nonsense, tough negotiator and litigator. He says she can be a fireball when pressed."

"Sounds like he knows quite a bit about her," Langston observed.

"He checked her out with other associates who do malpractice in the area."

"I'll get that name from you while you're here. I might do some of my own checking."

Erica shot him a glance, but Langston stared straight ahead. "Who do you plan to talk to?" she asked.

"Oh, maybe a friend with some influence."

"Influence? With CEF?" she asked.

"No. Did he say anything else?"

"He did mention the lawyer told him she has an important witness in the case, but if Kemp Anderson has a name, he didn't share it with me."

Langston's voice held an edge as he instructed, "And he won't. Look, Erica, this situation is more than I want you handling by yourself. Remember, I have a vested interest in that clinic. You wouldn't be sitting on the corner in Elston in that pretty stone building if I hadn't put in some cash. I'm not going to stand by and watch it go down. We've both got too much invested. You just keep practicing good medicine, and let me handle some of these other details."

Erica stopped her horse and waited for Langston to

follow suit. He continued about ten yards and pulled up. Looking back over his shoulder, he frowned. "Coming?"

She raised her voice. "Langston, I don't want you taking over this situation. If I'm being sued, then no one except a malpractice lawyer can do anything to alter or influence that process. Other than maybe a judge." She didn't see Langston's small smile as she coaxed her horse to close the distance between them. Coming alongside, she added, "You know I appreciate your involvement with the clinic startup. I couldn't have done it without you. We're a good team, but there are aspects you must steer clear of." His face softened. She explained, "It's early. I haven't been served papers yet. It may all blow over. So, I don't want you calling in any favors until we see what happens. Okay?"

Their eyes locked. He reached over to cover her hands and eased the reins from her grasp.

"I have a hard time waitin' around for others to act. To my way of thinking, best policy is act first, watch other people react. When something, or someone, I care about is in a mess or gettin' hurt, I act. You've got to understand that if you want to hang around with me. Now, let's get back to the house and enjoy some comforts there."

He gave his mount a gentle nudge and pulled Erica along a few steps. Smiling, he handed her the reins and let her know, "I've had a good meal brought in, a great bottle of wine sitting there, and my big bed just waiting for us to mess it up."

Comforted for the moment, Erica smiled and turned her horse in the direction of the house.

25

Monday

"I'll wait."

Canned music played in his ear. Langston gazed out his front window across the long circle drive toward the road. He wanted to get this call done before too much of Monday got away. Erica had departed late Sunday afternoon. The house felt empty after that, and his mood took a dark turn. He was impatient. Another issue he didn't need right then.

"Langston Carlisle, how the hell are you?" Prescott Hughes' voice sounded too jovial for a Monday morning.

"Doin' fine, Prescott, just fine."

"Well good. It's been a long time. What can I do for you today?" the state board president asked.

"Got a little situation I want to discuss. Have a minute?"

"Sure do."

"A friend of mine has a clinic out here in Elston, and she's havin' a problem with an unhappy family. Seems they hold her responsible for what happened to a man seen there at the clinic."

"Go on," Hughes prompted.

"The man died at KU, and the widow and son may go after her and the clinic, and I sure don't want to see that happen."

Hughes said nothing for several long moments, then offered, "I'm not sure, Langston, what I can do about that. Have they brought suit?"

"Not yet, but they've complained to her, and they have a lawyer. And they don't like the offer they've received."

"Hold on a minute, Carlisle, I can't just...offer?"

"Yeah, Kemp Anderson talked to them on behalf of CEF, and they just flat turned him down." Prescott Hughes fell silent on the other end, so Langston continued, "Now, you need to know I have an interest in seeing that clinic succeed. I won't have someone tearin' down what I helped build up."

Hughes expelled a noisy breath. "Look, Langston, I'm not in a position here to block some family from taking action if they believe they've suffered harm. That is not something I or the board can interfere with. Which practitioner or clinic are you referring to exactly?"

"Comprehensive Care Clinic in Elston. Erica Simons runs the show there. Started the place about a year and a half ago, after the bill passed."

"Oh, yes. And you had an interest in the start-up?"

"Yeah. Thought it was a good thing. What with all the doctors leaving, we need good people to fill the gaps. They do good work, know what they're doing."

"This situation sounds familiar."

"How so?"

"Matter of fact, about three or four weeks ago, I received a call from a doctor in Topeka. Said he'd seen several people recently at Memorial who'd been evaluated at a couple of those clinics. In fact, one of the patients went to the clinic in Elston before he landed in his ER. That wouldn't be the case you're referring to, would it?"

"Could be. Who's this doctor?" Langston demanded.

"I can't divulge that. But I will say, he also sent me and the board a letter about the advanced practice clinics. Expressed concern about missed diagnoses, patient harm. It's on the agenda for the next meeting. Didn't quite get to it this month."

"Look, Prescott, those clinics are a good thing. We need them. And you know CEF strongly backed them."

"And you're a member of CEF?"

"Yes, I am. It's a damn good group, works for the right things!"

"Okay, Carlisle, take it easy. Look, I do recall that group strongly backed the legislation which allows the nurse practitioners and PAs the right to practice without medical supervision. As you know, that comes with responsibility and accountability. It doesn't relieve them of the same malpractice worries physicians have." He paused, then continued, "I admit I was skeptical at first about what could happen after the legislation passed. Change isn't easy, but sometimes we have to accept it and move on. Though there are always consequences which come along with change. That was quite an aggressive fight they brought, and it went on for a good time before the bill finally passed—"

"I know all that, Prescott! And don't you lecture me!"

"Okay, Langston, listen. Calm down. What do you want to see happen here?"

Assuming a low, threatening tone, Langston answered, "Don't tell me to calm down, Hughes. I want that clinic and those nurses left alone. And I'll tell you who *will* care what happens...Dirk Benson, that's who. I know he voted for it. And he knows who to take care of in Topeka." He'd bully this bureaucrat if he had to.

Hughes didn't counter.

Langston went on, "You better be careful up there at the

board. When you show them that doctor's letter, they better come to the right conclusion and shut down that rabble rouser, whoever he is. Otherwise, I'll let our friend Benson know I think your leadership on the board is in question. Maybe your tenure is about up. You need to stand up for what's right in this state and not let some crusading doctor ruin everything!" Carlisle, out of breath from his tirade, paused.

Hughes cut in. "All right, Langston, I hear you. Give me a little time to work with the board members. Some of them are doctors, too, and some had the same concerns the ER doc expressed. But I'll see what I can do."

"Well, after that, you better get back to me. I'm not going to sit around and watch that clinic go down. And in the meantime, I think I'll just have a visit with Dirk. I'm sure he'll be interested in knowing what's going on."

Sounding weary, Hughes answered, "Of course, Langston, you do what you think is right. I know how to reach you. Good day." He disconnected before Carlisle could retort.

Langston stood in place staring at the phone. Hughes had just hung up on him. How dare the little wimp! Bureaucrats! Who needs them? He strode to his front window and scanned the horizon. He didn't have time for this nonsense. There were things needing his attention on the ranch and elsewhere. He should be out on the land right now, not standing there talking to an idiot!

He remained fixed in place, staring out the window. What had that woman dragged him into? He recalled he'd stood in this very place the day the sheriff made his way up the long drive, met him at the door, and informed him of his first wife's untimely death. That had been ten years ago—ten long years—when he was just forty-five with three kids to finish raising. She'd been the love of his life. A beautiful, strong woman, in love with the land, the ranch and him. He didn't think he'd ever find another woman like her. And he hadn't. What a mess he'd made of his second attempt at marriage, which only lasted three years. Why he'd married a woman who didn't go for ranching he'd never know. He'd assumed she'd get used to it eventually, but she complained he only loved his land, and himself, and had divorced him two years ago. Maybe he did only love his land. He sometimes wondered.

Then he'd met Erica about a year ago. How he'd been taken with her looks, and her spunk. He recalled throwing that ranch hand of his in his truck when he'd cut his arm real bad on some fencing, barreling down the road to the family medicine clinic where she worked, insisting she sew him up. He smiled at the memory of his pursuit. It didn't take long before they became lovers, and he became interested and invested in her future. He thought, *their* future. Could they make a success together, or were things going to blow apart?

Rubbing the back of his neck, he turned away from the window. It was time to stop tripping down memory lane. A call to Representative Benson was now a priority which he couldn't put off. He strode to his desk and picked up the phone.

26

Meredith pulled into a convenient spot in front of Fayth's school just before three. In a few minutes children would pour through the doors. She glanced at her rearview mirror again and noted the nondescript grey sedan parked down the street and around the corner. She had tried to ignore it all day, but it bugged her to be followed.

Her discussion with Brock the night before had not gone well. They had argued well into the evening about the need for a security detail. He admitted he'd spoken with local authorities on Friday, and had decided over the weekend it was a good idea. She voted 'nay'. He explained it was just a precaution, and he'd feel better if she agreed to it. From what he had said, though, she wasn't convinced the situation called for constant surveillance. Finally, to calm him down and stop the argument, she relented. Now, she felt watched...because she was watched.

How long was this going to go on? She picked up her cell to check texts she'd ignored while driving. Two messages waited from another nurse who was organizing a health assessment booth at a local mall set for next week. Meredith tapped in a quick response and put down her phone. She glanced up…the grey sedan was moving, coming around the corner. Looking for a better stakeout spot? She focused on her side window, just as the school doors burst open, disgorging children right and left. A black Honda, which had seen better days, eased past on her left. She caught a glimpse of the male driver, who also appeared a little worse for wear, and paid attention as the grey sedan followed the Honda. Both cars crept slowly down the street away from her position. A chill gripped her. Who was that in the beat-up Honda? Her heart thumped. Her neck muscles grabbed. She sucked in a deep breath, blew it out, and intentionally released her tight shoulders.

Fayth ran up to the car, suddenly hitting the passenger door with a thud. Meredith jerked and saw children swarming around the school's front lawn or making a beeline toward waiting cars. A school bus down the way ingested a small throng of excited kids.

Meredith mustered a strained smile as she leaned over to help Fayth open the car door. "Hi, honey." The youngster climbed into the passenger seat and dropped her pink backpack on the floor. She asked her daughter, "Was it a good day?"

"Yeah. My teacher liked my story, and we had a good lunch." Still distracted, Meredith barely heard the kindergarten report which followed. Fayth went on, "We went outside this morning, and I played with Danny and Chrissy on the slide. She has new Minnie shoes and they got dirty, then we did our letters and some new words. We got some new words today and the Easter bunny will come next week. Mrs. Thurston said we're having a party, and the Easter bunny will come. Can I wear my new shoes? Can I, Mommy?"

Meredith maneuvered her way out of the parking slot,

having lost sight of both bothersome cars. "Sounds good, honey. We'll have to find him when we get home."

"Find who, Mommy? The Easter bunny?"

Meredith slid into slow moving traffic and stopped behind the departing school bus. She looked over at Fayth, realizing she'd comprehended little of what her daughter had just said. She gave her a quick smile. "Mommy was paying attention to her driving. Why don't you tell me that again?" The little girl launched into her diatribe, anxious to make herself clear. This time, Meredith listened, and said, "Sounds like fun. We'll get out your new shoes and see what you might wear with them, honey. You aren't worried you might get them dirty at recess, like Chrissy's shoes?"

"No, Mommy, cause I'm more careful than Chrissy. She falls down a lot and plays in the dirt with the boys."

"Okay, we'll see. Now, let's get home. Need a snack?" Meredith asked, as she watched the school bus turn right and move out of the way.

"Probly."

She ignored Fayth's usual humming and drove through the next intersection at the green light, noting when the grey sedan fell into place again several cars back. The black Honda had vanished. She accelerated onto the main thoroughfare, taking the most direct route home. To her own safe and secure four walls. Brock was on until eight that evening, and now she wished for someone else at home besides her five-year-old daughter…and the dog.

~ ~ ~

Wolf greeted Meredith as she walked back into the house, mail in hand, a small package supporting the stack. The grey sedan was parked in the cul-de-sac down the street, in front of a house which was perpetually on the market and currently unoccupied. She hoped the adjacent neighbors didn't get too nosey and decide to call the police.

How would she and Brock plaster on fake smiles and nonchalantly fabricate stories about this predicament? She wasn't at all sure she could even define their predicament, if put on the spot. Bottom line, the fewer people aware of this mess, the better.

Fayth was upstairs fetching her dolls in advance of her favorite late afternoon TV show. Meredith put the mail on the counter, prepared a cup of coffee, and pulled various items from the fridge for Fayth's snack. Attentive, Wolf monitored the whole process, as he did every day.

"Come on down, honey. Your snack's ready," she called up the back stairs.

Settling on a countertop stool, she triaged the mail, setting aside several bills and throwing most of the rest into the shred or trash piles. Then she examined the small package which bore an unfamiliar return address. She couldn't quite make out the postmark, faint in places and smeared otherwise. She hadn't ordered anything recently and wasn't expecting a parcel from either of their parents. The typed address label read: Mr. and Mrs. Brack Stafford. From someone who obviously didn't know her husband was a doctor, or how to spell his first name. Fayth skipped into the room, a doll tucked under each arm.

"Mandy and Miss Carly want a snack, too."

"Hum…okay, honey. Why don't you eat yours first then see if they're still hungry. Here's some sanitizer for your hands." She absentmindedly handed Fayth the small plastic jar. Intent on completing her task, Meredith found a zippo and slit the top seam open. Perched on several sheets of pink tissue paper was a small, folded note. Opening it, her stomach lurched.

Squirting sanitizer on the counter, herself, and a nearby stool while rubbing her hands together, Fayth asked, "What's that, Mommy? A present?"

Shocked, Meredith pushed aside the tissue and stared at the small object in the box.

"Mommy, what's that? What's in the box?" Fayth quit rubbing her hands, wiped them instead on her clothes.

Meredith pulled out a small, pink hair bow of Fayth's...one they'd lost track of the week before.

"My bow!" Fayth shrieked.

Alarmed, Meredith stared at the bow, then dropped it on the counter as if it had bitten her. She stood, circled the island, then gingerly picked up the bow again and informed her daughter, "See honey, it's the bow we lost last week. Someone sent it back to us." Gently, she nested it in the box, took a deep breath, and leaned on the cold counter.

"I want to wear it," Fayth pleaded.

"Not right now, honey. Let's have your snack then we'll take care of the bow."

Apparently satisfied for the time being, Fayth ran over to the sofa in the adjoining family room, arranged her dolls there, then returned to the kitchen for her snack. She climbed onto a stool. By rote, Meredith prepared milk, apples, and peanut butter, while paying little attention to her daughter's actions. She frantically sorted various scenarios, which could have led to someone finding, or worse, taking the bow and mailing it to them as a threat. *How had they gotten hold of it in the first place?* Her stomach knotted. Her vision constricted—two pinpoints on the counter. Dizziness washed over as she envisioned someone watching, or worse, stalking Fayth. She leaned on the counter for support.

"Honey, do you remember losing your bow last week?" she mustered, her voice tight, registering an octave higher.

"I think so. When we went outside."

"Outside, where? On the playground?"

"Uh, huh." "

"Where were you on the playground when it came off?"

"It didn't fall off."

"Did you give it to a teacher?"

"No, a nice man needed it."

Stunned, Meredith sank onto the nearest stool. "What nice man, Fayth?" She heard her own voice tone—fake, singsong at best—which sounded far from reassuring.

"A nice man at the fence. He needed it for his baby."

"What baby?" she squeaked. "Was there a man at the fence with a baby?"

"No, just him. But he said his baby liked pink bows too and he didn't have one to give it so he asked me to give him mine, so I did."

Nausea swept over Meredith. She finally loosened her grip on the countertop, rose, and finding a handy glass near the sink, swilled a gulp of water, and spat it into the sink. She turned back to Fayth.

"So, you gave the man at the fence your bow. Did he leave then?"

"I think so."

"Did you see where he went, Fayth? Did he get into a car?"

"Maybe, I don't 'member."

"Did you tell your teacher?"

"No."

She stared at her daughter. Finally managing a calm voice, Meredith said, "Okay, honey. After you finish, why don't you watch TV?"

"Uh, huh, okay, Mommy."

While Fayth finished her snack and hummed tunes, with Wolf at attention close by, Meredith hurried to the large family room windows and frantically scanned the backyard. Nothing looked unusual. Who was out there? Who knew where they lived? And who watched Fayth at school? She shooed Wolf out. He immediately barked and raced across the yard in pursuit of a squirrel. Squinting, she watched Wolf tear around, protecting his territory. Shuddering, she yanked the draperies closed. It was time to call Brock.

Fayth slid from the countertop stool. "I'm all done. I don't want any more."

Jarred from her thoughts, she returned to the kitchen. "Okay, honey. Let's wash our hands. Then you can watch TV."

Fayth cooperated and stood on her small stool at the kitchen sink, dumping too many doses of hand soap on her hands and into the sink. Frustrated, Meredith hurried her along, helped her rinse, and quickly dried her hands.

"I want my bow now."

"Later, honey."

"No, now, Mommy," she whined. "My hair needs it."

"Fayth, your hair is fine." She found herself touching her daughter's hair—her long blonde curls resting undisturbed on her small shoulders. She jerked her hand back and forcibly suppressed an urge to shout. *Who cares what your hair looks like right now?* In a calm, firm voice she instead said, "Please go in the family room, now. I need to call Daddy."

Apparently appreciating her mother's tone, the five-year-old quit needling and skipped into the other room, scooted up on the couch and rearranged her dolls. Meredith headed for the study.

She closed the door, grabbed the phone handset and punched in Brock's beeper number. Waiting, she paced—one minute, three minutes, five minutes. No return call. She paged again. Not five more minutes passed before she frantically dialed the ER directly. An unfamiliar receptionist answered and asked if she would mind waiting.

"Yes, all right, I'll hold." Meredith stood in the study, staring out the front window at the neighbor's house. That she felt agitated was an understatement. Why hadn't he answered his beeper? If she could just jump through the phone and run find him herself. The package and its contents remained on the kitchen counter, along with the rest of the mail. Maybe she should have gone down the street and shown the officers assigned to keep watch. She figured they'd take it away, though, and she wanted to talk with Brock first, give him a chance to see it.

"Pick up, would you please pick up…"

A moment later, Nadine came on the line to inform her, "I'm sorry, Mrs. Stafford, Doctor is in a code. It'll be a while before he can come to the phone."

"Yes, okay, yes, I understand."

"Can I take a message? You sound upset. Is something wrong?"

"You could say that. When he gets done, please have him call me right away. At home."

"Is there anything I can do?"

"I wish you could. Just make sure he gets the message and calls back. Thank you."

Nadine paused for a moment. "Sure thing."

Meredith disconnected, beside herself that she couldn't reach Brock. But, she'd been in enough codes herself to know the routine. Nadine would be sure he got the message. Alone and afraid, she closed the shutters and tried to squelch thoughts of what might happen next. She took hold of the side of the desk and bent over, sucking in a deep breath, exhaling slowly. After a few moments, she straightened, squared her shoulders, and left the study.

No way would she let Fayth see her fear.

27

Brock walked through the back hall and stopped at the kitchen door. Dim and quiet. No Wolf to greet him. No TV show running in the adjoining family room. No 'Daddy, Daddy,' coming from another room.

He stepped into the spacious kitchen, flipped on the overhead lights, and looked at the island. There it sat. The other mail had been cleared away. He walked over, looked at the small box, opened the flaps, plucked the folded note, and read the cryptic message.

it's not worth it

He dropped the paper on the counter. Heat flamed his face; a foul taste rose in his throat. Slamming his fist on the countertop, he leaned over, slowed his breathing, expecting any moment he might retch. When the obnoxious taste subsided, he stood erect, pushed aside the tissue, and gazed at the small bow. Then methodically closed the box flaps.

Restraining himself, he stared at it. Instead of smashing the whole thing flat. He retreated to the back hall, and unloaded his pockets. Gripping his cell, he punched in Meredith's number. She picked up after two rings.

"Yes?"

"I'm at the house. Where'd you go?"

"We're over at the Lewis'. They asked us over spur-of-the-moment for burgers."

"Wolf with you?"

"Yes. We're all here. We've eaten, how about you?"

"Grabbed something on the way home. Sorry I'm so late."

"I'm sorry, too. Just a minute." He heard rustling noises as she changed places in the neighbor's house. He heard a door shut, then she came back on. "Brock, this is a big deal."

"Yes, I know."

"You have to take care of patients, I understand all that, but we had a serious problem, too. And I don't mind saying I was afraid, am afraid."

"Absolutely, honey. I'm sorry." He paused. Meredith remained silent. "What's happened so far? Have the police come?"

"Not yet. I wanted you to see the package and its contents before they took over."

"So, the guys sitting down the street haven't seen it, either?"

"No, I was afraid they'd take it away before you got home. Brock, what's this all about?"

"I've got an idea, hon, but don't know for sure. Why don't you come home, and we'll sort this out. Fayth's still up?"

"Yeah, she's watching a video with Trevor. She's fine. I'll be home in a minute."

As he disconnected, a thought struck. And he needed to act on it before Meredith got there. He strode to the basement door, flung it open, and flew down the stairs, flipping on a light switch when he reached the bottom. Turning the corner, he grabbed the keys in the adjacent bar drawer. Pushing the door open to the unfinished area, he rushed to the secured safe room door and turned the key. There was the locked case, on the upper shelf. Just where he'd placed it several years ago, out of Fayth's sight or reach. His other gun, his hunting rifle, had been relegated to the ranch, stored there for the rare opportunity he had to hunt with his father and brother.

He took a deep breath and stared at the case. Now it was time to resurrect its contents, maybe put it to use. Taking another deep breath, he pulled the case from the high shelf, opened it and picked up the weapon, its cold handle chilling his palm. Not allowing second thoughts to deter him, he pulled out the holster and sheathed the firearm. He closed and locked the case and left the safe room, turning the lock.

Suddenly exhausted, Brock climbed the stairs, killing lights as he went. The loaded holster felt heavy in his hand, but his mind spun. He'd need to find his permit, likely somewhere in his desk. Certainly not a good idea to get caught without it. He'd need to buy some ammo and, for sure, resume target practice. And maybe take Meredith with him. It had been awhile.

Without further delay, he went to the garage, placed his weapon under the front seat of the loaner car, and hit the car door lock. Exiting through the garage side door, he forced himself to slow down, and made his way around to the back patio.

The sun had set, the April evening cooling, dusk creeping in. Welcoming the fresh air, he flopped down on a chaise lounge on their flagstone patio. Large stone pots were prepped and stood ready for a new season of flowers. Redbud trees and a large dogwood held full buds, soon to burst open. Three mature hardwoods stood strong, their tiny buds barely visible. Chirping birds interrupted the quiet and faint laughter from a distant yard caught his ear. But none of it captured his interest. Everyone else's lives were stable, on course. His was blowing apart. Jittery and spent, he expelled a breath.

Moments later, the click of the gate latch quickened his pulse. Meredith's quiet footsteps on the walk brought him to his feet. She stopped and stood a short distance from him, arms straight down at her sides. He didn't recall ever seeing such a distressed look as she wore that night. He took a few steps toward her. She held up a hand.

He said, "I am so sorry I couldn't pick up. The code went on, even though it was hopeless. The family wasn't together about what was happening. I'm sorry."

"Please don't explain. I know all that. It's just...I was so scared...we've never had something like this...we have needs, too, Brock."

He gazed at his wife. "Come and sit down."

After a moment's hesitation, she moved to a chair opposite the chaise and perched on the edge, her sweatered arms wrapped around her waist. He sank onto the lounge and jerked the back upright.

"Where's Fayth?"

"She's still at the Lewis'."

Brock nodded. It was best that they could grab a few minutes alone for this discussion. He began. "I know I sounded clipped when I called back. Nadine said you were upset about something. Why didn't you tell her what was going on?"

"Oh, gee, I don't know. I guess I wasn't expecting a threatening package to arrive in the mail. Hadn't reviewed the manual on how to deal with that. Besides, it wasn't her business. You don't want everyone to know, do you?"

He didn't have a smart answer for that.

"After I got control of myself, and my thoughts, I just hunkered down, then we went to the Lewis', pretended to enjoy the burgers, and waited. I'm upset, Brock, and I won't deny it. I felt so alone when I couldn't reach you." She looked away.

He regarded his wife. There sat a very capable ICU nurse, one he'd seen handle many a patient emergency and who'd kept medical students and residents in line. He wanted to put his arms around her and give her back the strength she'd expended on this situation, his situation. It was time to level with his wife. He should have done so much sooner.

"You are right, on all counts. Let me try to explain what's going on, or what I think may be going on."

Meredith looked up. "Please."

"Okay. You saw how the car looked when we picked it up last Friday evening?"

"Yes."

"You remember the night my brakes went out, I told you about the highway patrolman's comments?"

She nodded.

"And this weekend I said the police had convinced me that surveillance was a good idea, as a precaution?"

She gazed at Brock, saying nothing.

"I guess I wanted to have the whole story together before I laid it on you, so initially I didn't tell you exactly what they found."

Meredith let out a long sigh, crossed her legs, and watched him.

"Last Thursday, the garage owner and the highway patrol let me know the brakes had definitely been tampered with. It wasn't just my bad driving last Tuesday."

Meredith looked horrified. "My God, Brock! So, they're sure?"

"Yes, they're sure."

"So, the security tail is not just a precaution."

"No."

"Why did you minimize this and not tell me

154

everything?"

"I don't know. I guess I felt out of control. And I didn't want to alarm you."

"Well, I'm good and alarmed now." She gave her husband a long look. "But, who?"

"I don't know that, either. First, the brakes. Now this. Obviously, not a coincidence."

Meredith abandoned her chair, stepped to his chaise lounge, and sat between his legs. He encircled her with his arms. "What *is* happening, Brock?"

"We're going to find out. Did the security detail stay with you all day?"

"Yes, wherever I went. I thought they'd left when I picked up Fayth at school, when they followed a beat-up looking Honda as it drove past. But they picked me up again after we crossed the intersection there. It's so weird."

"What do you mean a beat-up Honda drove past?"

"It drove by when I was parked in front of the school. I got a glimpse of the driver as he passed. But, he didn't look directly at me. The security guys followed it past the school, then it disappeared."

Staring across the darkening yard, Brock said nothing.

Meredith went on, "I'm sure the neighbors wonder what's going on. I know I looked strained when we went over to the Lewis'. They asked if something was wrong, so I told them it had been a hard day."

"Good. Here's what I think we should do. We need to get a hotel room for at least several nights. I'll call a place in a few minutes."

"You really think we can't stay in our own home?"

"Right now, we need to change venues. I think it's for the best."

She looked askance, finally saying, "Okay, but we need a place that'll take dogs."

"Right. Anyway, I've also been advised it may be a good idea for you and Fayth to go visit your folks for a time."

"Go to St. Louis? And leave you here?" She came out of his arms and sat bolt upright. "You're kidding."

"No, I'm not." He gently stroked her back.

She swiveled around to face him. "Who advised you to send us away?"

"Some individuals I'm working with on a related problem."

"Brock, what individuals? What kind of problem? So, you *are* involved in something."

"Yes, in a manner, I am. But I didn't think it would come to this. And now, it seems I've just scratched the surface."

Meredith gripped his hands. "Brock, tell me what you're involved in. Everything. Now."

He studied his wife's face, detecting a familiar flash in her blue eyes.

He nodded and shifted in his chair. "Okay. Here's the deal. There was this patient I saw in the ER one morning about six weeks ago…"

28

Tuesday

Erica Simons walked into her private office late
Tuesday morning and closed the door. She released
a pent-up sigh. Putting out the latest brush fire at the
front desk had left her irritable and hungry. Administrative
days wore her out. She glanced at her vintage wall clock.
Eleven-fifteen…nearly half the day already gone.

She dropped onto her desk chair and glanced at her
screen saver. Negotiating with several account specialists
about slow payments from two large insurance companies
had gobbled up hours of her time. More than one lost
connection hadn't helped. She had expended what little
patience she could muster for rigmarole. Turning to her
back table, she poured herself a cup of three-hour-old
coffee. It tasted strong and burned. She coaxed her EMR to
display the afternoon schedules for the three other
practitioners when her desk phone rang. The front desk
informed her the state board was on hold.

"I'll take the call." Her stomach clenched, and a wave of warmth spread over her. Why was Prescott Hughes calling her? She heard a few clicks before a woman's voice came on the other end.

"Ms. Simons?"

"Yes, speaking," Erica answered, hoping her voice didn't betray her alarm.

"Yes, this is Cheryl, Mr. Hughes' secretary."

"Yes, Cheryl, how may I help you?"

"Well, Mr. Hughes asked me to contact you about a situation."

"What situation is that?"

"He said you'd know."

"Oh? Well, you need to be more specific, please."

"Of course. It concerns the case of a man seen at your clinic, a Mr. Boyd Nettley."

Certain that feigning memory loss would produce no positive results, Erica strained to maintain an air of calm. "Yes, Mr. Nettley was seen at our clinic some time ago."

"Yes, well you may know he is deceased. That may also relate to several similar cases the board is now aware of."

"What similar cases, Cheryl?"

In a nervous tone the secretary continued, "Yes, Mr. Hughes wants you to write a letter explaining Mr. Nettley's case. They also want information about several other cases including an older woman and a teenage boy."

Erica's hunger pangs had transformed into a pit in her stomach. Hoping to end the call so she could either eat something or throw up, she set aside the horrid coffee. In a clipped tone, she managed to say, "I'd be glad to send you the information you're requesting, but I'll need full names, birthdates, and a release of information form for each one of the patients."

"Oh, yes, ma'am. I have a letter here I'll fax you. We're not asking for their medical records, so we don't need a release from the patients. He just wants a written report in your own words. I'll get your fax number when we're done so I can send you Mr. Hughes' request this afternoon."

"All right. When do they want this report or letter from me?"

"By the end of two weeks, ma'am."

Erica lost control of her smooth voice. "Two weeks? That soon?"

"Oh, yes, that's what he said. The board meets again then. And he mentioned they might need to schedule a hearing."

Erica, suddenly dizzy and nauseous, reached for her candy dish and retrieved a left-over Christmas peppermint. She tore off the twisted wrapper. "I see. Well, send those forms along, and I'll look into it. And when may I reach Mr. Hughes, personally?" She popped the mint in her mouth.

"I can tell him you wish to speak with him."

Talking around the hard candy, she said, "Please convey my strong desire to discuss the particulars with him."

"I will, Ms. Simons. What's your fax number there?"

The remainder of the afternoon's activities did not improve Erica's mood nor her physical symptoms. She'd barely been able to eat the potluck lunch brought in by the staff, and opted for Seven-Up and mints the rest of the day. She downed a few Pepcid, too, thinking that might handle the burning reflux which refused to let up.

Toward the end of the day she gave up. There was no sense in scrambling with future staff schedules, looking up any more obscure billing codes, or making other phone calls. Sapped of energy, she felt deflated, spent. As she sat at her desk, she heard the staff chatting, preparing to leave. The back door closed repeatedly, and an eerie stillness crept in.

She rose from her desk and stood in the door of her private office, listening. Was she alone? Nothing but absolute quiet surrounded her. And it was not a comfortable atmosphere. Always arriving after other staff had begun their day, she seldom experienced complete stillness in her own clinic. Then suddenly the silence broke with the annoying ring of the fax line. Was it another announcement or advertisement arriving, or maybe something else from the state board?

She stepped out of her office and embarked on a roam through the clinic, her clinic, unobserved and unobstructed by coworkers. The tall ceilings and windows reminded all who visited that the building—built in 1887—possessed a rich past, first as a small-town hotel before its conversion to various businesses over the decades. Then years of decline took over before good buyers—Erica and Langston—surfaced and snatched it up.

Bringing it up to code, though, as a medical office had been an eye-opener, and produced good, steady employment for various area tradesmen. With patience and enthusiasm, they had accomplished that and managed, in the process, to preserve its vintage charm. The second floor remained only roughed-in as she and Langston discussed various uses for the space, but had yet to put those ideas into action. Proud of their efforts, she loved driving to the small town, turning the corner and admiring the clean limestone structure so representative of that area. Hell, the whole town was constructed of limestone. But hers was the best!

She walked past empty exam rooms, standing ready for the cleaning crew. She noted the vacant, formidable old hotel front desk, papers secured away in locked drawers, screen savers scrolling. She went for the fax machine, retrieving a pharmaceutical rep's dinner invitation lying there and, with purpose, shredded it. Continuing on, she walked to the far end of the office suite, then uneasy, turned and hastened back to her private corner enclave. It suddenly seemed darker outside than expected. She glanced through her office blinds, noting an impressive bank of clouds obscuring the late afternoon sun. A storm front was advancing from the west. She needed to get moving before too long. Dropping onto her desk chair, she swiveled, stared at her computer, and considered what she should do.

Here she was, age forty-two, with one divorce under her belt, living in Topeka, Kansas, the mother of a twenty-one-year-old son away at college. Involved with a fifty-five-year-old twice-married rancher who basically owned the clinic. What were her prospects for the future? It scared her to realize she wasn't sure anymore.

She never forgot she had wanted to go to med school, how she had allowed her parents to dissuade her. 'Medicine was too demanding. She might never marry if she pursued medicine.' Arguments she had heard too often. Eventually, she had thought it would satisfy her to pursue her nurse practitioner education, to finish and secure a good position with a solid family medicine clinic. That had been a worthy goal. She was going to be so fulfilled and happy! So, why *hadn't* she just stayed there? She, at least, wouldn't be mortgaged to the hilt now, despite Langston's cash infusion, and in danger of losing everything. And involved with a man who wanted to run the show, and rule over her.

She knew why. Independence and proving herself had always been important. Bucking the constraints and expectations others put on her. And so, look around, honey…what have you finally achieved? Is it all going to go up in smoke? It just might.

Irritated, she hit restart, and killed the computer screen. No more ruminating. There was nothing more to do there. It was time to leave before the storm hit.

~ ~ ~

Having made her way from Elston to Topeka, and keeping one eye on the clouds in her rearview mirror, she maneuvered her Cadillac Escalade through traffic and past the capitol. Erica felt tempted to just drive to the state board office, instead of home, and barge in on Prescott Hughes. At a stop light, she reconsidered the wisdom of that idea. Over the drone of the NPR broadcaster's voice, she heard her cell ring. She muted the radio and picked up.

"Hello?"

Prescott Hughes said, "Hello, Ms. Simons. I'm returning your call. Sorry it's so late."

"Late is no problem, Mr. Hughes. Look, I'm in traffic. I may have to find a place to pull over."

"Make yourself safe."

Annoyed at his admonition, she began. "So, I received the call and fax from your secretary Cheryl earlier today. Can you explain a little more about that?"

"You mean our request for the report regarding Mr. Nettley and the other patients?"

"Yes, that would be it."

"Sure. We received information, a letter from a concerned party, a physician involved in the Boyd Nettley case at Memorial's ER. He also expressed concern about several other cases which have landed in their ER over the past one to two years. Several patients from your clinic, I believe, and one from another area clinic. We're looking into his complaints, are investigating the details."

"His complaints?"

"Well, concerns."

"Just who is this doctor?"

"I'm not at liberty to say at this time."

"I see." Erica paused, and turned into a Walmart parking lot, pulling into a remote position. She put her car in park and continued, "So, you're asking me to write a letter to the board, describing our interaction with this Mr. Nettley and the other two patients?"

"Three other patients, Ms. Simons."

"Three?"

"Yes, apparently another patient presented to the ER two weeks ago. A young pregnant woman. We're requesting information on that case as well."

Stunned, and now angry, Erica sat silent. What pregnant patient? She had seen no pregnant patients in months.

Hughes went on. "We want you to summarize your clinic nurses' interactions, or assessments, of those four patients and the sequence of their encounters at your clinic. We may wish to review their medical records at some point, as well."

"I see. And what is this about a possible hearing?"

"Yes, well, if after our review we believe we need to interview you in person, we'll notify you of a hearing appointment. You'll have two weeks to contact our office if you need to reschedule. Otherwise, it will go forward."

Erica listened.

"Ms. Simons? Are you still there?"

"Yes, I'm here. Does this have anything to do with the Nettley family retaining a malpractice attorney?"

"Not specifically. We don't get involved in malpractice litigation in the state. Other than bringing our records up to date on a physician or practitioner if they're found negligent in a suit. We don't chase down just-named defendants in medical malpractice suits."

"Then why am I being targeted by the board?"

"First of all, you're not being targeted, and yours is not the only clinic we're looking at."

"So, which other clinics?"

"I'm not at—"

"—liberty to say," she finished his sentence, no longer worrying about her obvious snippy tone.

"Look, Ms. Simons, this type of investigation occurs regularly. Many situations warrant the board taking a look. That's all this is, initially. You get us your report. Please divide the four cases in an organized fashion, and in narrative form summarize what took place at your clinic with regard to each of those four people. We'll look it over and get back to you."

"How long does that usually take?" she asked.

"It varies, but usually not more than sixty days."

"And then you'll tell me if you want a hearing?"

"Yes, that's basically how it goes."

"Okay, Mr. Hughes. I'll get the information to you, but at some point in this process I'd like to know the name of the doctor who's complaining to the board."

"Depending on how this goes, that information may be released. Right now—"

"I know, you're not at liberty to say."

"Yes, Ms. Simons, that is correct. I believe we understand each other. Do you have any other questions right now?"

"No, I do not, Mr. Hughes. I will say, I am not pleased with this situation."

"I wouldn't expect you to be. Have a good evening." He hung up.

The first cloud-to-ground lightning bolt flashed in the distance, just west of Topeka. Erica stared out the windshield, and dialed Langston's cell.

29

Wednesday

Brock swung the rented Ford Taurus around the corner and glanced in his rearview mirror. They were still back there. He was glad for the company but irked this mess had taken such an ominous turn. What was he doing? This was no way to live. Maybe he should back off.

Such thoughts plagued him regularly, of late.

Meredith and Fayth had just departed. After driving him to the body shop and on to the car rental agency, they pulled out, little Fayth's forlorn face plastered against the car window as she waved goodbye. They would be in St. Louis before evening, hopefully safely tucked in at his in-laws'. That is, if the long arm of this situation didn't reach that far. Meredith had fretted about involving her parents and ensuring their safety. Brock tried to reassure her they weren't widening the circle of danger. He hoped he was right.

And, thank God, Wolf's vet had a spot and could tuck him in at her kennel. He wasn't about to leave the dog alone in a hotel room, and trying to shepherd around a border collie would have strained a major effort. Still, he wished for his faithful companion's company.

They had handed over the perturbing package to the authorities Tuesday morning and hadn't heard anything more since then. Now, he needed to get back to the hotel where they'd camped out since Monday night, check out, and get some other things done. Going through his mental checklist, he turned into a Walgreens on the next corner. He needed to call Claire, but he certainly didn't intend to work in another jaunt to Kansas City that day or the next.

~ ~ ~

Even for such a vintage building, it was surprising the space still resembled something from the 1940s. Perhaps the renovators hadn't discovered it yet. Or, the school board wouldn't part with the needed money. Same original terrazzo floors in the halls, smoothed and worn in places. Same long, imposing wood desk in the front office, spanning the width of the room, obstructing anyone's passage to the inner sanctum. Same wooden chairs upon which visitors and young reprobates would wait. No smell of freshly mimeographed papers, though. And no clacking typewriters, now only silent computers emitting the occasional chime of an arriving email.

Brock hadn't been to the principal's office in probably thirty years. At least, he couldn't remember an experience after the time in third grade when he'd decked that bully Bobby Porter for picking on his little brother Alan. They'd both had their comeuppance with the principal over that scene. He remembered his dad giving him the eye over the dinner table that evening, but saying little to add to or relieve his misery. Later, perched on the upstairs landing while his folks did the dishes, he'd heard his father tell his mother how proud he was of Brock for standing up to the Porter kid. He remembered hearing his dad's warm chuckle as he'd said it. That now brought a smile to Brock's face while he sat. The reason for his visit to this principal on this day did not.

Lost in thought, he started when a door to his left suddenly opened, and a woman stepped out. "Dr. Stafford?"

"Yes, ma'am." He stood and gazed at the short, stout, middle-aged woman assessing him. Her hair stylist had apparently not convinced her to go with something new since the eighties, except perhaps the application of red hair dye. Her well-controlled coif framed her face in a neat bouffant style, which impressed him as some sort of soft helmet. She wore a green knit suit, stockings, and low-cut heels which cupped her thick ankles, reminding him of his high school German teacher from twenty years ago.

"I'm Judith Schwartz. Please come in."

Brock, marginalizing his thoughts, followed the principal into her office and took the offered chair in front of her imposing wooden desk. Clutter had been cleared away, or never existed. Though a small teapot and a freshly poured cup sat at her right hand, she offered him nothing to drink. Suddenly aware of his posture, he sat up straight.

"I understand you're here about your daughter, Fayth."

"Yes, I am."

"A concern about her progress in kindergarten?"

"No, not at all. A concern about playground and school security."

Mrs. Schwartz' brows shot up. "What exactly is your concern about security?"

"I'll come right to the point, Ms. Schwartz. Our five-year-old daughter Fayth was approached last week by an unidentified man at the playground fence who asked for her hair bow. She gave it to him, and he or someone, mailed it back to us just yesterday."

Judith Schwartz, having regained a calm expression, said nothing.

Brock went on. "Of course, we're alarmed that anyone would approach our daughter, or any child for that matter, and alarmed that a teacher would not, or did not, note someone hanging around the playground fence. We would like to know whether any of the teachers outside with the children at recess can recall anything from around that time."

The principal paused before answering. "You said that it occurred last week? Do you know which day?" She opened a leather notebook and glanced at a large calendar page.

"Yes, last week, but Fayth can't remember exactly which day of the week. My wife noticed one of her hair bows missing by about Wednesday and thought she might have left it here at school. But according to Fayth, a man spoke to her at the fence and asked for the bow."

"Where was she on the playground?"

"She said in the back corner near the slides."

"Was she with other children?"

"She didn't say."

"Is this the first you're aware of someone approaching your daughter?"

"As far as we know."

"Well, I share your concern that this is unsettling—"

"Not just unsettling. Dangerous, ma'am."

"Yes, of course, it would seem so." She paused and sipped tea. "For starters, I will need to speak with our security man, bring him in on this, and investigate further who may have been outside with the children at recess. Maybe someone did notice something, but didn't report it, which they are supposed to do. I can also speak with the district's security team."

Struggling to avoid an angry tone, Broak said, "We'd like to know you will do more than speak with various people. This type of thing should have been noted by an adult on the scene and reported to you and the police promptly...last week."

The principal leaned forward over her desk, offering him a patronizing smile. "Would your daughter be ready and able to give the police her story? You know, sometimes young children don't understand situations and embellish stories about something they've seen or experienced. When the police or anyone else questions them, the facts change or the whole story tends to fall apart. Or, they say nothing."

His aggravation apparent, he retorted, "I would remind you, we received her bow in the mail yesterday. With a rather cryptic message enclosed."

Judith Schwartz brows drew together, her lips pursed. "A cryptic message?"

"Yes, a four-word message. A threat."

"Oh, dear, well that sounds like there may be more to this story than I realized."

"There is. The police have the bow now. And, they've spoken with Fayth, and us. She did not forget or change her story."

"Well then..." Mrs. Schwartz leaned back in her chair.

"And, I'm told they'll be dropping by to speak with you also. I came today to alert you to the situation and their impending visit."

"Well, thank you, Dr. Stafford. I am very sorry to hear of your daughter's encounter. I wish I had more information about the incident you describe."

Brock stood. She rounded the corner of her desk, attempting a smile. He towered over the shorter woman and extended his hand. They shook. "I wish you did, too." When he reached her door, he turned and informed her, "And Fayth won't be in school for a while. She's leaving today for a safer place."

Not waiting for a response, he turned and left.

30

B rock rounded the corner, glanced at the building, and spotted an angled parking slot along the street. He pulled in, killed the car's engine and sat for a moment, gathering his thoughts. He'd noticed some miles back that he'd lost his tail. With all his tearing around, they may have needed to stop for gas, or developed more interest in food than his adventures. No doubt, they would pick him up somewhere, later. At any rate, they didn't need to be part of the next activity.

He took a few minutes and assessed the building. Quite a place. It looked refreshed, all the old blackened grime blasted from the limestone. New, darkly-framed windows sparkled in the sun. He was familiar with the town and its history, and was impressed that an advanced practice nurse could afford such a place. He wondered if she owned the whole building or leased space. That info could be easily found searching the county tax rolls, if he cared to. Maybe for another time. He climbed out of the Taurus and donned his hat and shades, his mission in mind for the next hour or so.

Once inside, he scanned the large lobby and advanced toward the imposing front desk, obviously a restored antique from the building's days as a hotel. Impressive, to say the least. A mature woman there, who manned a new computer, stood. "May I help you?"

He removed his shades. "Yes, I'd like to see someone about a problem. Do you take walk-ins?"

"Yes, we do. Your name, please."

"Adam Smith."

She studied his face, then glanced at her computer screen. "Let's see, Mr. Smith. Do you have an ID?"

Brock pulled out his wallet, opened it, and assumed a surprised expression. "Oh, gosh, I don't. It's not in here." He rummaged further then glanced up and grinned at the receptionist, who looked concerned. "My son must have been playing with my wallet again."

"Just a moment." She left her desk position and disappeared through an old oak door. Moments later she reappeared, smiled, and informed him, "We can see you, anyway. How do you want to pay for this visit?"

"Cash."

Her brows shot up and she smiled. "Well, okay. You may take a seat."

Brock removed his Stetson, settled into an empty club chair, and glanced around at the other patients, wondering if any of them had frequented the ER recently and might recognize him. The former lobby, now waiting room, was sparsely populated. The few people there sat at odd angles in small clusters of comfortable chairs and an occasional loveseat. The décor was decidedly vintage.

For his part, he was decked out in an untucked, rumpled, plaid flannel shirt, jeans, and well-worn boots still sporting a few chunks of dried mud. His appearance reminded everyone there he had just ridden in off the ranch. He feigned a dry cough, which he made no attempt to conceal.

Several others glanced up, then returned to their cell phones or magazines. The new, wall-mounted TV and Days of Our Lives captivated a few of those assembled. Picking up an out-of-date issue of Field and Stream, he pretended to read, and waited.

After approximately twenty minutes, a young woman in scrub clothes appeared in a doorway and called out his new first name. She guided him down a hall toward an exam room. He loped along behind her. As soon as he settled on an exam room chair, she took his vital signs and asked him to stand on the scale.

"Do you want me to take off my boots?"

"Probably should. How tall are you?"

He smiled. "Six-two in my sock feet." Taking a few moments, he finally pulled off his boots and tossed them aside, knocking off bits of dirt, and climbed onto the scale.

The medical assistant glanced at the small pile of debris he'd created, frowned, then turned her attention to the scale. "Okay." She fiddled with the scale and said, "One-ninety."

"Sounds about right." He stepped off the scale and turned.

"You can sit up there," she instructed him, waving toward the exam table.

"All right." He got up, swung one leg over the exam table edge and perched as instructed.

"Now, what are you being seen for. Your cough?"

"Well, I said that at the front desk, but I'm more worried about some blood I've had."

She looked at him. "Blood? Are you coughing up blood?"

"No." He cleared his throat. "Blood...you know, in my bowels."

"Oh. So, we're not seeing you for your cough?"

"No."

"So, how much blood and how often do you have it?"

"Oh, about every day or so now. It started maybe a month ago. I was busy with calving and didn't bother."

"Do you have a doctor?"

"No. I thought this would be quicker."

"All right. You can get undressed from the waist down and one of the providers will be in."

Brock, not anxious to disrobe, knew he'd have to play along but decided to stay put until the other nurse arrived. He only had a brief wait.

Shortly thereafter, the exam room door opened, and a petite woman entered. "Hi Mr. Smith, I'm Lindy Barnett, the nurse practitioner."

"Hi, I'm Adam."

"Okay, what is your concern today about blood in your stools?"

He cocked his head.

She clarified, "Blood in your bowel movements."

"Oh, yeah. I'm having that about every day or every other day now. Started about a month ago."

"How much blood?"

"I don't really look too close, ma'am, but you know, some on the paper."

"Any in the toilet water?"

"Ma'am, I don't look at that."

"Any pain with this?"

"Not really." He paused, then added, "Well, maybe sometimes."

"And where is this pain?"

"Down there." He waved his left arm around over his lap.

"Have you had this before a month ago? Any problem with hemorrhoids?"

"Don't think so."

"Well, you'll need to get undressed so I can take a look."

"Do I have to?"

"Yes. That's what we usually do. There's a cover sheet."

"Well, all right, if you say so." Brock stood.

Lindy turned her back, busying herself with her computer, tapping in the information she'd gleaned from him so far.

He dropped his jeans and shorts, got back up on the table, and placed the small sheet over his lap. *Here we go. This is going to be interesting.*

She stood and pulled out the lower portion of the table, instructing him to turn on his side. He paused, then dutifully assumed a side position for the exam, noting she hadn't bothered to examine his abdomen first. His long legs hung uncomfortably over the end of the table.

She donned gloves and said, "You'll need to pull up your knees."

Raising his head, he glanced over his shoulder. "What?"

"Please, pull up your knees."

He complied.

After a visual inspection, she gingerly palpated his anal area. "You may have a small skin tag here."

"What's that mean?" he asked.

"Oh, a piece of tissue or skin. It's pretty common. Sometimes it's an old hemorrhoid. But I don't see anything else. Hang on."

Lindy instructed him to relax, and proceeded with a brief rectal exam. He tensed and groaned appropriately for effect, but felt no discomfort, given her small fingers. She quickly removed her hand, and applied her finger to an Hemoccult card. Testing it with developer, she announced, "Negative. You can sit up now."

"What's negative mean?"

"No blood. It means you're going to be okay. It's probably just a small hemorrhoid acting up, or a fissure."

"A what?"

"Possibly a fissure. A small cut or slit in the anal canal. No big deal, but they can hurt, and they bleed sometimes."

"Okay. What can I do to get it to go away? Do I need anything else done?"

"Eat more fiber. And you could take a stool softener."

"What's that?"

"Oh, some Colace or Senokot. You can get them over the counter at any drugstore. Just don't get carried away and overdo it. The directions are on the box."

"Okay. So, I don't need one of those scopes?"

Lindy paused. She looked at the computer chart. "You're young, only thirty-eight. That's not usually required before you're fifty. We can hold off on that for now."

"Good. I was scared there, you know. I think my grandpa died of cancer of his bowels."

"Yeah. Blood always looks scary. You can get dressed." She headed for the door.

Brock stood, holding the sheet in front of him, and asked, "Do I need to come back?"

"Oh, I don't think so. Not unless it keeps up. Just see them at the checkout desk as you leave."

"Okay, thanks."

The door closed behind her.

Tossing aside the cover sheet, Brock smiled, and reached for his boxers. Decent then, he felt around under his shirt, and turned off the tiny recorder attached there.

31

She spotted him sitting alone at the bar, nursing a beer, watching NBA basketball. He had called her that afternoon and briefly informed her of the latest events, finally admitting he would likely land at the local Doubletree. No way he'd end up in a safe house, he could take care of himself. She readjusted her shoulder bag and shifted the heavy leather satchel to her other hand as she walked across the room toward him.

"Come here often?" she asked, moving up behind him. Brock looked surprised when he glanced at the mirror over the bar. She took the barstool beside him and laid the satchel in front of her.

"Well, Claire Randolph, what are you doing here?"

"Trying to find you." Brock sipped beer and didn't respond. "Just a hunch you wouldn't be sitting in your room alone. This is the most likely other place."

"How'd you know I wouldn't be at the ER, working?"

"Remember, you told me you might end up here."

"Oh, yeah, well I guess I'm having trouble keeping track

of things." He frowned as he glanced back at the TV.

"I doubt that. So, tell me how this all happened."

Brock turned toward her and stared for a few moments before answering. "Just as I told you, my wife Meredith opened a package we received in the mail late Monday, and there was one of our daughter's hair bows. With a very short message."

"Oh?"

"Yeah. 'It's not worth it.'"

Claire's brows shot up.

"She hunkered down, afraid as hell. So, off we went to the hotel, stayed there two nights. The police came yesterday, took away the evidence, and we haven't heard anything since. I bundled Meredith and Fayth off today to her parents' in St. Louis, and our dog is camping out at our vet's. And here I am."

"I got the gist of that when you phoned earlier." The bartender approached. Claire ordered a glass of white wine. After he retreated, she added, "Brock, this is terrible—"

"No shit," he interrupted.

"So, give me your thoughts."

"I don't know what to think. Getting your daughter's bow in the mail from some stranger feels like a gut punch. Someone's out there, watching her—talking to her— watching us, knows our home address, lobbing serious threats."

The bartender returned and placed the wine in front of Claire.

"Why don't we take one of those booths?" she suggested, swiveling around on her stool, and bumping Brock's leg with her knee.

He looked down at their legs, and waited for her to get off the stool. She picked up the satchel and her shoulder bag, and wove through the empty tables. He followed suit, carrying her wine and his half-finished beer. She zeroed in on a large corner booth, away from the few other patrons, and slid to the middle. He had to make a choice about appropriate spacing and settled on a sufficient gap between them, without hugging the end of the seat. Claire put the leather satchel to the side.

He changed the subject. "What's in your briefcase?"

"The records I'd asked you to review. I thought you might have some time to go through them while you're not working."

"I was only supposed to have yesterday off this week. But when all that happened, I traded away today for a shift this weekend. So, I don't know how much longer I'll be sitting around here. I may get Wolf out of hock and go back home."

"Wolf?"

"Our border collie," Brock clarified, offering her a fleeting smile.

"Sure." She returned his smile. "Look, I know you have a lot on your mind, and you look tired. But I brought you the copies of the records so you could go through them when you have some time. No real rush, but I'd like to hear back from you in a couple of weeks."

He gazed at her. Her shiny, dark hair hung loose at her shoulders, framing a face enhanced by scant makeup. Her green eyes glowed in the subdued lighting. She'd chucked the business suit for jeans and a silky looking, teal blouse. Several buttons had been left open at the neckline. She had shrugged out of her suede jacket while settling into the booth. Brock was paid to be a good observer, and his observations at that moment were causing a distinct discomfort. Where was this headed? He glanced at her left hand. The large diamond glittered at him. After a few moments, he said, "A couple of weeks, huh? Who knows what'll happen between now and then?"

"True. My timeline is somewhat flexible, but I won't file, of course, until we have your input. I've also got an outside emergency medicine expert witness who's reviewing the records."

"Why don't you just go with him…or her?"

"I could and I will, but you were on the scene, treating the patient. You have firsthand knowledge of the case. You're a fact witness, and the family trusts you."

"How're they doing?"

"Good. I think they're fine. The son John calls me about once a week. They've never been through this process before, so they expect things to happen quicker than they do. I explained to them the order of things, their petition, the defendant's answer, the interrogatories, all that. They're smart, they're catching on."

"Thank God."

"Thank God?"

"Yeah, thank God most people haven't been through this process. It's a bitch."

Claire placed her right hand on his arm. He looked down at her hand and raised his eyes to meet her gaze. He felt a familiar stirring, and diverted his gaze to his beer.

She withdrew her hand and, glancing at the bar, sipped her wine. Ending the uncomfortable silence, she asked, "You mean the lawsuit, or your current situation?"

"Either, actually."

"What do you plan to do about the mysterious package? Have you discussed this with anyone yet?"

"Other than the police, no. Have any suggestions?"

"Well, yes, I do. I think we'll want to let my KBI friend know about this latest development."

"Do you think he'll be that interested?"

"Yes. The local authorities may contact his office, anyway."

Brock looked back down at his nearly empty beer, and asked, "How did you come to be friends with an agent?"

Claire took a sip and tilted her glass back and forth. She smiled. "I've known him a long time. We go way back."

"What's his name again?"

"Fletcher Steele. We met in law school." Registering Brock's surprised look, she continued, "Yes, some agents have law degrees and end up in law enforcement. Not a bad idea, really. Anyway, we dated for a while, two years, actually. Then went our separate ways."

"Oh, and why was that?"

She smiled. "You sure ask a lot of probing questions, Doctor."

"I'm used to asking about personal things, I guess. Goes with the territory."

"Okay. We parted ways when he wanted to get married, and I did not. At least, not at that time. After a while, he met someone else and has been happily married for about twenty years, has two teenage sons. We occasionally cross paths at a meeting or on some case, but we haven't seen each other for several years. We're friends, nothing more."

He glanced at her hand. "And you found someone, too, and got married."

"Yes. I did."

"And what about him? He doesn't mind you taking road trips at night just to deliver some records?"

Claire shifted in her seat. "No, generally he doesn't. Besides, he's out of town right now on a big case in Chicago." She held his gaze, then added, "He's in the litigation division of his firm. It's a demanding career path."

"I bet. So, you don't work for the same firm?"

"No. I didn't want to join the same firm. There was no prohibition against it, but generally it's not a great idea. I prefer a smaller firm, anyway."

"So, tell me about Lewis, Bates, or Dunning? Are they still around?"

"No, all retired or dead. Well, Bates' grand-nephew practices with the firm."

Brock nodded and finished his beer. "Children?"

"Me? No."

He studied her.

Claire explained, "Oh, we tried. I found out I have an infertility problem, so we went through all the tests and a few attempts at in vitro, but after a while we gave it up. It was a big hassle. I'm forty-two and resigned to it, really. I figure it's for the best. I'm devoted to my practice, and realized I wouldn't give a child the time they need. It's okay, really. My nieces and nephews keep me busy enough."

Brock smiled.

"Now see, you have a knack for getting people to spill their guts and tell you everything."

"Everything?"

"Yes, just short of what gyn procedures I put myself through before we called a halt to it."

Brock laughed. "Do you want to give me that history, too?"

"No, thank you, Doctor. Besides, you already know all that." She finished her wine.

"Would you care for another?" he asked, gesturing toward her glass.

"Not if I'm driving back home tonight," she answered, lifting her eyes to meet his.

He paused for a moment, then hailed a waiter. "So, tell me what else you do besides practice law and play with your nieces and nephews."

The waiter came and went.

"Oh, we travel several times a year. Have to mesh our schedules and force ourselves to leave town in order to have any time off. Baird plays golf quite a bit, sometimes with me." She smiled when their waiter returned, and took a sip of her refreshed drink. "I play more tennis than golf. And I ride."

"Ride?"

"Horses, Brock."

"Good. I thought you were going to say cycles."

"Never. Though, I tried once. Scared me to death."

"Good choice."

"So, what about you...other than trudging around the ER, what else do you do?"

"Spend as much time as I can with my family. I like to be outdoors. Hunt, fish. I play a little baseball in the spring and summer. Help my father and brother with our family ranch when I can. And I ride. There's a stable full of horses to tend. We run cattle, breed a little."

"I thought you only had the one brother?"

Brock looked away, then replied, "My youngest brother Tom is five years my junior."

"I see. You hadn't mentioned him when you told me about your other brother." He looked at her again. "Brock, you gave me an overview, but what exactly *did* happen to Alan?"

Several moments passed. He sat back against the booth, and rubbed his hands on his thighs. "Alan was thirteen when he got very ill one day, very quickly. Had a fever and a severe headache. Mom called his doctor, but he was out of town. The office nurse told us to give him some Tylenol, and that the headache would probably get better. She never contacted the doctor covering for our family doc while he was gone. Alan progressively worsened. He was out of it. My folks knew something was seriously wrong. About six hours later, we took him to the ER. He was admitted, tests were run. They started treatment, but before we had all the results, he died. Meningococcus...bacterial meningitis. Tore my parents up. My brother Tom was only eleven. We were both in shock. We were just kids and didn't know what to think."

"Oh, Brock, I *am* sorry. That's so sad."

"Yes, it was. Is. I was sixteen. It's been twenty-two years, and I thought I'd gotten over it. Put it in perspective. But I guess this whole deal with the clinics resurrected something."

"Yes, I can see why."

"And now I've poked around where I probably shouldn't have. Maybe just scratched the surface."

"You may be right there." She paused and sipped her club soda. "Tell me about your own family now."

"I've already mentioned our daughter Fayth, who's five."

"And your wife?"

"Like I said, she's a temporarily-retired ICU nurse. Likes having time with Fayth right now, but she's talked about getting back into active nursing. She organizes volunteers for community health assessments and stays busy. Hates sitting around the house."

"Have any pictures?"

Brock produced his wallet and flipped it open to several small pictures of Meredith and Fayth, and the three of them together. He smiled.

Claire studied the blonde, classic beauty staring back at her. Long straight hair, straight nose, wide-set blue eyes, and a generous smile. Fayth was a darling, blonde five-year-old wearing an impish grin. Brock looked relaxed and tender in the photo. She observed, "They're beautiful. You make a handsome family. I'm sure it was hard sending them away, even for a short while."

Brock looked at her. "Yes, it was, but it's for the best right now." He refolded his wallet and stuck it in his back pocket. "So, you think your friend Steele is interested in all this?"

"Yes, I do. I seriously doubt these two incidents are coincidental, and I'm concerned something else may happen. Aren't you?"

"Damn right, I am. Other than sending off my family, and the dog, and hiding out in a local hotel, there's not much I can do until someone makes another move. Oh, and I have a security tail, and I now drive a tan Ford Taurus."

"Fletcher may have other ideas, or further suggestions."

"Can't wait." Brock glanced at his watch. "Look, it's getting late, and I'm sure you want to get back to KC. I'll try to look over those records in the next week or so. Then, I'll give you a call."

Claire hesitated, then said, "Okay, sounds fine." She turned and unloaded a large manila envelope from her satchel and passed it across the near divide to him. "Here they are."

He picked it up as well as the bar receipt and got to his feet. She scooted to the other end of the large booth, slid off and stood. When she picked up her jacket, he assisted then ushered her toward the door. Only one other patron remained at the bar, observing their egress in the mirror. Once in the lobby, Claire turned to Brock and offered her hand. It felt small and cool enclosed in his warm grip.

"I enjoyed this evening. Thanks for the drinks. I hope both situations become clear and improve soon."

"I do, too. Thanks for making the evening more pleasant than sitting here alone." Their gaze didn't break. Still gripping her hand, he added, "I'll stay in touch. You okay to drive?"

"Sure." She smiled, eased her hand free of his, and turned toward the main entrance.

He watched her move through the automatic doors and disappear. She did not look back.

As he made his way to the bank of elevators, he failed to notice the stranger from the bar slink through the revolving door after her into the dark, cold night.

32

Claire accelerated after she passed through the Turnpike's toll booth on I-70, west of Kansas City. It was just shy of eleven o'clock. She changed to the outside lane and resumed her ruminations concerning the evening just concluded.

She'd taken a chance going to Topeka to track him down. He hadn't seemed put off, but had she been too presumptuous? Would he avoid her now? She absolutely needed him on board for this case. Yes, the attraction was real...and disquieting. And she hadn't been able to ignore or shelve it. Tonight turned out the way it should have, but she'd have stayed if he had invited.

Headlights glared in her rearview mirror. Reaching up to adjust the mirror downward, it surprised her to see a vehicle so close behind. She tapped her brake and slowed a bit. No change. She sped up. They kept pace.

Realizing she was fast approaching a double-trailer semi, she quickly changed lanes to pass, without signaling, and accelerated. The trucker flashed his lights to let her know she could scoot in. Sliding into the right lane again ahead of the huge truck, she checked her mirror, only to see the same car pass the semi and ease in right behind her. The truck driver laid on his horn and flashed his lights at the obnoxious driver. Her new tailing friend apparently didn't care. With his lights glaring in her mirror, she couldn't tell the make or model of the vehicle. Taller than a sedan, it had to be an SUV or pickup. She changed lanes again to pass a slower-moving car. The driver behind her followed suit. *Who on earth is this?*

As the miles sped by, nothing changed. Nearing the exit for southbound I-435 on the west side of Kansas City, she glanced again at her mirror and noted the vehicle hanging back behind another car. Maybe this game was over. Hopefully. She took the exit ramp without signaling, and accelerated again to merge into the inside lane on 435. They took the slow curve, as well, and continued a short distance behind. It was obviously a dark-colored SUV. Not white or gold—she confirmed that as they passed under a tall road light. There was no doubt they were still following. Was she being paranoid or what? Should she just drive to the office where security comes by regularly? Stop and hang out at an all-night QuikTrip, or go home? Keeping one eye on the rearview mirror, she sorted her options. She could call Baird, but what could he do? Plus, she was too busy driving and watching to safely use her phone. They dropped back a few more cars, but never left her.

Fifteen minutes later, she exited south from the interstate onto a well-traveled suburban street, accelerated, and sped through a yellow light. Her tail maneuvered through traffic in an effort to keep up, but was boxed in by several cars and caught the red light. Thank God. She continued south and on impulse turned left at a short cross-connecting street. Hopefully, they would assume she went straight. *But what if they already know where I live?* Such terrifying thoughts would not leave her alone.

It was nearly midnight. Tense, she turned right on a four-lane parkway and sped south toward the next major thoroughfare, meeting the light there as it turned yellow. Not heeding the caution, she quickly turned left and drove east again, numerous streetlights providing generous pools of illumination, whether good or bad she wasn't sure. The few vehicles approaching from the west didn't look familiar, but she doubted she would recognize the car until it was again upon her.

Turning south onto a familiar neighborhood artery, she drove and watched. An SUV suddenly appeared a distance behind her and sped up as she crested a hill. Frantic, she gripped the steering wheel, breathing hard, her heart thumping. She'd have to figure out how to cut through one of the neighborhoods near hers, or just speed home and fly, actually crawl, through the security gate. Both dumb ideas. What other options did she have? She reflexively mashed on the gas.

Moments later, a white cruiser turned out of a side street and slid in behind her, its rotating red and blue light piercing the darkness. Suddenly relieved, she braked and pulled over, expelling a pent-up breath. She pressed a hand to her chest. Thank God! Deliberately slowing her breathing, she lowered her side window as the officer approached. A black Mercedes SUV crawled past and, not signaling, turned at the next residential corner. She strained to see around the rotund officer and read the rear plate, but it lacked any illumination.

"Evenin', ma'am. In a hurry to get somewhere? May I see some identification?"

Spent, she slumped in her seat. "Of course, Officer."

33

Thursday

The ER doors slid open and two EMTs maneuvered a gurney through the door. A stocky, ruddy-appearing man lay supine on the cart, eyes closed—the patient they had received a call about twenty minutes earlier. The triage nurse directed them to an open bay. Brock watched as they quickly pulled the cart into place and stamped on the brake pedals. Another nurse joined in, and a flurry of activity ensued. Brock closed out the chart open before him, and strode across the ER. The wall clock read 8:45 p.m.

It was nearly a quarter past eleven when he next sat down, parked his fresh coffee, and pulled out his cell. Things had quieted down, for the time being. The man brought in by paramedics had gone to the cardiac cath lab over an hour ago, and several other patients had been discharged. Another ER doctor and an extender attended to a couple of kids with minor conditions. They were covered. Brock wanted to talk with Meredith before the night slipped away.

"Hi there," she answered.

"Hi. How're you both doing?"

"Fine, I guess. Fayth's finally down."

"It's kind of late for her."

"Well, some nights it's hard to get her to bed. She misses her daddy tucking her in."

"I miss her, too."

"Overall, she's settled in fairly well. Mom and Dad are great with her." Meredith paused, then said, "They're worried, Brock. I had to tell them something about what was going on."

"I know. I just don't think we should burden them with many details for now."

"I told them Fayth and I needed to get away because of a case you were involved in that had taken an unusual turn. Things are a little tense right now, but under control. Out of an abundance of caution, you'd been advised to send us away for awhile. They seemed skeptical at first, but accepted my explanation without too much argument."

"Good. I think that's about all you should say for now."

"You sound tired. *Are* things under control?"

"I am tired. Didn't sleep too well last night. Tossed and turned 'til about two. And I was busy all day before I came in." He paused, then added, "I hope things *are* coming under control. Late this afternoon, the detective called. Didn't say much, no news from the schoolyard yet. So, I think I'll go back home tomorrow, after I get off in the morning, and pick up Wolf at the vet's."

"I wish they had some leads."

"Me, too. Maybe they know more than they're telling us."

"Do you feel safe staying at the house?"

"Yeah."

"Well, at least Wolf will be happy to be home chasing squirrels again. And don't forget to use the alarm." She paused, then changed subjects, "Are you busy tonight?"

"Yeah, we were at first. Things have quieted down a bit. I'm sure it'll pick up later."

"Brock, you sound distracted. You're worried about all this."

"Yeah, and other things. The clinics. The malpractice lawyer I told you about has a friend with the KBI. She's discussed this with him."

"The KBI? Have they spoken with you?"

"No." A silence stretched between them. "I especially miss you."

"Oh, Brock...how long do you think we need to stay here?"

"Honestly, Meredith, I don't know. I think we should give it a few more days, maybe a week, just in case something else happens."

"Oh, please don't say that. Do you really think you should go back home so soon?"

"I'll see. I'll let you know tomorrow."

The intercom crackled with static noise, then the clerk's voice informed Brock, "Dr. Stafford, you have a call on line four."

"Thanks." He waited until the intercom clicked off. "Listen, I need to get this other call. Try to get some sleep, hon. I'll talk with you in the morning."

"Sure. Hope it stays quiet. Love you."

"Yeah, love you, too. Bye."

He clicked off his cell and reached for the desk phone, wondering if he'd hear a woman's voice. His heart beat hard. "Dr. Stafford here."

Instead, a gruff male voice announced, "Dr. Stafford, this is Sheriff Delaney from Saline County."

"Yes?"

"We've got a situation out here tonight at your family's

ranch."

Brock's stomach flipped. Delaney was silent. "Situation?"

"There's been a fire."

"A fire?" Brock stood and stared out the lounge window into the huge ER bay.

"Haven't been able to locate anyone. Don't your folks live out here?"

"Yes, but they're gone right now. And my younger brother's in Colorado. How big a fire? Is it out?" The doctors' lounge suddenly felt hot and cramped.

"The fire department's working on that. Looks like it started at the house. The winds we're havin' spread it to the barn before we got here."

"My God…" Brock's heart pounded.

"There's a good bit of damage between the house and the barn."

"Anything else burned?"

"There's one small outbuilding that's partly burned."

"And the horses? We stable six horses there." Brock sank into the nearest chair.

Sheriff Delaney cleared his throat and paused before answering. "We know of one horse that's been lost."

Six hours later, and just before dawn, Brock sat hunched over at the main desk and pounded computer keys. Nadine was elsewhere, searching for first pastries. He saw his colleague Dr. Anne Goodwin approach from the lounge.

"Glad to see you here."

"Long night?" she asked.

"You could say."

"What do we have?" She glanced around at the sparsely populated patient rooms.

Brock proceeded to give her a rundown on the few patients remaining from the night shift. When finished, he informed her, "And, I had a family emergency."

She frowned. "Oh?"

"Yeah. Someone tried to burn down my family's ranch outside Salina."

"My God. You're sure it was intentional?"

"It sure looks like it, but they're just starting to investigate. We lost at least one horse."

"How terrible."

"Yeah, pretty bad. I need to drive out there today, soon as I leave here."

"Are you sure you want to do that? You look like you could use some sleep."

"Don't have a choice. My family's out of town and can't get here 'til the weekend. So, it's me."

"You're back on tonight?" she asked.

"I was, but Bennett's covering tonight. I'll need to pay him back Sunday night. I'm already working another shift Saturday."

"Can you handle all this and work the weekend? Maybe you need some time off."

"We'll see. I hope not. When the folks get back and my brother arrives, I should be able to work my scheduled shifts."

"Okay, but keep us informed. Several of us could probably trade around and cover you. Sounds like a complicated situation to me."

"And to me."

He signed off the computer terminal, rubbed the back of his neck, stood, and walked to the doctors' lounge. Grabbing his jacket, he waved back at Nadine, who'd arrived from the cafeteria with a loaded tray. She frowned as he headed for the staff door empty-handed. She'd found his favorites, fresh and warm.

When he broke through the door, the early morning sun hit his face. Squinting, he punched in Meredith's cell number.

34

Friday

Small groups of men walked back and forth staring at the ground, hunched over, picking up various bits of debris, and scribbling notes. Some took pictures.

Brock stood a few steps from his car and surveyed the scene. The damp spring air and brisk wind made it feel colder than it was. Clouds raced across the sky and partially obscured the sun. He flipped up his jacket collar, and stuck his bare hands in his pockets. His scrubs provided practically no warmth. The bacon egg McMuffin and coffee he'd grabbed two hours ago were fading. The pit in his stomach gnawed. The stench of charred wood and animal flesh swirling on the breeze nauseated him. He needed to get moving and change from his downwind position. But, where to start?

He walked toward the house. The remains of the tall, proud-appearing log home stood, the roof partially burned off, sections of log walls missing on the back and the west sides. The garage, now gutted, appeared as a charred cavern, its blackened doors lay haphazardly, one inside, the other forward onto the drive. The wood and stone fence adjacent to the garage now crumbled into a rubble pile at one end. Several blue spruce and other tall cottonwoods surrounding the house appeared untouched, their newly budded branches waving in the wind. Brock avoided looking directly at the barn. A uniformed man broke away from a small group and approached him.

"Dr. Stafford?"

"I am."

"Sheriff Ralph Delaney." The two men shook. Delaney regarded Brock for a moment, then said, "I'm real sorry about this. We've been here since last night, and I'd like to ask you a few questions."

"Can we go around first?"

"Sure." The sheriff and Brock walked closer to the house. "Did you just get off?"

"At seven."

Delaney studied Brock. "Probably worn out."

"Pretty much."

"Sorry you have to go through this. Let's start over here." They took a few more steps, then Delaney paused and gestured toward the house. "As you can see this end of the house sustained the most damage. The garage is pretty much gone."

Brock stared at the burned out remains of a late model Ford F-350 sitting on one side of the decimated garage.

"Looks like you all have a basement here," Delaney observed.

"We do."

"There's goin' to be some water down there. Anything valuable stored there?"

"Yeah. There's a rec room, some furniture and game tables. One bedroom and a bath. We also have an unfinished storage area and a safe room—cement walls, steel door—with a couple of file cabinets and a gun case. I'm not sure what else."

"That may be okay. We're still working on the inside." He paused. "Looks like the fire started back there," he said, pointing to the kitchen portion of the house adjacent to and behind the garage. "Anyone been there yesterday cookin'?"

"Not that I know of. The woman who cleans doesn't come on Wednesdays."

Delaney seemed satisfied with Brock's answer, scribbled a few notes, and continued. "Then the wind carried it across that part of the yard, to that there small outbuilding, then to the roof of the barn." Pointing to the outbuilding, he added, "Found a small John Deere and some tools in there."

"Yeah." Brock, full of dread, stared at the small building, wishing he could avoid the next stop.

"Let's go over to the barn."

Without answering, Brock steeled himself and trod across the damp ground with the sheriff. The charred barn loomed larger as they approached. Brock's stomach churned the closer they got. How fast could he run if he suddenly were overcome and hurled? Not to worry…there was plenty of wet grass and mud all around.

Before they reached the destroyed barn door, a man emerged and came toward them, his face strained, his black Stetson pulled low. As he neared, he pushed up his hat brim and stuck out his hand. A neighbor from the adjacent ranch.

"Charley Ross, down the road."

Brock knew of the man who'd bought the nearby ranch after he had left for college, but wouldn't say they were well-acquainted. Courtesy demanded he restate his name. "Brock Stafford, George and Liz's son."

"It's a damn shame," the man said, shaking his head.

"Sure is," Brock agreed.

The neighbor stared at Brock for a few minutes, then informed him, "We got the rest of the horses out last night.

Me and my hand. They're at my place. Had some extra room. Don't you worry about them." He paused. "Except the one."

"Which one?'

"The palomino. They took him away before dawn."

The ground shifted. His head swimming, his eyes stinging, Brock averted his gaze and bent over at the waist, staring at the ground.

The neighbor laid a steadying hand on Brock's back. No one spoke. Fairly certain then that he wouldn't retch, he regained his composure and after a few minutes straightened. Ross' hand shifted to his shoulder, where he delivered a firm, supportive squeeze.

His voice husky, Brock informed them, "Nicholas, my dead brother's horse. Beautiful animal. Had him a long time."

The three men stood silent.

~ ~ ~

Delaney and Brock sat in the cruiser, out of the wind, drinking lukewarm coffee from a thermos. They'd covered the basics about Brock and his contact information, his parents' contact information, the insurance carrier for the ranch, when the remaining family would likely arrive, and so forth.

Brock had spoken with his father several times since the first call in the middle of the night. Furious didn't adequately describe George Stafford's deteriorating mood. With each subsequent conversation, he'd asked more probing questions. Brock knew he wasn't going to escape explaining the obvious connection to the crazy cases he'd been chasing. Obvious, in his mind. The prospect of revealing all to his dad ushered in a range of emotions, but surprisingly, welcome relief accompanied those feelings. But when would that fateful discussion occur? He also knew, once calm, his father would prove supportive and do anything to protect him, Meredith and Fayth, and the ranch. They all just had to stomach the initial shock and get through this.

Having completed the tour and the basics, it was time for more detailed questions. Delaney began.

"Ever had anything like this happen before?"

"Never."

"No maintenance issues, wiring, so forth? No recent work done?"

Brock stared at Delaney. "Not that I know. Dad keeps the place up."

The sheriff nodded, and shifted gears. "Any idea of someone who may have wanted to do this?"

"Specifically, no."

"All right. Your dad have any problem with suppliers or disgruntled hands?"

"Not that I know of."

"Any money issues?"

"Look, you'll need to ask him some of these questions." Brock stared at Delaney. "But, the answer is no."

"Any bad blood between him and someone…any enemies?"

"Doubt it, but you'll have to ask him."

"Anyone after you or your brother?"

Brock stared out the side window of the cruiser.

"Anyone?"

Brock didn't answer.

"Son, you got somethin' you're holdin' back?"

Hesitating, Brock looked back at the sheriff. Delaney stared back in silence.

"Yeah, okay. I don't know if it's related, but there may be something." He huffed out a breath. "Ever since I got involved in this case in the ER almost two months ago, things have happened."

"Things, huh? Why don't you tell me exactly what *has*

happened?"

Brock nodded, then launched into a selective review of events since meeting the now deceased Boyd Nettley, his widow Karen, and their grown son John.

35

"Burned down?"

"Yeah, Claire, that's what happened."

"I'm shocked. I don't know what to say."

"There's not much to say."

"Only one horse was lost?"

"Yeah, but that's one too many. He was my brother's horse. Beautiful palomino stallion. He was twenty-three."

"Alan's?"

"Yeah." Silence stretched between them.

"What are you doing right now?"

"Driving back to Topeka. Can't stay out here."

"Of course. You sound tired, Brock."

"Now why would that be?" After a beat, he unleashed. "I've been up all night in the ER, drove one hundred twenty miles out to the ranch after I got off at seven. It is now one-thirty. I've got another hundred miles to go to get back home. I've been chugging cold coffee with the sheriff, haven't eaten anything since Mickey D's early this morning. I'm tired—no, let me rephrase that—I'm exhausted, hungry, and in need of a good shower. Other than that, I'm just fine."

"You sound mad. Is there anything I can do to help?"

Brock gunned the tan Taurus and passed a semi on I-70. "You're right, counselor. I am damn mad." He hung up.

~ ~ ~

Claire dropped her cell phone on her desk and stared at it. She glanced at the wall clock and her appointment book. Another client was due at two. Agitated, she stood and paced the confines of her office. This Nettley case and the concentric circles of damage had spun totally out of control. Control she had to regain. Her secretary rapped and cracked open her door. When she saw Claire's expression, she stood in place and said nothing.

"Yes, what is it?" Claire snapped.

"Ms. Randolph, ma'am, your two o'clock cancelled. He rescheduled for next week. Anything I can get you?"

"No! Any other calls, just take a message. Right now, I need some time." After a brief pause, her secretary turned to leave. Quickly regrouping, Claire added, "And thank you, I'm sorry I snapped."

"No problem. If Mr. Randolph calls, should I put him through?"

"Yes, of course, put him through."

The secretary silently eased the door shut. Claire heard the door plaque slide over as she sank into her chair. Yes, she was 'in conference', with herself. Glancing at her framed photos, she picked up her cell.

~ ~ ~

Fletcher Steele cradled the receiver on his shoulder and fiddled with his ink pen. He'd been on the phone three times already about this situation and was tired of talking.

He glanced at his watch, and finally broke in.

"Seems that way."

Claire added, "I don't know how else you would look at it. He's on his way back now from the ranch, obviously worn out, and angrier than I've ever seen him."

"How many times have you seen him?" Hearing no answer, he observed, "I wasn't aware you knew him that well. Thought you'd only interviewed him once for the Nettley case."

"You've got a good mind for details—"

"That's what they pay me for."

"I've spoken with him on several other occasions, and dropped off medical records for him to review."

"Okay, look, I got a call from Delaney in Saline County this afternoon around one-thirty. Since you first told me about the brake failure, I've heard from the highway patrol. When I called the Topeka police earlier this week about that, they relayed the information about the squirrely package and note."

"Good."

"May only be good, Claire, considering that they're in possession of it and working to scratch up leads. Someone out there watching and approaching a little five-year-old girl is very concerning and should be considered a threat."

"Of course."

"What do you want me to do, Claire?"

"Keep him safe, Fletcher."

"I got that. But it seems absurd to me that a doctor involved in some malpractice suit is a target. Maybe you need to tell me more about the circumstances surrounding that suit. Who goes after someone like that?"

"Someone who has something to lose. At first blush, it looked like a fairly standard, straight forward malpractice issue, except that it involves an independent nurse practitioner clinic. That's a new twist. Now, it seems it's morphed into something bigger. When he told me about the brake failure, I was concerned he'd struck a nerve. At the time, you said you wondered if he was making some important people uncomfortable."

"Yes, I did."

"So…"

"So, what important people would he agitate?"

"Perhaps people at those two clinics I told you about. Maybe someone with a financial interest in those clinics. Perhaps a creditor. Maybe a politician here or there. You could probably tell me more than I'm telling you, Fletcher."

Ignoring her prodding, he said, "I understand he's gone to a hotel. We know his wife and kid went to St. Louis to her folks'. We've been following him, and them, around. Short of carrying him off to a safe house, I'm—"

"He won't go anywhere like that."

"How do you know?"

"He told me Wednesday night when we spoke. Said he was probably going to get his dog from the vet and go back home either yesterday or today." She went on, "There's something else, Fletcher. I'm convinced I was followed home late Wednesday night. Out on I-70 coming back from Topeka and all along 435 on the south end until I exited. I think they might have picked me up again as I got closer to home. Thank goodness, I finally got stopped by the police."

"Did you tell the cop about it?"

"I started to, then the car turned into a neighborhood. I wasn't sure it was the same car and couldn't see the plates as they passed by—no light. The officer's considerable girth got in the way. I felt stupid saying anything."

"What make and model of car?"

"A black Mercedes SUV, I believe."

"And, what were you doing in Topeka late Wednesday night? Did you call Baird?"

"I took records to Dr. Stafford. He's in Chicago."

"Stafford?"

"No, Baird."

"I see." Steele paused. "So, you just went on home, ticket in hand, and hunkered down?"

"Basically, yes. I felt like a fool. Who would drive a notable black Mercedes SUV to tail someone? I set the alarm and stayed up and read. I didn't sleep very well."

"I bet you didn't. Why didn't you call me yesterday about this?"

"I don't know. When the sun came up, it seemed silly. I didn't want to bother you."

As Claire finished her explanation, Steele heard a light rap on his office door. A younger man stuck his face around the door jamb and Fletcher motioned him inside.

"Listen, I'll take a look at a few more things here and see what we can do. We'll contact Stafford and get his story. Don't tell him you've talked with me today. In fact, you need to stay focused on the suit, Claire, and watch your back. Let me know right away if you're followed again or harassed. I'll be in touch."

"You don't need to lecture me."

"Apparently, I do, and I like to lecture you, Counselor."

"Shut up, Steele," she retorted and hung up.

Fletcher looked up and saw the younger agent smirking. "Feels good to tell off a lawyer every once in a while."

"Sounds like it, sir."

"Tell you what, Grayson, we need to get this guy, this doctor, and make sure he stays safe. He's touched a nerve somewhere, and I think we're close to finding out who he's pissed off."

"Yes, sir. Where is he now?"

"On his way back to town, from out by Salina. His family's ranch. It caught fire or someone torched it last night...and ended up killing a horse."

"Sounds like there's more to the story," Grayson observed.

"There is. We'll have a briefing at five. Meanwhile, we

keep an eye on him. He's probably picking up his dog at his vet's and heading back to his house. Tomorrow he's on duty in the ER again. We'll pay him a visit there toward evening. I hope we don't have to manhandle him to get him out of there."

"Yes, sir."

Grayson turned away, slipped through the door. Fletcher waited a moment then picked up the phone. He didn't like what Claire had just told him. Not at all.

36

Saturday

He awoke to the smell of bacon. Savoring the aroma, he rolled over and felt for his wife's pillow. Obviously, she was up and around, busy with breakfast. Something they rarely shared these days. He pulled the pillow close and caught a whiff of her scent. He wanted her back in bed, but he couldn't deny the bacon calling. Soon, two teenagers languishing in the lower level would catch the aroma, emerge, and the day would get underway. Baseball practice was at ten.

Fletcher hadn't discussed any details of the case with her yet. And he wouldn't, couldn't. She knew he was preoccupied with a long, drawn-out investigation, and that it might involve field work, which she wished he would give up. She had made that very clear. Hence, the full, home-cooked breakfast, laden with bacon. He pushed the pillow around and shielded his eyes from the daylight seeping in around their shutters.

But sleep would not return. His mind was awake, harassing him with career thoughts. Thoughts which intruded more frequently of late. He'd been with the Bureau seventeen years and had ascended the ranks swiftly to the position of Director. He had never missed practicing the law. But after ten years at the helm, he, at times, missed the excitement of being out with the younger agents, in the hunt, there for the 'takedown.' It brought relief from dealing with the bureaucracy, and renewed his vigor for pursuing law and order.

This case, though, had been a mixed blessing from the start. He had immediately been fascinated with the possible players involved and soon had realized it would require finesse to maintain control, prevent leaks, and guide the younger agents through the morass of potential political fallout. Rather than off-loading the investigation onto a junior agent to manage, he'd maintained a controlling hand in the dealings from the start and now looked forward to bringing it to conclusion. They had been close for a long while, watching and waiting for something to clench their case. When Dr. Brock Stafford arrived on the scene, crusading about the independent clinics…well, what a gift!

Fletcher's stomach growled. It wouldn't be denied. He quit fighting his thoughts, rolled over and out of bed, and headed into the bathroom. Maybe his phone would stay quiet for the whole day.

Pam was in the kitchen, her back to him, when he padded in. He sidled up and wound his arms around her waist.

"Bacon, huh?" He planted a kiss on the back of her neck. "I'm surprised there's any left. The boys must not be up yet."

"Won't be long, I'm sure." She turned around and regarded his T-shirt and baggy flannels he insisted on wearing around the house. She hugged his neck. "What's your day look like?"

He grabbed a piece of bacon and jammed it into his mouth. "Thought I'd take the guys to their practice and help out a little."

"You don't have to go in today?"

"Not unless I'm called."

"So, we get you for a whole weekend?"

"Can't guarantee that."

She turned back to her counter and poured two cups of strong coffee, then cocked her head toward the adjoining outdoor deck.

They adjusted the table umbrella and settled in for a quiet beginning to their morning. It was cool and calm. The sun filtered through the tall trees framing their backyard. He felt her gaze settle on him.

"You're preoccupied, I can tell."

He smiled. "Can't get away with anything, can I?" He took a sip of steaming coffee and surveyed the back lawn. "So, it's past time for the pre-emergent. Maybe later I'll get the guys to help with that."

"Dream on." Pam paused then asked, "So, come clean. Are you going out on a case soon?"

"How'd you figure?"

"You're restless, distracted, excited."

"Guess I'm not a very good actor, huh?"

"Not around here, you're not."

"Guess I need to brush up on my skills." He smiled, "Okay, yeah, we have a situation heating up and it's likely I'll go out some time this next week."

She frowned. "Can't you send someone else?"

"Not on this one, Pam. We've been over this before. I know you don't like the field work, but I need to control what happens in this case, or we may lose the footing we've gained. And, we're dealing with individuals who are major players in several important arenas. Plus, honey, I love getting back out there. It makes the work real, makes me feel real."

"Real…and safe, huh? Look, Fletch, I don't want to end up a widow with two sons to finish raising. And I want you around so we can grow old together, then you can regale me with all those tall tales you've stored up."

He closed his hand over hers and smiled. "I like the sound of that, too." He leaned over and planted a kiss on her mouth. "But, I doubt anyone on this one will greet us brandishing weapons. It's more likely they and their lawyers will bore us to death with their uppity attitudes." He didn't add that, meantime, he'd prepared for various outcomes and had placed beefed-up security over her and the boys. Just in case.

The back door slid open, and their eldest stuck his head out and squinted. "Any more bacon?"

His mother turned and answered, "That was a whole package. But yes, there's more if you must."

Fletcher and Pam exchanged smiles and stood, picked up their cups, and headed for the back door.

"Better get inside and survey the destruction," Fletcher advised.

37

Nadine looked up from her computer and regarded the two gentlemen staring at her. The security guard Chuck, wearing a stern expression, stood with them.

"Yes, may I help you?" she inquired.

Chuck answered, "Nadine, they asked for Dr. Stafford."

She eyed the men suspiciously. Who wears business suits to the ER on a Saturday night? The harsh, overhead fluorescents cast unappealing shadows on their faces, accentuating their chiseled features, especially their noses. "He's in with a patient. And, who are y'all?"

They removed their shades and flashed their credentials. "We'll wait, ma'am." Neither offered a smile.

Nadine's eyes widened. "Well now, is there a place y'all'd like to wait?"

They stared back at her, surveying her name tag. "Some place close by, Nadine. Where would you suggest?" Todd Grayson asked.

She dismissively gestured toward chairs near the triage

area, hoping they'd get discouraged by noisy kids and leave. Chuck smiled at her and showed them to the seats. They both glanced around at the various patients and assorted families awaiting triage.

The gathered cohort stared back at them. What an exciting place the ER had turned out to be!

Nadine fiddled with her computer and peered over the desk, willing Brock to return to her territory before the men caught sight of him.

No such luck.

~ ~ ~

Brock emerged from a patient room, spoke with a nurse entering, and made his way to the desk. The gentleman rose and silently approached. They obviously knew who to look for.

"Dr. Stafford?"

Brock turned and observed the two fit-appearing, suited men. He stuck out his hand. Grayson looked at his hand, apparently decided to oblige, and the two shook. Brock smiled. "What can I do for you?"

"We need to speak with you."

"Okay, can this wait?" He glanced at the wall clock over Nadine's head, which informed him it was 6:30 p.m., and added, "I finish at seven."

"We know."

Nadine broke in. "And the family in five asked to speak with you, Doctor."

"Thanks, Nadine." Grayson looked at Nadine, then turned back to Brock, who said, "I need to finish with a few more patients before my relief comes in. Is this an urgency?"

"We'll explain," Grayson advised him.

"Look, would you mind waiting in the break room and I'll meet you there as soon as the other doctor gets here."

Grayson nodded. "Would Chuck mind showing us there?"

Nadine offered, "I will." She rose, pulled herself up to all of her five feet two inches, and motioned them to follow her. "And you can help yourself to the coffee if you want. I just made fresh."

Twenty minutes later, after giving report, Brock fetched the agents from the staff break room and ushered them into the doctors' lounge and closed the door. He made sure the intercom was turned off.

"Now, what is this about?"

Grayson and his partner flashed their cred packs at Brock. "Dr. Stafford, you will need to come with us."

Brock stood, gripping a surgical towel, and stared at their credentials. "Come with you where?"

"You'll know soon enough."

"I'm not going anywhere 'til you tell me why you've come here and where we're going."

"Director Fletcher Steele asked us to escort you to a meeting with him."

"I don't believe I've made his acquaintance."

"Perhaps not."

"So, why don't you two just tell me where to meet him and I'll drive myself there."

"No, sir."

"What?"

"Dr. Stafford, we've been instructed by Director Steele to bring you safely to him. We are instructed to withhold the location from you or anyone else."

"Oh, for God's sake! This is ridiculous." Brock snapped the edge of a chair with the towel, punctuating his statements.

"Sir, Doctor, you need to come with us."

"I need to go home and let my dog out."

"We'll get someone to do that."

"Incredible." Brock wadded up the surgical towel and threw it at the recliner. No one flinched. "Answer one question for me...does this have to do with my family's ranch burning down? Or my failed brakes? Or the stupid package we received?"

Heat suffused his face and his carotids pulsed. He took deep breaths and struggled to control his reaction.

Grayson answered, "I can't say."

"Damn!" Brock stared at the floor, then looked up and met their steady gaze. "Do I have a choice?" No answer. The three men stood silent for several long moments. "Okay, I'll go with you...under protest. You can phone ahead and tell him that." He grabbed his jacket from a nearby hook and stomped toward the door.

As the trio left the lounge, Brock turned to Grayson. "So, do you want to leave through the back door or out the front, past security and all those people?"

"That's up to you, Doctor."

Brock hesitated, then strode across the ER toward the main entrance, flanked by the two suited agents, their eyes obscured by shades.

Everyone present stared. Indeed, the ER proved more entertaining that evening than anything else they might have done.

38

Dusk had settled in when the SUV pulled into the driveway of a nondescript, mid-century brick ranch on a quiet cul-de-sac. Streetlights flickered on here and there. Other similar homes lined the avenue, displaying neat lawns and trimmed shrubbery. Various makes and models of vehicles stood parked in a few driveways. He noticed no children playing outside or running the street. One agent rounded the vehicle and opened Brock's rear door. The other agent climbed out of the driver's side and scanned the scene. Two dogs barked in the distance.

"So here we are, huh?" Brock asked. No answer from either agent. They walked up the front walk. "Don't forget about my dog. Wolf's his name."

"No, sir."

One agent stood behind Brock while the other rang the bell, knocked twice, and the door opened. Someone had to have been right behind it, waiting and watching, Brock concluded.

"This way," Grayson instructed.

Brock obeyed and followed him down a short entry hall—bedroom wing to the right—which opened into an updated, minimally furnished living room. All new matching contemporary pieces, the grouping resembled a furniture showroom ensemble. Several sleek lamps provided subdued lighting. Wood blinds, slanted down, covered the large picture window. He assumed there was a fenced back yard beyond the window, probably crawling with other fully armed men pretending to tend the lawn and landscape. A tall man pushed up from a leather club chair and walked toward Brock. They locked eyes.

"Dr. Stafford? I'm Fletcher Steele, Director with the KBI here in Topeka."

Brock extended his hand. "Finally, we meet."

"Yes. I hope we didn't cause you too much disruption in the ER this evening."

"Some, but they'll recover."

"Why don't you sit down? Are you hungry? Would you like something to drink?" Fletcher reclaimed his chair and gestured to another opposite him across a sleek, glass coffee table.

"Food would be nice sometime this evening. Right now, I'd like some water." Brock watched as Grayson disappeared around the corner, presumably into the kitchen. He looked at Steele. "So, what brings me here?"

Steele didn't answer right away, taking measure of the man. "I believe you likely know why we want to speak with you."

"I can imagine all sorts of things."

Steele smiled. "All right. I believe you're acquainted with Claire Randolph, an attorney with whom you have some dealings in a malpractice case. And for matters peripherally related to that case, we have reason to believe you have stirred the pot, so to speak, and may be in some danger."

Brock said nothing.

Fletcher continued, "We're aware you sent your wife and young daughter to St. Louis to her parents' and that you housed yourself at the local Doubletree Wednesday and Thursday nights—now checked out—and prior to that at the Residence Inn with your family before they departed. We're aware you kenneled your dog at your vet's, and have removed him to your home again just yesterday."

Brock stared at Steele who added, "We're aware of the brake incident ten days ago. We also know of the package and letter you received six days after that. And now the ranch fire two nights ago. Obviously, we think there's a connection."

Grayson returned with a tall glass of ice water, handed it to Brock, and retreated to a corner of the room. Brock gulped water and looked back at Steele.

"You know a lot. Tell me if my family is safe…in St. Louis."

"They are."

"You're keeping an eye on them?"

"We are."

"Would someone go let my dog Wolf out…and back in? And make sure he has some food and water for the night?"

Steele motioned to Grayson who approached. "Your keys, Doctor?"

"Don't you already have a copy?"

Steele shot him a retiring look, then smiled and extended his hand. Brock reached into his jacket pocket and plopped the keys into Steele's hand. Grayson said something in Steele's ear, who nodded, and the younger agent left. Brock shrugged out of his jacket then, draping it over the chair arm.

The two men eyed each other. Steele broke the silence. "I understand you're upset. And angry. I would be. This is not the type of situation anyone wants to get involved in."

His conversational tone helped, and Brock leaned back in his chair. "Damned right, it's not."

Fletcher smiled and continued, "I'm married, have been for twenty years. Have two sons, both teenagers. And a dog. Wolf is a ..."

"Border collie," Brock supplied.

Fletcher nodded. "Good dog, I'm sure." He paused. "At any rate, we believe these incidents are not coincidental and that you've raised some hackles."

"Raised whose hackles?"

"We have some promising leads. Nothing I can specifically discuss at this time. But, needless to say, we want you and your family secured and safe."

"So, they need to stay in St. Louis for now."

"Yes, they should." After a moment, he prodded Brock, "Why don't you start from the beginning and give me the Cliff Notes version of how this all began. I may ask a few questions as we go."

Brock said nothing for a few moments. He figured Fletcher Steele already knew the full story, but decided to oblige the man. If he wanted to spend his evening listening to a repeat account, he would humor him. Then maybe he could go home. "Why not?"

"Early in the morning of March first, about seven weeks ago, Boyd and Karen Nettley came to the Memorial ER. He had a perforated right colon from an undiagnosed colon cancer, and was very sick. We ended up shipping him to KU Medical Center, at the family's request, and the story goes on from there."

Brock glanced at his watch. "Can I go now?"

"Just a few more minutes," Fletcher answered.

They'd spent the better part of an hour and a half going over the events of the past month and a half. Brock heard a racket near the front door. He turned just as Wolf bounded through the front hall. He ran up to Brock, squatted at his feet, and laid his head on Brock's thigh. Surprised, he petted his dog and turned back to Steele.

"What's going on?"

"Your dog will be safer here. That is, unless you want to take him back to the vet."

"Here?"

"Yes, with you."

"Now, wait a minute, I'm not staying here."

"It's wise if you do so," a familiar voice advised him.

Not having heard anyone else approach, Brock turned, surprised to see Claire Randolph standing in the doorway of the living room. "What the hell?"

"Agent Steele, can you explain to this hard-headed doctor why he needs to calm down and just cooperate with us?"

Brock frowned, Wolf barked, and Fletcher smiled. "I've been trying, Ms. Randolph."

Claire walked toward the couch and sat. "Good evening, Dr. Stafford. I trust your day has gone well."

Brock stared at her. "Passable, up to this point."

"Good. I'm glad you two have met and had a chance to chat this evening." She paused and exchanged looks with Steele. "You've probably gathered this is a safe house. I would advise you to stay here until this whole situation gets under control. Director Steele is working on accomplishing just that. You and I need to submit to his guidance and his protection." Her green eyes flashed when she smiled at him. Wolf walked over and licked her hand. "Your dog, at least, knows who to listen to."

Brock shook his head. "Do I have a choice?"

"Not really. If you're as smart as you appear to be, you'll agree. It's too hard to chase you and your dog around," Claire said.

"For how long?"

Steele answered, "Can't give you a definite time frame, yet. Soon, I hope, we'll break this whole thing open."

"Days? Weeks?"

Steele shrugged. "Probably days."

"I can't just lie around here. I have to cover my ER shifts."

"We know that. And we'll accompany you to work."

"Now, hold on...I can't have a couple of guys hanging around the ER while I—"

"Doctor, we have a plan all worked out," Steele informed him.

Claire smiled.

39

Sunday

From his vantage point at the main desk Brock had an unobstructed view of the wall clock. He'd only been there an hour, but it seemed much longer. The rest of the night lay ahead. The doors slid open, a gurney rolled in, and he reflexively looked up. The EMTs didn't appear too stressed.

A triage nurse greeted them and began her assessment. Brock turned away and resumed charting. The ER tech Russ Jackson checked equipment in one of the open patient cubicles. In an adjacent room, Dr. Clancy was evaluating a young boy with a probable acute appendix. All seemed calm that Sunday evening, given the setting.

Twenty minutes later, Brock settled into the doctor's lounge—recliner extended, coddling a fresh cup of coffee—when Russ stuck his head in the door and informed him, "The guy in room two is ready."

"How's it going so far? Enjoying yourself?"

"Feels like old times," Russ answered.

"How long were you a paramedic?"

"Five years."

Brock nodded. "So you've jumped from the frying pan into the fire."

"You might say," Agent Jackson replied.

"Well, let's go see what this is all about." Brock set down his coffee and climbed out of the recliner.

As they approached the patient's bed, the man raised his head and studied the two of them. Brock glanced at the monitor, taking note of the patient's pulse and blood pressure tracing. "I'm Dr. Stafford, and this is Russ Jackson, an EMT. How're you tonight, Ken? Ken Jones, right?"

"Yeah. Been better. My stomach hurts."

"About what time did this start?"

"Oh, maybe around ten. When I got up this morning."

"Show me where it hurts now."

Ken pointed to his mid abdomen and winced.

"Did it start there or some other part of your abdomen?"

"Pretty much same place."

"Any nausea, vomiting?"

"Not really. Don't feel like eating much."

"When was the last time you ate or drank anything?"

"Last night I ate some pizza."

"Any drinking, any alcohol last night?"

"Few beers."

"How many's a few?"

"Oh, you know, not all of a six-pack."

"Okay. Anything else?"

"Couple shots."

"Of...?"

"Tequila."

Maintaining a bland expression, Brock asked, "Okay if I examine you?"

"Sure, Doc, that's why I'm here."

Stafford efficiently examined Ken under Russ' watchful eye. Instructing Ken to turn from side to side, Brock examined his back and undertook a thorough rectal exam before Jones had much chance to protest.

"Hey, what the…?"

Flipped on his back again, the patient stared hard at Brock during the remainder of the exam, occasionally glancing at Jackson, who busied himself rearranging equipment and supplies in the adjacent bedside cabinet.

"Did you have to do that?"

Brock slung his stethoscope around his neck, looked at Ken Jones, and said, "Yes." While he mashed around on Jones' abdomen, he asked, "So, does this hurt?"

Ken cocked his head off the pillow, purposely tensed his abdominal wall, and squeezed his eyes shut. "Yeah, Doc, right there." Letting out a huff, he dropped his head back onto the pillow, rolled his eyes upward.

Brock assumed a concerned expression and turned to Russ. "Let's get the usual lab, and would you ask the clerk to order a CT, with and without?"

"Sure, Dr. Stafford." Russ whipped out a tourniquet and multiple vacutainer tubes from a drawer.

Ken's eyes, now recovered, widened. He raised his head. "What're you gonna do?"

"Get some blood samples."

"You gonna stick me, and do all that?"

"Yes. It's routine. We don't know what might be causing your pain until we check a few things," Brock informed him and resumed mashing Ken's belly. He distracted the patient with conversation about the previous night's activities, any female contact he'd had, and current sports news. Ken had no trouble keeping up his end of the conversation.

As Russ turned toward the cart to draw blood, he took a hard step and kicked the cart's wheel. "Oh, sorry."

Ken didn't flinch. Brock smiled and turned to leave the

enclosure.

"You gonna come back, Doc?" Ken asked.

"Sure. We'll talk when you're back from CT."

"Can I have something to drink?"

"No."

The wall clock informed Brock it was nearing ten. Several other patients had come and gone in the meantime, and a few newcomers awaited triage. Taking a few moments, he had just procured fresh coffee—determined to enjoy at least part of it—when the intercom crackled, and the clerk announced that Ken Jones had returned from CT.

Jackson stuck his head in the door. "He's back."

"I know. His lab's all normal, including his liver functions. No pancreatitis. Maybe we should get a cathed urine."

Jackson smiled. "Just say when."

Brock lowered the footrest and scooted out of the recliner. At a desk computer they viewed Ken's abdominal CT images together, both contrast and non-contrast images. Brock observed, "Looks normal to me. We'll see what radiology says."

"What do you think?"

"I think he's not in as bad a shape as he puts on. No peritoneal signs. Probably just too much fun last night. Let's go see him and you can get that cathed specimen."

"Hey, thanks."

Brock and Russ approached the patient, who lay supine on the cart and appeared to be sleeping. Brock purposely bumped the cart and Ken's eyes popped open. No complaint, no wincing.

"Mr. Jones, how're you doing?" He didn't wait for an answer. "I've looked at your CT and your lab work. Nothing jumps out at us, but I'd like a surgeon to have a look."

"What?" Jones asked.

"It's a good idea to get their opinion with a case of belly pain, especially if it's not obvious what the cause is. In most ERs, it's routine to ask surgery to check out abdominal cases." Brock went on, "And we'll get a urine specimen to check for blood or infection."

"I don't think I can pee."

"No problem. Jackson here will help you with that."

Ken cocked his head. Brock retreated, asking Russ to get a quick urethral swab also, and the EMT-turned-KBI agent took over.

The patient sat up. "What the hell you gonna do?"

Jackson reassured him, "You just relax and lay back there."

Leaning over the central desk, Brock informed Clancy, "I need you to see the guy in two. Complaining of abdominal pain since this morning. All his studies look normal. We're getting a UA and swab right now. He's not too happy. See what you think of his exam. Not too impressive."

"Fever? Vomiting?"

"No."

"Any blood?"

"Nada."

"Okay. Be with him in a minute. They just called me from the OR on that kid with the appendix."

Meanwhile, raised voices emanated from room two. Brock nodded and headed back to the lounge.

Fifteen minutes later, Clancy stuck his head in the lounge door. "I don't think he's got anything. I looked at the CT, and it's negative. The report just came back, and they agreed. But I wouldn't mind if you want to keep him in overnight on obs. We can see him again in the morning."

"Might not be a bad idea," Brock said.

"I'm off to the OR. Let me know if you get anything else."

"Sure will."

Brock reclined and dialed Meredith's number.

One hour later, Jackson opened the lounge door and a shaft of light hit Brock's eyes. He blinked and squinted, at first not realizing he'd dozed off after talking with Meredith.

It had taken some time to explain to her where he was staying and why. She was obviously alarmed. He'd tried to sound reassuring, adding that Wolf was safe and sound with him. In the heat of their exchange, she'd said she didn't care about Wolf, then apologized over and over for her harsh words. They'd discussed the ranch fire again, and the loss of the palomino. He told her his parents had arrived home and were staying with their closest neighbor. Meredith broke down and cried. Weary and overwrought, Brock tried to soothe her, but found himself close to losing it. She finally admitted the separation, intrigue, and uncertainty were getting to her. Her parents were asking more questions than she cared to answer. Fayth was happy to be there with Grandma and Grandpa, and their two cats, but kept asking when they could go home. She missed school and her daddy. Feeling lousy after the long conversation, Brock had closed his eyes for just a few minutes of rest.

"Got the UA and swab back. Normal, no blood. Swab negative for Chlamydia. He's gotten over it and is quiet."

"Okay, I'm coming."

"Oh, by the way, we ran his name and demographics. Bogus name. No such residential address exists. It amounts to a spot on the Walmart parking lot. His stated phone number's not active. And the car he drove here has expired Reno County plates. Probably lifted."

"Interesting. Anything else?"

"Yeah, for being in such pain, he's been real talkative and nosy. Asking a lot of questions about you."

"Oh? What kind of questions?"

"First, about how long you've been here, how long you've been a doctor. Where you trained. If you always work nights. Then, he asked whether you had a wife, or any kids. If you lived here in town."

Brock frowned and pried himself from the recliner. Could this be the guy from the school playground? Brock suppressed a momentary urge to run to his car for his piece. "Then, Agent Jackson, let's go pay Mr. Ken Jones another visit."

Stafford and Jackson exchanged glances as they stepped into room two. Brock stared hard at the man, then plastered on his professional face. Jones lay semi-reclined, watching TV. His color appeared good, and the monitor showed normal cardiac rhythm, pulse, temperature, and blood pressure readings. Brock strolled over, ran a cardiac tracing, and pretended to study the normal pattern.

He then looked directly at Jones, informing him, "Mr. Jones, you look more comfortable now. In fact, everything we've ordered tonight has come back normal."

"That's good, right? The CT and all the blood?"

"Right. The CT, the swab, the urine, the blood work, including liver tests and labs for pancreatitis. All normal."

"So, I can go? When are you gonna give me somethin' for the pain?"

Brock went on, "But sometimes these situations evolve, and things change several hours later." The patient gripped the handrails. "After Dr. Clancy saw you, he suggested, and I agree, that you need to stay in overnight for observation. Surgery would like to see you again in the morning, and make sure you're doing okay before you're discharged."

Ken Jones bolted upright, hands still glued to the side rails. "No way!"

Brock stood silent. Russ moved closer to the cart.

"I'm not stayin'. I just need somethin' for the pain and I'm outta here."

"I'm not able to discharge you with pain medication

tonight. If you stay in overnight, the nurses can monitor your pain and let the doctor on duty know if it gets worse."

"You mean I wasted time and money on tests and you're not givin' me anything?" His hands now unglued, he glared at Brock.

Russ stiffened, leaned in.

"That's correct, Mr. Jones. I'm advising you to stay for observation."

The patient slammed his right fist on the cart rail and yelled, "I'm not stayin' in this fuckin' place all night!" Shaking his sore hand, he thrashed around, trying to lower the side rails.

Brock stepped back and drolly observed, "Your abdominal pain must be improved. But maybe we should give your hand a look."

"No way. I'm outta here!"

Brock went on, "The nurses will give you a form to sign. It states I advised you to stay, and that you're leaving against medical advice."

"I'm not signing some stupid form!" With that Ken vaulted off the end of the cart, popping off various monitor leads in the process, grabbed his shirt, jeans, and shoes and, still sporting the patient gown, headed for the ER door, his bare back and red bikini briefs clearly visible under the flapping gown.

"Hey, just a minute, buddy," Chuck barked. "Leave that gown here!"

Brock and Russ stood outside the cubicle and watched the scene unfold. "Let him keep the gown," Brock advised the security guard. "He may need it tonight." Smiling, he turned to the agent. "Got all the information you need?"

"I think we did, Dr. Stafford. And we've got someone to stay on his tail."

"Good."

As he turned, Brock noticed something on the floor, partially obscured by the gurney wheel. He bent down, rolled the cart aside, and recognized it to be a small brown envelope. He picked it up, and turning it over, was shocked to see his name and Capital Memorial ER typed in an unusual font across the front. No completed address, no return address, and no postage.

He turned to Jackson. "Look at this. He dropped it as he jumped off the cart."

The agent cast an eye on the envelope then Brock. "I'd better examine that first."

"Why don't we both take a look?" Brock strode toward the doctor's lounge, Jackson following.

When they'd sequestered themselves inside, both donning surgical gloves and masks, agent Jackson carefully opened the envelope and frowned. Apparently assured it contained no questionable substance, he pulled down his mask, and handed it to Brock. "Maybe you should take a look first."

Brock glanced inside, pulled out three photos and a small note stuck on top. In the same weird font, it read, 'haven't gotten the message yet?' He looked at Jackson, handed him the terse note, and gazed at the pictures. He dropped onto the recliner, holding the photos face down on his chest.

Jackson said, "Care to share?"

"Not really. But, hell, why not?" He held the three pictures up to Jackson, who grasped them, studied them for only a moment then stared at Brock.

"So, I'm sure you can explain these."

"Of course. And it's no big deal. But there are people who might think otherwise." Brock eased them from Jackson's hands.

"All right. You know we need to give those to Steele."

"At some point, maybe." Brock leveled a look at the agent. "I'm not losing control of these pictures." His tone was sufficiently firm to silence any counter Jackson might offer. Though Brock was certain the agent hadn't given up yet. Jackson sank into a nearby chair and Brock added, "Look, I'll do what's absolutely necessary, but I don't want these wandering around." After a long pause, he said, "That's the malpractice attorney Claire Randolph I'm working with on the Nettley case. When I was staying at the Doubletree last Wednesday, she came by to give me his medical records. Apparently, someone had an eye on us and snapped those pictures. She left and I headed to the elevator. Nothing happened...at all."

Wearing a worried look, Jackson said, "Yeah, Steele knows Claire Randolph very well. Look, I believe you, man."

As if thinking out loud, Brock added, "There were only a few people around when we left, but I can't remember anyone who stood out. And I'm pretty sure I didn't see that Ken Jones fella from tonight."

"Obviously, this is intended to intimidate. I don't have a choice. I need to let Steele know." Jackson got up and walked toward the door. Brock closed his eyes, his hands clasped over his chest, protecting the envelope. He heard the door click shut.

Agent Jackson pulled out his cell. Walking toward the back of the ER, he dialed Fletcher Steele's number.

40

Monday

Stafford signed off the computer, gave Nadine a nod, and headed to the doctors' lounge. It was 7:30 a.m. Inside, Agent Russ Jackson waited. Brock closed the door and picked up the desk phone, a call he had put off making until last night's scene forced his hand.

Dr. Frank Bennett, chief of ER services, answered, "Bennett here."

"Hi, Frank, Brock Stafford."

"Aren't you gone already?"

"On my way out. Listen, we had a situation here last night I need to discuss with you." He glanced at Jackson.

"Shoot," Bennett answered.

"About eight last night a forty-year-old man came in under an alias with bogus belly pain. Workup was entirely negative. Had Clancy see him to put his blessing on it. After about three hours, I informed him of his results and advised him to stay overnight. He pitched a fit and left without signing out AMA."

"So, what's so unusual about that?"

"He gave a nonexistent address, and non-working phone number. And he asked too many questions about me."

"Questions about you?"

"Yeah. Look, you know about the ranch fire. Some other things happened before that, and various officials are involved. Investigators."

"Stafford, what are you trying to say?"

"Hell, Bennett, I'm saying I think the guy came in to find me and check out the scene. Here, there's someone I want you to talk to." Brock handed the receiver to Jackson and sat down.

"Agent Russ Jackson here."

"Agent who? Where's Stafford?"

"He's here, Dr. Bennett. I'm with the KBI. We're working with Dr. Stafford on a case. I accompanied him to the ER last night for his shift due to concerns we have about his safety."

"Safety?" roared Bennett.

Jackson held the receiver away from his ear. "Yes, safety, sir."

"What's this all about, Agent, what did you say your name was?"

"Jackson, sir. I can't give you details right now, but Dr. Stafford is right. The man who came in last night was not a real patient and may pose a danger to the doctor and his family."

"Give me Stafford back. And who's in charge of you?"

"Director Fletcher Steele, sir, at the KBI office here in Topeka."

"I'll be calling him today. Now give me Stafford."

Jackson smiled and handed the receiver to Brock.

"Now look, Brock, if people are traipsing in the ER, looking for you, and it's posing a danger, then it's a danger to our staff and patients. We can't have that. You need to take a leave. How long does the KBI think this will go on?"

"They're not sure, probably not too long."

"Are Meredith and your daughter here?"

"No, they're in St. Louis at her folks'."

"Good God. How'd you get yourself into such a mess?"

"It has to do with that case I told you about some weeks ago. I can explain later. Do you have enough staff to cover my shifts?"

"We'll have to make it work. Where are you staying?"

"I can't say."

"Oh, for God's sake!" Bennett coughed, then continued, "Look, just keep yourself and your family safe, and keep me informed. I hope for your sake this gets resolved quickly. They letting you use your cell?"

"For now."

"Call me when you know how long you'll be off."

"I will. Sorry this has screwed up the schedule."

"We'll work it out." Bennett hung up.

Brock turned to Russ Jackson. "Let's get out of here."

41

On patrol, Wolf tore around the fenced backyard, barking. Quarrelsome squirrels scattered and scurried up large oak trees. One agent threw a frisbee and, distracted, the border collie obliged, leaping in the air to fetch it. Satisfied his dog was entertained and exercised, Brock slanted the blinds down at the sound of a woman's voice.

"Do you want any of these eggs, Dr. Stafford?"

"Sure, sounds good," he called back, as he made his way to the kitchen.

"And there're some waffles if you'd like." The older woman gestured toward a toaster on the counter.

"I can eat anything you've got. I didn't know you all had to cook for your prisoners."

Agent Margot Blake smiled. "We're trained in a lot of skills."

"I'm sure," he said, straddling a bar stool. "Jackson fit right in last night at the ER." He picked up the poured coffee. "Thanks."

"He's good, and it comes in handy having someone who's been an EMT."

"I bet. You on for the whole day?"

"Yeah. I'm here 'til six. Grayson will be around, too. Steele may come by later."

"When will I get up to speed on what's actually happening?"

"When you have a need to know." She smiled and put a full plate in front of him.

"Smells good. When do I get some bacon?"

"When I care to cook some. Maybe tomorrow."

Tired of cable news and Sports Center, Brock muted the sound, stretched out on the couch, and closed his eyes. He'd spent some of that Monday morning after breakfast reviewing the medical records Claire delivered to him the previous week. It hadn't taken long. Boyd Nettley's stay at KU Medical Center only encompassed three days. Not a surprise, the records from Comprehensive Care weren't included. Wolf stretched out as well on the floor, his back pressed against the sofa.

Then the left-behind photographs came to mind. He knew Jackson had notified Steele, but nothing more had been said, nor had Steele contacted him yet. At some point they would talk. He suspected it wouldn't be long before he was paid a visit. Unless Steele's gang had staged the whole thing for show, and to let him know they were in charge. It never hurts to maintain some degree of skepticism, does it? He tried to limit such thoughts.

Not realizing he'd dozed, Brock roused when he heard noise in the front hall. Wolf's tags rattled. Recognizing the voice then, Brock remained in place. Someone walked into the living room, paused, and dropped into one of the club chairs. He opened his eyes. Wolf walked over and smelled her shoe.

"I hope I didn't wake you."

"You did, but it's okay. I don't want to sleep all day, since I don't work again tonight. Don't work again 'til whenever." He knew he should discuss the whole photo thing with her, but he sure wasn't going to blurt it out right then. First, he'd see what she had come for.

Claire smiled. "I see you've been looking at the records."

"Yeah. I've gone through them. Made a few notes in the margins. Hope you don't mind."

"Not at all. Those are your copies."

He studied her. She wore tailored slacks, a silk blouse and a soft pastel pink jacket. Her hair was pulled back loosely at her neck. She didn't look like a day in court was planned.

"Don't you have other work to do? In Kansas City?"

"Are you saying you want me to leave?"

Brock sat up and looked at her. "No, just seems this one case is dominating most of your time."

"It is, but I'm an organized, efficient person. Besides, you're an important witness, and you find yourself in an unusual position. So do I, actually."

Unusual was an understatement. "That's for sure." He ran his hands through his hair. "Sorry about how I look. I need to get out of these dirty scrubs and clean up."

"You look fine, Brock." She smiled. "Did they bring you some of your things?"

He felt warm and his heart thumped. "Yeah, and I think they're going to take me by the house later to pick up more clothes."

"That's good."

"So, what do we need to discuss? You must've had some reason to come by here, other than checking on your witness-in-hiding."

"Okay. Let's get down to business then and discuss the case. After reviewing the records, do you think we have a solid position?"

"Yes. Nothing in those records I've seen so far has changed my mind. What about the other clinic's records?"

"I got a call from their counsel last Friday. Those records are on their way. The expert we've retained has also given me his preliminary feedback. So far, you're both in agreement. After you see the remaining chart, we'll have a more thorough discussion again."

"So, it's moving forward."

"Yes. It's begun."

"How're the Nettleys?"

"They're holding up. John said his mother's exhausted but is staying determined. It's hit her how much there is to do with the ranch, and how long this legal process may take. And of course, she's grieving and misses Boyd terribly."

"Do they know about any of the other stuff?"

"No. I thought it wise not to tell them about this situation. The less they know the better. Still, Fletcher's concerned and watching over them. I suggested to John that Karen stay with him and his wife in town. We don't want her out there on the ranch by herself. They'd already convinced her to do so, several weeks ago."

"Right. Has anyone else been in touch with you?" Brock asked. Maybe that would prompt her to bring up the photo issue, if she'd also received copies.

"No. Kemp Anderson, the CEF lawyer, is laying low. Hasn't called back again."

"That may not be good. Do you think they have anything to do with this situation?"

"I've wondered, but I don't have any evidence of direct involvement...yet." She stood, then joined him on the couch. Wolf escorted her and plopped down at Brock's feet. "I did a bit of digging and found this material on the organization. I thought you might want to look it over." She scooted closer and Wolf sat up, on alert. Brock didn't move. "There's information here that details how contributions flowed from CEF to at least two state representatives and one senator. Not necessarily illegal, though that's not been determined yet. Depending on the types of contributions, the activity may or may not be considered ethical. We're examining the money trail." Claire leaned toward Brock, extending the documents to him. Wolf let out a low growl.

"Hey, boy, it's okay," Brock said, rubbing the dog's head. The border collie whined and jumped onto his lap. "I'll take a look. How did you get hold of this?" Brock asked, maneuvering his arms around Wolf and accepting the papers she offered.

Claire scooted back, giving the dog ample space. "Through the CEF site to begin with, and two campaign watchdog sites which monitor and detail how the money flows. And through another source."

"Another source?"

"Yes."

"But you won't say which source."

Claire redirected, "Did Prescott Hughes at the board ever call you back?"

"No, not after their early April meeting. My letter may not have been added to that agenda. They'll have another meeting the first part of May. I've thought about checking in with him again to make sure he hasn't conveniently lost it. Or, I might call one of the other board members, one of the physicians."

"Sounds reasonable." Claire eyed Wolf, who covered Brock's lap and stared at her. She gave him a faint smile. The dog cocked his ears and watched her.

"You remember the other patient I told you about from the Northridge clinic, the one who came in coughing up blood?" Not waiting for her answer, Brock continued, "Anyway, I looked up the cancer center he and his wife went to. The one the Northridge clinic recommended, and for which they picked up the Spencer's tab. Turns out, the

Center for Diagnosis & Treatment-Ca is part of a chain of six clinics scattered around the country. It's a franchised operation, started about four years ago. But interestingly, the larger corporation is also developing subspecialty clinics for heart disease, lung disease, chronic renal conditions, and neurologic disorders."

"That sounds like quite an undertaking."

"No kidding. It's a very big project. They're not all up and running, and are not advertising much yet, but the concept is in place, and it looks like they're close to recruiting physicians for the other specialties."

"Do you think they're in cahoots with CEF, or just ended up on the receiving end of Northridge's generosity?"

"I don't know, but I suspect they're oblivious to CEF and their involvement, maybe purposely so, and are just glad someone—anyone—is paying in full for Lamar Spencer's care."

"That's certainly interesting information to keep in mind as we go." She paused, then pivoted. "Is your Jeep still in the shop?"

"Yeah, it's at the body shop. Should be done later this week or early next week. I'll garage it and keep driving the Ford or change to another rental if these guys insist."

"Any problems at your house?"

"Not that I've heard. They're keeping an eye on it. And the ranch." He added, "My folks got back late Saturday, are still stunned and angry. They've gotten Nicholas taken care of, and the other horses are fine. The neighbor's been a big help. In fact, they're staying with him, to be closer to the ranch." He paused, then added, "I want to get together with them this week and bring them up to speed."

"You probably should talk with Fletcher first. He'll be sensitive about how much you tell them."

Brock, his temper flaring, gazed at Claire. "Someone torched my family's ranch, killing a horse, possibly intending to hurt anyone who might have been there. Not to mention the other two *incidents*. My parents have a right to know how we became a target. It's not fair to keep them in the dark."

"I'm not saying keep them in the dark. Just watch how much detail you reveal. At least, run it by Fletcher before you see them. And he'll want someone to go with you. You know they can't come here."

Brock cast a glance around the room. Here he sat in a safe house. How the hell did that happen? Never, in all his wildest imaginings, did he ever picture himself in such a situation. What exactly had he become, anyway...a concerned doctor on a mission, a whistleblower, a nosy snoop who should have minded his own business, practiced medicine and kept his big mouth shut? This is the stuff books and movies were made of—surreal, for sure. He looked at her when she spoke.

"And your family's doing well in St. Louis?"

"Yeah, they're fine. Fayth's keeping Grandma and Grandpa busy. They miss being home, though."

Claire touched Brock's arm. "I'm sure." Wolf whined and laid a paw on her arm. She withdrew her hand. "He's being very protective today."

A smile softened Brock's face. "He's a smart dog. He knows when things are out of kilter."

From the kitchen, Blake called out, "Anyone in there hungry for lunch?"

"Sure, any time," Brock answered. So, they'd just have to wait until after lunch to have the reveal.

"Well, I should be going."

"You might as well eat before you leave. Margot's a great cook. I have something else I want to tell you, anyway. But it'll keep. It's not suitable table talk." He grinned, eased Wolf from his lap, and stood.

Claire rose. "Well, okay. You've intrigued me."

Wolf barked, danced in a circle, and led them to the small dining room.

"That's incredible. You were very brave. I can't imagine you were pleased to have such an exam."

He smiled. "No, but hey, anything for the cause, right?"

After finishing lunch, they had retired to the living room again for the story about Brock's spur-of-the-moment visit to Comprehensive Care Clinic the previous Wednesday. He decided he'd spring the other topic on her after the less tense and more amusing subject of his clinic adventure.

He described how they'd taken him without proper identification, were glad for his one hundred twenty-five-dollar cash payment, and shuttled him out the door without expressing much concern or suggesting further workup. He outlined the essentials of his purported history they failed to elicit, the disregarded family history, and the abbreviated exam performed, which ignored his chest and abdomen completely. Claire perked up when he admitted he'd worn a small recorder.

"So, where is that recording?"

"I have it locked up at home, in my study." Just a minor fib. The copy he had made was locked in his safe room, the original secured in a new safe deposit box at the bank. He'd keep that for later.

"I'd like a copy of that, please."

"Sure. Maybe when they take me by I can get it. Unless someone has broken in and run off with it."

"Perish the thought."

"Do you think it'll help?"

"I don't know, but it can't hurt, either, with our negotiations during the proceedings. Things like that have a tendency to alter the defense's attitude and recollection of the truth. Of course, your clinic visit there and Boyd Nettley's case have only indirect bearing on each other."

"But, it may show they haven't changed their nonchalant attitude or approach to rectal bleeding. And abdominal complaints. Same practitioner, and she didn't ask me about belly symptoms, and she didn't touch my abdomen. She did not do a thorough job, Claire."

"I hear you, Brock. Get me that recording, and I'll make a copy of it."

"I want to keep the original."

"Sure."

"Can I submit the clinic charge for reimbursement as an expense for the case?"

She smiled. "Get me a copy of your receipt. I'll consider it, although I didn't ask you to do that. You just went off on your own on that one."

"But you're glad I did."

She smiled and stood. "Well, I should be going."

He nodded and patted Wolf's head. Getting to his feet, he said, "Here're the records," and handed her the oversized envelopes.

"There'll be more where those came from."

He glanced around. In a low voice he said, "Look, there's something else we need to discuss before you leave. Please, sit back down."

Claire looked surprised at his tone. She perched on the edge of the couch. "What is it, Brock?"

He sat down and picked up a smaller brown envelope from the coffee table where the records had lain. He handed it to her. "Take a look at that."

She carefully opened the flap and glanced inside. Tension tightened her face. She gingerly slid the photos—two of them in the bar, one of them standing in front of the elevators—and the enclosed note. It registered after only a few seconds. She looked at him. "Where did these come from?"

"Technically, from the floor of the ER." He studied her worried face. "A bogus patient who came in last night dropped them as he fled. No idea where he got them. But I'm absolutely sure I didn't see him at the Doubletree last Wednesday night."

"You may not have seen him, but it doesn't mean he wasn't there somewhere, perhaps not in the bar."

She had him there. Good 'ol Ken Jones could have been hanging around anywhere. Admittedly, he hadn't been exactly scanning the scene while engaged with Claire. "You're probably right. At any rate, Agent Jackson who accompanied me to work last night notified Steele, but I haven't heard from him yet." After a pause, he said, "So, you haven't received a set of these?"

"No, not yet." She glanced around, then focused on Brock. "Look, we can't let this pressure us. We both know nothing happened."

"Convincing everyone else of that could be a challenge."

"Of course. You haven't told your wife yet, have you?"

"Oh, no…no, no."

"You'll need to, and soon. Nip this in the bud. Let's see what Fletcher has to say, before we overreact. I'm sure he'll talk with you soon. Give it a little more time, then you bring it up, if he doesn't. We have to keep him in the loop, Brock. And secure those, don't share them with anyone else, for now."

"You can be sure of that."

"Well, I should be going," she said, getting to her feet. He stood as well and stretched his lower back.

"You need some rest."

"Yeah, I may take a nap. That's sounding more appealing since lunch."

As they ambled toward the front door, escorted by Wolf, Claire said, "You know this thing will work out. I trust Steele. And I think we should stay calm. I'll let you know if I receive a similar package."

Margot Blake appeared and joined them in the front hall. With a quick nod, she stepped outside. They watched as she fetched the empty trash container from the curb and glanced up and down the street. As she approached the garage door, she again gave them a curt nod. Claire emerged and made her way down the walk.

"Stay in touch," Brock called after her.

"Of course."

He watched as she got into her Lexus SUV, rolled down the street, and disappeared around the nearest corner.

A nap sounded really good, but restful sleep would likely elude him.

Who would make the next move?

42

Tuesday

Brock stood on the wide porch that afternoon, wind whipping around the corners of the solid stone and cedar ranch house. He rang the bell and glanced back at the two men in the navy SUV. Claire had been right. If he was going to come at all, he had to bring them along for the ride. They kept an eye on him, not playing with their phones, yet. He heard heavy footsteps approach and the lock turn. The door swung open, and Charley Ross' tall, lanky frame filled the opening. He glanced over Brock's shoulder at the vehicle, didn't smile as he looked back at Brock, and cocked his head as his signal to enter. Brock stepped over the threshold and the two men shook hands.

"They've been waitin' for you to come," Charley said.

"I know. I appreciate you letting them stay, Charley. You're a good neighbor."

"Well, we have to take care of each other out here." A

tight smile accompanied his comment.

Brock nodded crisply, his neck muscles tense and tender.

"Brock, is that you?" his mother called out from an interior room.

"Yeah, it's me."

Within moments George and Elizabeth Stafford emerged, stepped into the front hall, and studied their son. How much older they looked. Their faces wore new lines etched by the strain of the past five days. Suddenly, Brock realized he hadn't seen his folks in over a month. Just about the time he reviewed the first batch of patients' records and first heard from Claire Randolph. How far things had slid since then. He attempted a smile and stuck out his hand, which his father grabbed and held firmly.

"Glad you're here," George said.

"Me, too." Brock stepped forward and the two men embraced. Elizabeth laid a hand on his arm. He turned and hugged his mother, tighter than he'd intended.

"Well, I've got to get out and check that fencing. Be back later," Ross announced. "You all take the family room. I made some coffee. If you want anything else, just help yourselves." Charley headed straight through the large, beamed room, his adjacent kitchen, and out the back door, leaving them alone in the suddenly quiet house.

Strained, they fussed over pouring coffee and finally settled themselves in the great room. George and Liz on the huge leather couch, and Brock across from them in a generous chair, they sipped and regarded each other.

Brock began, "You both look tired."

George answered, "We are. Very. And I bet you're worn out, too."

"I can't claim otherwise."

Ending that brief conversation tract, his father reached forward, set his coffee on the table and said, "Tell me once more when Delaney called you."

Brock shifted in his seat. *Why is he asking me that again?* He felt uneasy and hated it. Hated feeling this way with his own father. No doubt his dad remembered every conversation they'd had from the past Thursday forward. It had only been five days but seemed more like a month. Apparently, George wasn't going to jump in and go right for the jugular and ask him what the hell was going on. Brock reminded himself to take it easy, just sit there and let this conversation unfold in whatever manner his father desired. Let the man regain any measure of control he could muster. Brock, at least, owed him that.

"I was in the ER working nights last Thursday. It was around eleven-thirty or so when he called."

George nodded and said, "Delaney's been to see us a couple of times. He seems to think you may be involved in something…something, shall we say, which has caused you some distress. Why don't you tell us what all's happened?"

"Okay, fair enough." Brock shifted again in his seat and set his coffee cup on the table between them. "So, I got the call Thursday, late evening while I was on in the ER. Since Delaney and the Fire Marshall had things under control, I finished my shift around seven in the morning then drove out to the ranch. Besides, in the middle of the night, I couldn't find anyone to come relieve me."

"Had things under control," George interrupted, glancing at Liz.

"As best they could," Brock interjected. "Anyway, you know the story from there. I don't need to go through all that again. Friday, after they finished with me, I drove back to Topeka, decided to pick up Wolf at the vet, and went home."

"Okay, fine. So, how is it that you now find yourself in some secret location? Sounds like you're in the middle of some bad stuff."

"Last Saturday evening, just before I got off at seven, two agents from the KBI showed up at the ER to fetch me.

I had no idea they were coming. I guess they figured surprise would win my cooperation. They didn't give me much choice about going with them, to what boils down to a safe house. There, I met Director Fletcher Steele. We had a chat and he basically told me I had to stay there. They brought Wolf over, and that's where we are now. Safe and sound."

"Fetched you. Safe house. Son, what on earth compelled them to take you into custody and stick you in a *safe house*?" Brock hadn't seen such an expression of stern consternation on his father's face in a very long time. "And was this after you'd already sent Meredith and Fayth away to her folks'?"

"Yes sir, they left for St. Louis early Wednesday."

George stared at his son. His mother placed a hand on her husband's arm. "George, just let Brock tell us what's going on."

"I'm trying, Liz." His father pushed back against the sofa cushions and expelled a long breath. "Okay, I'm sorry I sound angry with you. I'm not. I'm just trying to understand how all this fits together."

Brock leaned forward, elbows on his knees, and looked directly at his father.

"I know, Dad. I can give you the basics, but there are some details I can't discuss right now with anyone outside the investigative team."

After a pause, George waved his hand in circles and said, "Okay, go on."

"On March first I saw this man in the Capital Memorial ER. He was sick, had a ruptured bowel from what turned out to be a tumor. We transferred him to KU to see a surgical specialist, and he didn't do so well after surgery. He died and his family decided to bring a lawsuit."

"Oh, God."

"But, in the meantime I got concerned about the clinic he'd gone to, and started digging around about the care he'd received. After that, things started happening."

"What clinic did he go to? One around here?"

"Sorry, I can't divulge that."

His father frowned. "Okay. So, how about this…what things started happening?"

"Well first, on April twelfth, someone apparently tampered with my brakes while I was at work. Failed on my way home causing me to run off the road near my exit on I-70. That was…"

"Oh, dear," Liz uttered, before he could finish his statement.

"And you didn't see fit to tell us?" George asked.

"That was after I'd first met the family's malpractice lawyer. I thought it was a one-time deal, and figured it could have been a coincidence. And afterwards, I was busy taking care of the details and didn't want to worry you all."

"Malpractice lawyer. So, let me get this straight…someone tried to injure you because you're being sued?"

"No, I'm not being sued. I'm a witness in the case. But before I knew about the suit, I had contacted the state medical board president and my state rep about my concerns."

"I'm not sure I follow but, anyway, who's your rep?"

"Yates Garwood."

"So, you were going around stirring up things at the capitol. Who else did you talk to?"

"That's about it."

"Who's our representative, George?" Liz asked.

"Bob Benson. He's got a cousin a coupla counties over who's a rep in Sixty-eight, if I recall correctly. Wonder what 'ol Bob would think of this?"

"Please don't call anyone, Dad. Let me finish and I think you'll see why."

George extended his hands, palms up, as his only response.

"About a week after the brakes, on Monday the eighteenth, we received a weird package, an anonymous package in the mail with one of Fayth's hair bows inside. She said some man had asked her for it on the playground at school."

"Oh, lord," Liz exclaimed, covering her mouth with her hand. Simultaneously, George muttered, "God almighty."

"Exactly."

Liz rebounded quickly and threw questions at Brock. "She's okay, isn't she? He didn't hurt her, did he?" Shaking her head, she asked, "Poor little Fayth told you this?"

"She wasn't hurt. He apparently spoke to her through the fence and, strangely, no teacher on playground duty noticed it. Fayth admitted to the encounter when Meredith questioned her, confirmed by me, and then the detectives assigned to the case. Her story hung together. That's when Meredith and I decided to pull her out of school for the time being, go to a local hotel for a few days, then very soon after that I sent her and Fayth to St. Louis. The situation had gotten too strange and dangerous."

"That's an understatement," George added.

"Even before the ranch fire, I think the KBI had decided to pay me a visit, because…the malpractice attorney is friends with Director Steele."

"So, you think he knows what he's doing?"

"Fletcher Steele? Of course, Dad."

"No, the malpractice lawyer."

"It's not a he, Dad. It's a she."

"God almighty."

"George," Liz reprimanded.

"Dad, let's leave that lay. She's with a good firm in Kansas City, is very experienced and competent in malpractice law." He'd leave out *and beautiful* for the time being. And with whom he'd been photographed at a hotel in the absence of his wife. That would probably not help this conversation progress. Out of the corner of his eye,

Brock noted his mother's head bobbing affirmatively. "So, then on Thursday, the twenty-first, the ranch burned. And Nicholas…"

"Yeah, well…" George looked away, his eyes welling.

The three fell silent.

George finally asked, "So, where's this investigation now? I still don't have a handle on how a malpractice case could explode into all this mess. Who do they think is after you?"

"Don't know yet. But I feel like they're getting close. They haven't shared specific evidence with me, or who they suspect."

"I don't like the idea that politicians may be involved, Brock. That can be a tough crowd."

"I didn't say politicians are involved, Dad. I just said I contacted my legislator."

"About what?"

"About a piece of legislation which passed several years ago giving nurses and physicians' assistants the right to practice without direct doctor supervision. That's what I meant about the clinic the patient went to. My poking around may have scratched the surface of a very big issue."

"And you think that was why the man you saw didn't do well?"

"I think that's part of it."

"Brock, why did that bother you so much, other than the obvious?" Liz asked. "That doesn't sound right. I mean, I know you care about your patients, but why did that particular case get you going?"

Turning to his mother, he didn't miss her worried eyes, her lined forehead, her furrowed brow. Trying to hold a steady gaze, he answered, "Honestly, I didn't know at first why it fired me up. I'll tell you what I told the malpractice lawyer the first time I met with her, which was about a month ago. I said my younger brother died when he was thirteen and I was sixteen, 'because a diagnosis was missed. I guess it made an impression on me.' It just came out. And since then, I've uncovered four other cases with less-than-optimal outcomes. All from the same or similar clinics."

His folks sat silent, looking stunned, obviously not expecting their deceased son's memory to be resurrected, and pushing into Brock's present predicament.

"I don't know what to say," George admitted. "We haven't discussed Alan's situation in years. How did that come to mind just because this man did poorly and died? That's bad enough in its own right. But why did that make you think of Alan?"

"Initially, I didn't think of Alan or make that connection. But after I dug around for other similar cases, I realized that if I was honest with myself, it had conjured up recollections of Alan's situation. Of how he didn't get diagnosed in time. I guess how I hadn't made any difference. In either case."

"Oh, Brock, you were a child," his mother said. "No one expected you to have figured out what was wrong, much less do something to stop it."

"I know. When you're young you can't avoid the impact a horrible experience has on you. It just imprints, then you go on." Brock paused. "But, it doesn't mean you've dealt with it. Or sorted it all out." He noted tears streaking his mother's face as his father's arm encircled her shoulders. "Then when the ranch burned and Nicholas died..." Pressure gripped his chest, tears threatened as he watched his parents. Struggling to regain some modicum of composure, he said, "I am so sorry this has involved you all. I thought we could keep it contained, that it wouldn't disrupt other lives." His voice caught. "It's affected too many people already." He stopped and gulped a quick breath. Having a complete meltdown wasn't going to help.

"Son, that's not your fault. Whoever did this is to blame. Is flat wrong. We don't hold you responsible. Nor, did we with Alan's deal. They told us at the time none of us could have done anything for him when we finally realized how sick he was. It happened so quick."

He looked up at his folks. "I know that, Dad. I do know that. I guess the similarity struck me. I thought I'd dealt with Alan's situation years ago, particularly during medical school and residency. Thought I had put it in perspective. I've taken care of plenty of meningitis cases in the meantime. I never expected to be side swiped by a case like the one I'm involved in now."

Lost in thought, they fell silent. Minutes passed. Their coffee had long since gone cold.

"Well, maybe we've all said enough," George concluded, glancing at his wife. "Obviously, this is a complicated predicament you're in. And we understand why you can't tell us all sorts of details. But, we're concerned, son, that you stay safe, that Meredith and little Fayth are safe. And that her folks are not dragged into this. We'll rebuild the ranch. That's what people like us do. It'll take some time, of course, but we'll get her done."

"Where will you stay in the meantime?"

"We'll be here with Charley through the week. Probably find a place to rent in Salina, stay close out here to watch over things."

"I was going to suggest you come stay with us in Topeka, but I know it would be too far to drive on a regular basis. Let me know if you change your mind. We have plenty of space." He paused, then informed them, "You need to know Steele may put protective detail on you all, and Tom as well."

Looking annoyed, George said, "We don't need a babysitter."

"If Steele decides you need it, I'd appreciate you all cooperating. Someone made a pretty hard statement when they torched the place, whether they knew you were gone or not. I think you should go along with it. Until this thing gets resolved. They'll stay out of the way and fade into the background before you realize it."

"Which we hope is damn soon."

A knock interrupted. Brock rose and strode to the front door, opening it to find the two agents on the porch, one facing away, scanning the landscape to the east.

"Dr. Stafford, we need to get you back to Topeka. About done?"

By that time, his father had joined them at the door. "Gentlemen, George Stafford." He extended his hand, and the three men shook. "You all take real good care of my son here, and his family." His voice stern, he managed a tight smile.

"Yes, sir. We intend to, sir."

"Good. That's what I want to hear."

Brock turned, embraced his father again, and hugged his mother who had made her way into the foyer.

"Take care, son. And call us later this week with any news and let us know how your family's faring. Now you get on out of here and stay out of trouble."

Brock's chest pressure suddenly released. He hadn't felt that relieved for some time. Now, also glad he wouldn't need a side trip to the Salina ER on the way back for a chest pain evaluation. There was certainly no reason to think his folks had seen any photographs of him and Claire, as evidenced by their comments and behaviors. They would be the last to know about that situation if at all, ever. He shook hands with his dad, turned and crossed the porch with the agents, and headed to the SUV.

~ ~ ~

George and Liz watched as the vehicle rolled down the gravel drive—dust swirling in its wake—turned onto the county highway at the bottom of the hill, and sped away. He pivoted and regarded his wife as he shut the front door.

"Well, what do you make of that?" It was more of a

statement than question. Not waiting for Liz's reply, he added, "That's the damnedest thing I've heard in a good long while."

43

Wednesday

"Come in, Yates, come in." The older representative projected a jovial mood that Wednesday afternoon.

"Got your message, Dirk. Sorry I was held up in committee."

"Want some coffee?" Benson asked, swiveling toward the cluttered credenza behind his desk. "Or maybe something else? It's not too early," he said with a wink.

"No, I'm fine, thanks." Yates Garwood glanced at his watch.

Benson turned back to his desk and rearranged several piles of papers. "Is the work on the tax bill goin' okay?" he asked.

"Making steady progress. Devil's in the details," Yates answered, his gaze fixed on his colleague.

Benson nodded, eyeing the younger legislator over his reading glasses. "Isn't that the damn truth?" He took a sip of stale coffee, then said, "Say, I just wondered if you'd heard again from that doctor in your district about those clinics? Came to mind the other day, is all."

Garwood took a moment before he answered. "No, I don't know of any more calls from him. Why?"

"Oh, nothing in particular, I'm sure." Benson leaned back in his chair and explained. "Thing is, I heard from a man about a week or so ago. A constituent, a rancher down in Morris County. He was pretty worked up about how those clinics are being treated."

"Oh?"

"Yeah, says he has a friend who runs one in Elston. He called Prescott Hughes at the state board. Tried to find out who the complaining doctor was. Hughes wouldn't tell him. So, he turned around and called me. The rancher did. I obliged him and finally called Hughes. And he wouldn't tell me, either." Benson leaned forward and shuffled papers on his desk. "Did I hear you correct back…when was that, Yates, when we talked about that doctor calling you?"

"Maybe the first of the month, I think, Dirk."

"Yeah, that's right. I lose track of time when there's so much goin' on. Anyway, back then you didn't tell me that doctor's name, did you? Cause for the life of me, I couldn't remember whether you'd even said it."

"I'm not sure, Dirk. I think I did. I know we talked about him being a doctor here in Topeka."

"Yeah, I remember that now. You've got a good head for details, Garwood."

Yates said nothing, glanced at his watch, and prepared to stand up. But Benson wasn't done.

"You know, that rancher expressed concern—he was real ticked off—that those clinics might be closed down if some rabble rouser talked to the right people about a few folks having problems. He made a real good point that, with so many doctors quittin', we need those clinics. They fill a gap. I can't fault his reasoning, Yates."

"I'm sure not, Dirk."

"So, I'm just concerned that it looks like we're addressin' our constituents' concerns here, and not fanning the flames."

"Fanning the flames?"

"Yeah, adding fuel to the fire, so to speak. Helping the wrong people. Helping an overzealous crusader. Hell, you asked me how I voted. I told you at the time, and I don't mind sayin' again, I cast my vote for the nurses' independent practice. At the time, I agreed with their position. Still do."

"It's not an unreasonable position." Yates paused, then asked, "Where do you go for your care, Dirk, if you don't mind me asking? That is, if you need a specialist's opinion?"

"Got a family doc in Emporia. But if I need to, I go to Wichita or Mayo."

Garwood nodded and stood. "Look, I'm due in another meeting in a few minutes. Anything else?"

"No, just wanted to touch base with you again. Make sure we understand each other."

"Good talking with you, Dirk. Take it easy."

"You do the same, Yates." Garwood reached the door and turned the big brass knob as Benson added, "And let me know if that guy's name comes to you."

Garwood didn't answer as he stepped into the outer office.

Melissa, Benson's aid, looked up from her computer screen, threw him a knowing smile, and a piece of advice, "You have a real good day, now."

~ ~ ~

"Darlin', what's the matter?"

"The case, Langston, the case. It's not going away…it's getting worse. My lawyer called Monday, and I have to hand over the chart."

"Really. I thought the board called you and only asked for a report."

"That was last week. This week it's the firm in Kansas City wanting the chart. Things are falling apart at the seams, Langston."

"Now, don't you fret, hon. It may seem like that, but I've got some wheels in motion to stop this."

"Yeah, it feels like wheels are in motion and coming off!"

"Do you want me to come up there?"

"No. I don't want anyone to see you coming and going from the clinic."

"Suit yourself."

"Have you heard back from the friend you were going to call?"

"Oh, I called him."

"Well? What did he say? Can he help?"

"Don't you worry about what he said. He knows who to work with. These things take some time."

"Time I don't have, Langston."

"You need to concentrate on work, Erica, and leave the negotiatin' to me. When the time comes, I'll pull the right strings tight enough."

"Concentrate? How can I concentrate with all this going on? It's hard to see patients and not think of everyone suing. I worry about what the other nurses may be doing, or not doing. I'm responsible for the whole kit and caboodle, Langston."

"You're gettin' yourself all worked up, Erica."

"Damn right, I'm worked up! Who wouldn't be?" After several moments, Erica added, "Maybe I should take a leave, go away for a while."

"Now listen, Erica, don't go runnin' off. Looks suspicious. Here's the bottom line…your clinic took care of a man who ended up dyin'. The burden of proof is on them to show that your nurse did somethin' wrong. It'll probably all turn out in your favor. That's why you've got insurance. Calm down and let the lawyer do his job." He paused, then asked, "Why don't you come down here for the weekend? We can take the horses out, relax, fool around, and talk about this again."

"I don't know, Langston."

"Probably would do us both some good."

A few moments passed. "I'll think about it."

44

Friday

Coral-hued clouds streaked the eastern sky. What was the old saying? Red sky in morning...? Flushing that thought, she glanced to her right as the first rays of sun breached the bluff to the east, a rise of land, dark and indistinct—even foreboding—just a short while ago when she had turned onto this county road. Daylight savings time had made for an unpleasantly dim departure when she left home that morning, at o'dark-thirty. But witnessing the brilliant beauty of a prairie sunrise made it worth the trip. Hopefully. Glancing at the dashboard clock which read seven-fifteen, she let off the gas a bit. It was right up ahead, at least if her GPS was correct.

She figured he was up and around. Ranchers never sleep in. This conversation likely wouldn't take too long—a somewhat reassuring thought. Since Monday, she had known what she must do. Sleeping on it for several nights had only solidified her determination. With Baird still in

Chicago, no one was around to monitor her comings and goings, which made this a whole lot easier. And, she had apparently eluded the security detail Steele had arranged. They were nowhere to be seen when she left her neighborhood.

Reaching down, she felt the hard, cold object attached to her belt, hopefully concealed by her long jacket. It had been a while since she'd thought she needed it, much less picked it up, but it seemed wise to bring it along in this situation. Never wrong to come prepared. She slowed, turned, and headed up the long, well-tended gravel drive.

~ ~ ~

In his study, Langston turned from the front window. *Who the hell is coming at this hour…in an expensive SUV and a cloud of dust?* The hall clock struck the quarter hour. He checked his desk drawer for his handgun, always there, and loaded. The gun cabinet, stocked with various rifles, sat across the room on the opposite wall, locked. The ranch hand had stayed busy in the barn since before dawn, mucking out the stalls. The buzzer under his desk was handy if this actually turned into something, which he doubted. Striding to his front door, he released the deadbolt and stood silent, waiting.

The bell rang. Whipping open the door, he propped his right shoulder on the jamb, leaning casually and smiling at Claire, and gave her the onceover.

~ ~ ~

His posturing wasn't lost on her, either. She knew he was sizing her up. She'd left her hair down and had chosen the wool, sage green jacket over tan slacks and silk blouse for that reason. Hadn't thought it appropriate to ride out to the ranch in a dark, skirted suit, looking ready for the courtroom. And no heels, of course, only flats in case she had to make a run for it. This man is capable of about anything, without a moment's notice. She had reconsidered over the miles whether jeans and boots would have proven a better choice. But there was no turning back now.

She returned his smile. "Mr. Carlisle? I'm Claire Randolph, from Lewis, Bates, and Dunning in Kansas City. May I have a word?"

"I know who you are." He dropped the charming smile and glared. "You want a word, huh? Why didn't you call for an appointment? I'm a busy man and this is a little early in the day, do 'ya think?" He pushed off the jamb and opened the massive oak door a bit further, crossing his arms over his chest, feet planted apart.

"I apologize for not calling. This was rather spur of the moment. May I come in?"

He paused, then twitched a sly smile. "Well, never say I forgot my manners. Since you're here, might as well come on in." He swung the door wide and stepped back, extending his arm gallantly toward the interior.

Claire stepped over the threshold and glanced around. The rustic interior oozed money and quality, and was eerily quiet at that early hour. No television news program nor radio in the background. She hadn't considered whether someone else might be there inside. That was certainly an oversight. But apparently, they were alone.

"We'll have our word in here," he said, motioning to his right and walking into his study before her. "Have a seat."

Claire followed and, taking in the spacious room, chose a chair in front of his desk. He propped his right hip on the desk corner and continued eyeing her. She held his gaze and didn't squirm.

"Mr. Carlisle, I'm here to discuss a situation with which we are both familiar."

"Oh?"

"Yes. I believe you are well acquainted with a nurse

practitioner, Erica Simons, who owns a medical clinic in Elston. As you may know, I represent the family of Boyd Nettley, a patient seen at her clinic."

Langston, his expression impassive, sat motionless and said nothing.

"I am here due to concerns regarding harassment of one of my witnesses. I suspect you may have some knowledge of the witness and may also have some knowledge of the incidents directed toward that individual."

"And what individual would that be, exactly?"

"I don't intend to discuss witnesses by name."

"Then I can't help you with my knowledge of any incidents you refer to."

"Perhaps that is the position you wish to maintain. But I will tell you that several serious threats have been lodged against this witness in the Nettley case, and the authorities, including the KBI, have undertaken an investigation regarding the connections between said incidents, your friend's clinic, and people of position in this state."

A frown creased his face.

Claire went on, "People in rather high places, including the legislature, the state medical board, and a certain business organization."

Langston stood and walked to the front window, giving her his back. Claire followed his progress across the room, fixing her gaze on his muscular frame. He was a fit, formidable foe. She sat forward in her chair, alert.

"I don't know what you're referring to, and I don't like what you're implying," he said, pivoting to face her.

"I believe you do. In fact, I misspoke earlier, saying your friend owns the clinic in Elston. We both know you own the clinic, which you assisted Ms. Simons to open after the independent practice legislation passed two years ago. And we both know you two are closer than just business partners."

Langston took a step toward Claire, a fierce expression

distorting his face. She stood from her chair, stepped behind it and gripped the top edge, maintaining only a minimal barrier between them. But it was better than nothing.

"Now, you look here. My financial dealings are no business of yours. And my personal life is definitely not your concern. How dare you come in here uninvited and basically charge me with doing something malicious to one of your witnesses, acting like my support of a friend in whatever manner I choose is somehow illegal." He took another step forward, his voice lowered to a threatening tone. "Matter of fact, I know your witness is some crusading doctor from Topeka. And for all you know, I might already have a name."

"My point precisely. I believe you do know who it is, and that you have engaged in harassing behavior to intimidate that individual. You, or other people you're acquainted with." She had said enough; it was time to go. He was obviously in no mood to have a reasonable discussion, but what had she really expected?

As she started for the study door, he reached out and grabbed her right arm, whipping her around. Fighting to keep her footing, she looked up at his menacing face, then down at her arm. Firmly, she demanded, "You will let go of my arm, now." He clenched it tighter. "Now!"

He flung her arm against her side, still hovering over her. "I don't know what you thought you'd accomplish coming here, but you better get out of my house and off my property." Taking only three long strides, he was at his desk, pulling open the top drawer, the glint of metal clearly visible.

Her heart pounding, she said, "I intend to. And I'll see myself out."

Restraining herself from running, she walked briskly through the study door, wishing she could sprout eyes in the back of her head. He didn't follow, remained at his desk. She stopped just short of the front door when she heard Langston pick up the phone. Then more interested than fearful, Claire crept back toward the study door, hand poised on her weapon, and listened to Langston issue a command.

"Come in here. Got something I need you to do. Now!"

Claire took the turn too fast at the bottom of his drive, spun onto the two-lane blacktop, and laid on the gas. She had thrown her gun on the floor the minute she'd leapt onto the driver's seat. Didn't want to touch it again. No traffic interfered with her speeding back to the main highway. She left the radio off and let her thoughts run.

What had she just done? Why did she take such a risk? Did she really think she could pressure Langston Carlisle to lay off Brock? She knew all the answers to those questions and didn't want to face them. Glad all he'd done was grab her arm, she rubbed her throbbing upper limb, realizing she should examine it when she got to the house. Turning on the A/C full blast, she glanced in the rearview mirror as a large pickup crested the hill not far behind. Another rancher heading to town? Hopefully not a pursuer. She decided to ignore them and her fears.

Fifteen minutes later, after considering what lay ahead that day, she checked her mirror again, alarmed to see the truck still behind her, in fact drawing closer. Having already passed through Council Grove, she had assumed whoever it was would have turned off there. Following her for twenty miles? Her gut told her this wasn't right. There was no choice now but to continue on Highway 56 to the Kansas Turnpike, less that twenty miles away. There she could put the pedal to the medal and get back to Topeka ASAP. Surely, they wouldn't follow her all the way.

What on earth was she thinking, coming out here? She then recalled Fletcher Steele's admonition to call him if she found herself tailed or felt threatened. She glanced down at her cell phone. Feeling foolish, she didn't pick it up. Fletcher would at least get on her case, but, hey, his men hadn't done their job, either.

She sped up. Without warning, a hysterical laugh escaped her throat. Maybe she'd get lucky, and the highway patrol would stop her again!

45

Steele sat in the front seat of the Suburban and watched. Agent Jackson, behind the wheel, and the two back seat passengers, said nothing. Fluffy clouds raced across the sky, partially obscuring the early morning sun. The forecast called for a windy, balmy day ahead of a storm system. No telling what the afternoon would bring.

Steele perked up when he saw two young women cross the street and enter the brick building on the corner. He checked his watch—7:45—waited five minutes, and pulled out his cell.

Adopting a smooth tone, he asked, "Good morning, is Mr. Scanlon in?" He paused, then answered, "Yes, this is Ron at Representative Benson's office calling. When do you expect him?" Steele looked out the side window. "I see." Pause. "Yes, that would be fine. Thank you." He hung up.

Jackson asked, "All set?"

"All set. He's due in ten minutes." Steele dialed another number. "Steele here. Ten minutes." Pause. "Okay, sure."

The four men sat and sipped cooling coffee.

On cue, ten minutes later, they watched as a black Tahoe approached the intersection, turned left, and took a quick left again, disappearing behind the brick building.

"That's him," Steele announced. "We'll give him five minutes or so to get inside."

Jackson put the SUV in gear, rolled across the intersection, and pulled into a spot in front of the vintage brick building.

~ ~ ~

Two suited men walked into Representative Dirk Benson's office at 8:05 and flashed their credentials at Melissa, who smiled and greeted them. "Good morning."

"Good morning, Miss. Would you mind stepping into the hall?"

"Of course not." Melissa stood and quickly passed through the door into the hall where two other agents waited. Congressional aides in the hall stared, some scurrying to their offices to spread the word. Another man arrived. He escorted Melissa down the hall and around the corner. The foursome from the KBI then re-assembled in Benson's outer office.

The intercom buzzed, and Dirk's voice asked, "Melissa, would you please bring the calendar and come in?" Receiving no answer, he repeated, "Melissa would you come in here?"

A few moments later, the door swung open. Benson, obviously shocked to see four men there and no Melissa, stood speechless. The agents produced their cred packs. Benson stared at his visitors.

"What's going on?"

"Representative Dirk Benson, we're with the Kansas Bureau of Investigation." They stepped forward. Benson backed up, gripping his office door. Without further explanation, or invitation, the foursome entered his office where a stunned young staffer jumped to his feet. One agent motioned for him to leave, and escorted him to the outer office to keep him company.

"What's all this about? I'm due in committee in a few minutes," Benson informed them. "Will you please schedule with my secretary, and we'll discuss whatever you have on your mind then? And, where in hell is Melissa, anyway?"

"She stepped out for a moment. Representative Benson, you need to come with us."

"Now?"

"Yes, now."

"You can't just come in here, disrupt my day, and take me away."

"Yes, we can, sir."

Benson marched to his desk. "I'm calling my attorney."

"He knows we're here, sir."

"Are you sure?"

"Yes, sir. He'll meet us at our destination."

"What destination? How long will this take?"

"We can't say, sir."

"Do I have any choice?"

"No, sir."

The most senior agent stood in front of Dirk Benson, while two others fell in behind the legislator. Benson looked to his right and left, then stared at the man in front of him. The foursome turned and moved as a unit to the door. Once in the outer office, Benson held his head high and turned to his staff assistant.

"I'll be back before too long. Hold down the fort. Call Chairman Ford, and tell him I've been detained and cannot be in committee this morning. But don't tell him why."

His assistant, nodding vigorously, could only say, "Yes, sir."

Two agents flanked the legislator. They made their way

down the house corridor, while the third agent peeled off and joined his associate in the representative's outer office.

"You can help us," they instructed the young man.

"Where's Melissa?"

"She's been relieved. Now, we need you to open those files."

~ ~ ~

Witt Scanlon stood behind his desk and glared at Fletcher Steele. Steele stared back.

"What are they doing out there?"

"Picking up files and paperwork we need."

"Are they messing with our computers?"

"That, too."

"What's this about?" Scanlon demanded.

"You'll find out when you need to know. Right now, you'll come with me."

"What do you mean, come with you?"

"I mean you will walk out of this office with me and come along to another location."

"I'm not going anywhere until I know what this is about."

"You'll know in good time, Mr. Scanlon."

"You can't just barge in here and order me around. I'm calling my lawyer."

"Go ahead, if you'd like. He knows we're here. So does Mr. Kemp Anderson."

Scanlon lost his smart expression. He swallowed hard, and dropped onto his desk chair. "I'd like to call my wife, let her know what's going on."

"You can call her later when you know what's going on."

Witt muttered something unintelligible and stood. He jerked on his sport coat from the back of his chair, and picked up his cell phone and briefcase.

Steele stuck his hand out. "Your cell?"

"You've got to be kidding."

"I don't kid." He motioned for another agent to take Scanlon's briefcase.

"Now, wait a minute…"

"We'll help you with your load."

"Can I at least go pee?"

"Later."

46

Claire slowly rolled down the street toward the house. It was a relief to drive without keeping an eye on the rearview mirror, to have time to settle her thoughts and compose herself before arriving at her destination. She was exhausted, done for the day, and it was only ten-thirty.

She lost her tail shortly before getting on the Turnpike heading northeast. He apparently had completed his assignment, had given up and turned back. It was just too coincidental to be anyone other than Carlisle's ranch hand turned pursuer. Her anxiety had eased a bit about being followed—twice now—but not about the case. If her managing partner got wind of these activities she would be taken off the matter, if not relieved of her position and partnership all together. She was ashamed she had given in to her feelings, had compromised her professional judgment and comportment.

She turned into the driveway and killed the ignition. A single Ford sedan sat there. She knew another was usually in the garage. After taking several slow breaths, she got out of her vehicle and embarked on the short walk to the front door. Her hair whipping in the wind, she felt disheveled, and her right arm throbbed. A few neighbor dogs barked, but no other activity was evident along the street. The house seemed too quiet as she approached. What would he think? As she pressed the bell, she wondered what, if anything, she was going to tell him. Hearing no footsteps or activity from within, she startled when Margot Blake pulled open the door a few moments later. She wore a serious expression and didn't offer Claire a smile. A different side of Margo she hadn't seen before.

"You look worked over. Come in here." She stepped back, giving Claire wide berth. "What happened? Come in the kitchen. I bet you could use some fresh coffee."

Definite command mode. Something has shifted. Claire trailed her into the kitchen without protest and stood at the counter's edge. "I *would* appreciate some coffee. Thanks."

Margot's skepticism was obvious as she poured coffee. "So what's been going on?"

"I went on a little errand early this morning which proved more difficult than anticipated, then raced back to Topeka."

"What sort of little errand?" Claire failed to answer, and Margo continued her questioning. "Why did you race back here? Did Steele send you somewhere?"

"Not exactly."

"Look, Claire, evasive won't work with me. Why did you have to race back here? What happened? You look...well, messed up."

Claire gave her a mirthless laugh. "I am messed up. You are right about that." She absentmindedly smoothed her jacket and leaned forward on the counter, steadying herself on her elbows. Taking a sip of hot coffee, she squinted at Margot over the rim of the cup. This woman wasn't going to let her off the hook. "Okay, all right, I went out of town to meet with someone early this morning, to discuss some things. It hit them the wrong way, we had a bit of a scuffle, I guess you'd say, and I tore back here to safety. I think I was followed, at least part of the way." Over her steaming coffee mug, she noted Margot's frown, glanced around the kitchen, and observed, "By the way, it seems awfully quiet around here. Where's Dr. Stafford?"

Margot informed her, "Oh, he's not here today."

"Released back to his house?"

"No."

"Back at work?"

"No."

"Look, Blake, he's my witness, a key figure in my case. Tell me where he is."

"I can't tell you, or anybody. Steele's orders. But I will say this much…he's left town."

Stunned, Claire sat down hard on a countertop stool. Suddenly discombobulated, she felt herself sway on the small perch.

"Are you okay?" Margot asked, rounding the corner of the counter, apparently expecting to render assistance.

"Can't say that I am. Mind if I take my coffee into the living room? I may need to lie down. I got up way too early this morning."

She stood from the stool. Margot, at her elbow, escorted Claire as she made her way to the living room and plopped down on the couch, barely placing her hot mug on the edge of the coffee table in time. She let out a long sigh and leaned back against the generous cushions. Margot took a seat across from her.

"And you might need to take a look at my arm. It's been squeezed a little too hard."

"Sure. Now, are you going to tell me who put the squeeze on you?" After a few moments, Margot pressed her. "Why don't you tell me exactly where you went, what you did, and what happened?"

"Okay, I will, if you'll tell me where Dr. Stafford is."

47

"**P**lease have a seat," Steele said, motioning to the opposite side of the conference room table. He scrutinized Witter Scanlon, who glanced around and chose a chair near the door. Steele placed a sheaf of papers on the table and sat down across from the businessman, facing the door with his two agents planted on either side of the escape route. He smiled at Scanlon.

"May I call my wife now?" Witt asked.

"In a while. Would you like anything? Coffee? Water?"

"Water would be good." Scanlon swiveled and looked at the two younger men flanking the door, then whirled around and faced Steele.

"Let's get started," Steele suggested. "I'm going to ask you a few questions about your organization first, then we'll go into more particulars as to why I brought you here."

"Where's my attorney?"

"He'll be along a little later."

Someone handed bottled water through the door to one

of the agents who placed it in front of Witt. He scrutinized the young man, unscrewed the cap, and took a swig. Scanlon then pivoted and informed Steele, "I'll only answer your most basic questions until he shows up."

"Suit yourself."

"Is this being recorded?"

"Yes. That'll keep us both in line," Steele said, smiling. He dictated the necessary introductory details into the recorder. That done, the two men regarded each other then Steele prompted Witt, "Why don't you tell me a little about Citizens for Economic Freedom and how you came to be the CFO."

"Don't you already know?"

"Refresh my memory."

Scanlon held his gaze, shrugged, and began. "CEF was founded about seven years ago by a group of concerned citizens. They believed the state government was not adequately representing or addressing business interests in the state. They formed a governing board and appointed me the first CFO." He took another swig of water and added, "I have my MBA, Mr. Steele."

"I'm aware. Was Jack Leggett a founding member of CEF or did he serve on the board?"

Scanlon paused. Fletcher knew he'd surprised him at mention of that name. "He was and he did."

"You worked for his company Leggett Industries, didn't you?"

"At one time, right after college."

"And you pursued your MBA during the period of your employment there?"

"Yes."

"That must have been a busy time for you." Witt said nothing, and Steele continued, "So, Leggett appointed you CFO?"

"He and the board did."

Steele prompted, "Go on."

Witt Scanlon spent the next fifteen minutes outlining the basic structure and tenets of CEF, from its founding to the present time. All information Fletcher Steele already knew, which was readily available on their website, and further gathered through his own investigation. Nothing new or particularly illuminating. He allowed Scanlon to ramble on, describing lofty ideals of free enterprise and individual liberty, none of which bothered him and, for the most part, with which he agreed.

"That's all I can say at this time," Witt finished, and fell silent.

"Okay. Thank you for that. Now, just a few points of clarification. Your position as CFO requires you to handle sums of money and conduct all necessary business operations for the organization, right? It also puts you in touch with various legislators, all CEF members, and possible donors, correct?"

"That, broadly speaking, describes my position, yes."

"Would that have included contact with Langston Carlisle? He's a CEF member, isn't he?"

Witt's jaw tensed. "He is. I have made his acquaintance but can't recall any recent contact with him."

Steele let that lay and redirected. "So, from time to time you interact with state representatives, senators, and with donors."

"Yes."

"Tell me a little about that process."

Scanlon waited, apparently collecting his thoughts before answering, "I contact legislators who agree with our basic positions, and some who are on the fence about an issue. We offer to provide them with detailed reports and statistics regarding an issue on which they may vote."

"Would you call that lobbying?"

"Yes, it can be considered lobbying. There's nothing wrong with that."

"I'm not saying there is anything wrong...with

providing information."

Scanlon took a quick sip of water.

"And how do you interact with donors?"

"Several ways. I review and edit our quarterly newsletter and make sure our staff sends that to our members and other interested parties."

"Do you call donors?"

"From time to time. Usually, to return a call from them."

"Now, Witt, what is considered a major donation?"

"Oh, around a thousand and up. But we stay in touch with all donors."

Steele made notes, well aware of Witt's fixed stare upon him. He looked up, met his gaze, and asked, "What else do you do with donors?"

"Periodically I make trips around the state and speak at meetings when I'm invited, such as Rotary, Chamber, groups like that."

"And CEF members or donors are also members of such organizations?"

"Yes, for the most part. But we have members who are not attached to such groups."

"Do members or donors also contact legislators?"

"I don't coordinate their individual efforts, if that's what you're asking. They can contact their legislators if they want."

"Did you provide the legislators anything else, any funds or perks to help their decision-making?"

"I don't like what you're implying, Steele."

Steele smiled. "Any assistance with their campaigns?"

"On occasion, we make campaign contributions, which are also legal."

"I'm aware of that. Any other incentives?"

"I'll answer that question only with my attorney present."

"Of course." Steele studied several papers in front of him, aware of Scanlon straining to see the contents.

"Mr. Scanlon, do you own a business in the state?"

Witt shifted in his seat, shot his cuffs, then answered, "I do. Creative Business Solutions."

"And you formed that entity immediately after you left Leggett Industries?"

Witt leaned forward, propped his arms on the table, and said, "Yes, I did, Agent Steele."

"Director, if you will." After a brief pause, Steele said, "Can you bring us up to speed on that business? Exactly what product or services do you offer?"

"Consulting services, business consulting, Director Steele."

"That should keep you very busy, I would think, holding down a CFO position and running your own business." He paused. Hearing no answer from Witt, Steele went on, "Does Creative Business provide such services to CEF, Mr. Scanlon? Or work with CEF in a coordinated manner?" Witt sat silent, staring at Steele, who pivoted and out of the blue, asked, "Are you familiar with a medical clinic called Comprehensive Care?"

Scanlon went pale, then countered with, "Are you asking me if I've ever been there?"

"No, I'm asking you if you are familiar with that clinic, know about that clinic in Elston, Kansas."

Witt swallowed, took a swig of water, swallowed again, and said, "The name sounds vaguely familiar but can't say I know anyone at that clinic. Who's the doctor there?"

"No doctors, just nurses, Witt. Advanced practice nurses."

"Can you be more specific, Mr. Steele? What exactly are you asking me about that clinic?"

"How are you acquainted, Mr. Scanlon, with a Dr. Stafford?"

"I'm not sure I am, Mr. Steele. Is he a doctor at that clinic? I thought you said there weren't any doctors there."

"He's not a doctor at that clinic, Witt." He paused for a

moment then asked, "As far as you know, has CEF or perhaps Creative Business Solutions ever provided financial support to that clinic or other similar clinics?"

Scanlon's eyes flickered. "Sitting here right now, I can't say. I would have to analyze our records. We have an accountant review the books semiannually. You can check our accounts—"

Steele looked up from the table. "We already have, Witt."

Scanlon went for his tie, stopped before loosening it, smoothing it instead. "What exactly are you saying?"

"I'm saying we've looked into CEF's and Creative Business Solutions' accounts at various financial institutions. And we've spoken with the accounting firm. They provided us with this detailed report."

"I'd like to see that."

"In due time, Mr. Scanlon."

"And who gave you permission to obtain that private information?"

"The Attorney General." At that, Witt Scanlon's face fell. Steele added, "The accounts are frozen, Mr. Scanlon."

"I'm done here, until my lawyer shows up."

"He's right outside the door."

48

A young agent left his post by the door and came up behind Steele. He delivered a whispered message and stepped back.

Steele, now in another conference room and tired of sitting, abruptly stood, excused himself, and left. Once in the hall, an agent waiting there spoke in low tones.

Steele frowned. "No trace?"

"No, sir. She's gone. Went to the clinic and to her home."

"And no sign of disruption or struggle?"

"No, sir. Clinic's open with patients there. Full complement of staff. No one seems to know why she didn't come in today."

"Did you complete the search, including getting her records?"

"Yes, sir. And two laptops."

"Were they ready for us?"

"Didn't appear to be, sir."

"Anyone try to stop you?"

"A bossy receptionist, but in the end, no. Element of surprise helped."

"I'm sure. And the same at her house?"

"Yes, sir. Her cat's gone, too."

Steele looked at the agent. "Cat's gone?"

"Yes, sir. And the pet dishes, but left behind an unopened bag of cat food and a litter box."

"Cleaned out?"

"No, sir."

Steele frowned again. "Okay, thanks. Have the sheriff put out an APB. And stay on it."

"Yes, sir. They have, sir."

"Good. Keep me informed."

Steele turned and entered the conference room. Closing the door, he said, "Sorry for the delay, Representative Benson. Let's pick up where we left off."

Dirk Benson stared at the KBI man.

"So, tell me how you came to be acquainted with Mr. Witter Scanlon at Citizens for Economic Freedom."

"Hell, we make lots of acquaintances, Steele. Once you're elected, everyone wants to meet you."

"Do business with you?"

"I don't like the tone of that question."

"Sure. So, you get to know a lot of people when you're in office. People who probably want to ask a favor or two, or get you to listen to their concerns."

"Of course. Part of representin' the people."

"And you have people or organizations who want to contribute to your campaigns."

"Of course. That's how it's done. Nothing wrong with that. Haven't you ever sent a check to someone running for office?"

"No, I haven't."

Benson looked surprised. "Guess you fellas can't do that, huh? Well, lots of other folks do, some big, some small. Nothing illegal about that."

"No, there isn't, in most cases."

Benson schooled his expression. "Where're you goin' with all this?"

"I'll get to the point, Mr. Benson."

"Please do. And I'm not answerin' all your questions without my lawyer here."

"I'm aware of that. Now, you became acquainted with Witter Scanlon at CEF after you were elected to office. Did you see him a lot?"

"We talked from time to time."

"Okay. You talked now and then about business issues in the state, and they provided your office with information you needed to make various decisions?"

"Basically, that's correct."

"And they contributed now and then to your re-election campaigns?"

"That's right."

"To what extent?"

"It's all in my donor records."

"Which we have right here."

Benson glanced across the table and frowned. "How'd you get hold of that information?"

"There are lots of individuals who are happy to help us, Mr. Benson."

"Who are you referring to, Steele?"

"That'll be made known in due time. Any other donations they made?"

"Like what?"

"Perks, you know, like Chiefs' tickets, various trips, free use of private Lear jets?" Benson remained silent. "I don't see anything like that here in these reports, Representative Benson."

"If we're going to discuss any reports you have, I'll insist on the presence of my lawyer."

"You've made that clear, Mr. Benson." Steele paused a moment. "Does the name Doctor Stafford mean anything to you?"

Benson's eyes narrowed a fraction before his face went blank. "Not that I recall."

"You don't recall discussing him or his concerns with anyone? Any other legislators or executives at the state medical board?"

Dirk Benson didn't answer. "Okay. How did you vote, sir, on the Advance Practice Act?"

"You probably already know that, Steele. It's part of the house record."

"Yes, we do. You voted 'yes,' correct?"

"Correct. And I don't regret it."

Steele pushed several sheets of paper around. He looked up at Benson and asked, "Sir, one more thing…" He paused, then asked, "Tell me how you're acquainted with Langston Carlisle."

Benson worked his jaw, held Steele's gaze. "He's one of my constituents, Mr. Steele, and we're friends. Owns a big ranch down in Morris County, but I'm sure you already knew that, too."

Fletcher Steele didn't smile.

Benson asked, "What does Carlisle have to do with any of this?"

49

The navy SUV slowly traveled the long gravel drive and pulled to a stop in front of the generous wraparound porch. Four men got out and, their backs to the vehicle, scanned the area. Two tall, wooden rockers flanked the large east-facing front window. Similar rockers sat on the south veranda as well. A huge, hostile-appearing cat lounged on one chair near the front door, eyeing them. When he had apparently seen enough, he jumped down and sauntered away.

The humid wind whipped around the corners of the house. Fifty yards to the south, they noted a well-cared-for barn—door open—and a late-model Chevy Tahoe parked outside, obviously unoccupied. Nearby, a small John Deere tractor stood idle. Half a dozen horses grazed leisurely in an adjoining pasture. Curious, they raised their heads, regarded the visitors, then resumed grazing.

Two of the men climbed the broad front steps. Two others stood sentry below, their backs to the porch, scanning the expanse down the hill to the road. One man rang the bell and knocked. No answer. All four pulled their weapons, while they repeated the sequence of ringing and knocking. Only the brisk wind answered. They called out the owner's name. Again, no answer. Noting no evidence of door damage, they tried the knob which resisted. One agent put his shoulder to the door while the others covered. The door finally gave way, and two KBI agents leapt into the front hall. Stillness greeted them.

Joined by a third, they methodically swept the foyer and adjacent large dining room just to the right of the hall. To their left a closed pocket door caught their attention. Moving further down the main hall they glanced in the large great room straight ahead and toward the kitchen in the rear, noting a lit range-hood light. One agent covered that area while two others returned to the closed door. They slowly slid open the heavy pocket door and scanned the quiet, well-appointed study. A lamp cast light on the leather desktop where the man lay slumped over, his head resting in a pool of blood. His lifeless eyes open, he stared at the agents who stared back.

~ ~ ~

Fletcher Steele pushed his sandwich aside and picked up the receiver. "Steele here."

"Director Steele, sir, we have a report."

"What is it, Grayson?"

"Sir, we're at the Carlisle ranch. We have a situation."

"Go on."

"Sir, we found Langston Carlisle. He's here, sir…dead."

"Dead?"

"Yes, sir. Shot in the head once. Close range. No weapon found, sir."

"You've checked the whole house?"

"Yes, sir. Whole house, yard, barn. His Tahoe's here. Hasn't been driven in the last couple of hours. There are fresh tire tracks on the gravel drive in front, not the

Tahoe's. Appears to be two different sets."

"Can you tell what type of vehicles?"

"Larger tires, sir. Both. Most likely an SUV or a truck. Maybe one of each."

"Take care they're not disrupted."

"Already did, sir. And there are two sets of footprints on the front porch, in the dust. One looks like boot tracks, cowboy boots. One looks smaller, like a woman's shoe."

"Can you tell roughly what sizes?"

"Boots look like about a twelve. Shoes, maybe women's size eight. About that."

Steele's stomach knotted. "A woman's size eight?"

"About that."

"Okay. Keep those from being disturbed, too. No ranch hands there?"

"Not right now. Only animals here are horses in the pasture, minding their own business."

"Nothing looks disturbed inside?"

"Nothing we've found yet, sir. Locked gun cabinet in his study. Untouched. Loaded handgun in his desk drawer, not recently fired. Front door wasn't forced until we entered."

"You forced it?"

"Didn't take much. Only the doorknob was locked. Deadbolt was off."

"Anything of interest?"

"Only his desk records and his computer."

"Copied them?"

"Yes. And downloaded his computer files."

"Anything else, Grayson?"

"The usual personal effects, nothing appears missing. Still wearing his watch. Cell phone in his shirt pocket. And a small tortoise hair comb on the rug in the study."

"What?"

"A hair thing."

"What kind of hair thing?"

"One of those small curved-looking things. Not to comb

hair with. I guess to hold your hair back."

"Don't need one to hold my hair back. Do you need one, Grayson?"

"Can't say that I do, sir."

"I'd like you to bring that to me today."

"Right. And we found some women's things in the master bedroom and bath."

"Women's things? You know he's not currently married."

"Yes, sir. Toiletries, few pieces of underwear, and a pair of riding boots."

"What size riding boots?"

"Small. Probably about a six."

"Okay, Grayson. Have you contacted the sheriff yet?"

"Yes, just before calling you. They're on their way now."

"Good. Stay where you are. Keep searching until they get there, and watch that they take care with the scene. And have them call me when they arrive."

"Yes, sir."

Steele re-cradled the receiver and leaned back in his desk chair. He gazed at his notes and took a swig of water. He had hoped that wouldn't happen, but wasn't entirely surprised it had.

While several other agents tended to Representative Benson and Mr. Witter Scanlon and their attorneys, Steele had taken lunch in his office sorting through material they already had. Letting everyone take a breather, he would reconvene with the lawyered-up gentlemen in about an hour. Armed with this new information he would approach the afternoon a bit differently. He expected it would be productive. But first he had to place a phone call. He picked up his cell and found the number he wanted. Three rings and a pleasant voice answered.

"Lewis, Bates, and Dunning. How may I assist you today?"

50

Fletcher pushed off the handrail as the elevator doors slid open. The hall was quiet, not busy that Friday afternoon. It was late, though, and most business had concluded for the week. He approached the double doors at the end of the hall, removing his cred pack from his inside pocket before gripping the doorknob. Hopefully, the waiting room was empty. Opening the door, he quietly closed it behind him and proceeded toward the main desk.

A mature woman looked up from her computer screen, obviously surprised at the late-day visitor. She smiled, though, and opened her mouth to greet him. Before she could utter the usual verse, he said, "Claire Randolph, please," and slipped his cred pack over the edge of the counter for her eyes only. She nodded and said nothing. He flipped it closed and walked to the interior door, which buzzed just as he took hold of the handle. A hushed, empty hall greeted him. He embarked on the long walk to a back, corner office. He knew the way though he had been there only twice before.

Composing himself when he reached the door, he rapped once and took hold of the handle. There was no response from within. Turning the lever, he opened the door just enough to gain view of the desk and the woman sitting there. She looked up and smiled faintly. Light filtered through angled blinds and cast a warm glow over her brunette hair.

"I wondered when you'd show up."

Stepping inside without invitation, he stood before her desk. "Your secretary said you'd probably be in all afternoon. You didn't answer my call."

Claire looked away. Steele took a convenient chair in front of her desk, leaning back and propping one ankle across his other knee. His tie had long since been discarded, his slacks well-creased from hours of sitting through interviews with recalcitrant persons of interest. He felt relaxed now, though a bit weary.

"So, are you going to tell me what transpired?"

"I suppose I should. Do I really have a choice?"

"Of course, if you want to lawyer up first." After a pause, Fletcher added, "You look like you've had a long day. Not your usual demeanor."

With a sidelong glance and a faint smile, Claire straightened in her chair and brushed back her loose hair.

"I have had a long day. You're probably surprised I'm still here. This seemed the safest place to retreat to, gather my thoughts, and decide my next best move. I apologize for not taking your call. I knew you'd try again."

"Why don't you give me some details?"

"Don't you already know everything?"

"I doubt I do, actually. I need your version to complete the picture."

"Would you like something to drink?"

He smiled. "Sure, why not? Have some club soda with a lime?"

Claire stood and moved toward a large cabinet on the

opposite wall. "Fresh out of limes." There, she opened two doors which revealed a well-stocked built-in bar, crystal glassware sparkling under a small overhead light. "I remember your usual when you want to avoid alcohol. Mind if I indulge in a whiskey?"

He said nothing, noting her wrinkled slacks, well-creased jacket, and bare feet. *She probably needs a whiskey, maybe more than one.* Then her discarded, dirty shoes off to the side caught his eye. Her hair looked a mess, askew on one side, held back on the other with a tortoise comb. "Not if you'll let me drive you home. Little sleep and strong drink don't mix too well on the road."

"Always-responsible Fletcher, my good 'ol straight arrow."

Ignoring her comment, he watched her deliberate movements. He knew this woman well, but it had been years since he'd seen her in such a state. He feared he already had a clear picture of what her day had entailed.

She crossed to him, smiled, and handed him his club soda. "Cheers," she said, raising her glass and sipping the rich amber bourbon. Returning to her desk chair, she sank into its soft leather confines and gazed directly at him. "So, okay, I'm ready to fess up."

"Why do you think a confession is in order?"

"Oh, Fletch, please don't play your sly spy games with me. Figure of speech, that's all."

"Fair enough. Let's hear it, then."

She swirled her drink, brushed back her hair, and began.

"Earlier in the week, I decided I needed to clarify some issues regarding Brock's situation as it related to the malpractice case, the widening circle of the other clinics' involvement, and the harassing incidents directed at him. Last Thursday, after the ranch fire, I thought things had gotten totally out of whack and I needed to do something to re-establish control."

Fletcher, impressed by her articulate recovery, broke in,

"And you didn't think we were doing enough?"

"I did, but felt I had to personally do something. I know that seems inappropriate. I realize now that it was an exercise in poor judgment. But, so be it. I jumped in."

Focusing on her, Steele said nothing in return. She seemed anxious to continue.

"So, I called Prescott Hughes at the state board. We are peripherally acquainted. Of course, I've known about Erica Simons since we initiated the lawsuit. Previously, I'd googled information on her and the clinic, and I've snooped around a bit. Interesting history, actually." Steele gave no sign of affirmation, so she continued. "That conversation with Hughes was Monday morning. Anyway, we chatted, and after a bit he seemed willing to provide more detailed information on Erica's clinic start-up in Elston, which, as it turns out, materially involved Langston Carlisle. Feeling comfortable, I guess, with the tenor of our conversation, he waded into personal territory about them as a couple. He more or less told me they had been an item, even before Carlisle helped her set up the clinic. Our conversation ended on a positive note."

Fletcher smiled.

She went on, "So, as Monday progressed, I developed this idea that paying Carlisle a personal visit might be productive. Maybe I could pressure him to back off, quit harassing Brock."

"How did you know he was the one initiating those activities?"

"Well, I didn't. But from what I'd found out about his financial interest in her clinic, and his temperament, which Prescott gladly described, I figured he was a major player in this whole mess."

Fletcher noted her absentmindedly rubbing her right arm. "What's wrong with your arm?"

She gave him a questioning look, then said, "Oh, it's a bit sore, that's all."

"Sore from what? Doesn't sound like you've had much time lately to engage in any heavy lifting or new workouts."

"You *are* good, Fletch."

He extended his hands, palms up.

"Okay, the encounter with Carlisle didn't go exactly as expected. He attempted to bully me, and, at one point, grabbed my arm as I was trying to leave his study. He certainly has a strong grip."

"Had…," he mumbled.

"What?"

Fletcher ignored her question and asked, "Did he injure you? Manhandle you?"

"No, not exactly. Well, not badly."

"Have you had it looked at?"

"No. Well, yes, Margot Blake at the house took a look."

"When did you have time to go by the house? And why?"

"On my way back. She, of course, recommended I get it x-rayed. It's just a bruise. It'll heal."

"You didn't answer my *why*."

She sipped her whiskey, then said, "It was a safe place to go. And I went by there to speak with Brock about my visit with Carlisle. Margot then informed me you'd sent him away."

"We did…to St. Louis, to his family."

Claire nodded and, saying nothing, turned and stared at her picture wall. "So, anyway, what would you suggest I do, press assault charges against him?"

"No, I wouldn't suggest that." He paused, then decided it was time to drop the bomb. "Doubt it would go very far. Claire, Langston Carlisle is dead."

She spun around and sat bolt upright, looking as if she'd been slapped. "Dead?"

"Yes, dead. Shot in the head." Her hand jerked to cover her mouth. *Surely, she isn't going to throw up right here all over her expensive furniture and carpet.* Noting the handy wastebasket behind her desk, he added, "Sometime this morning."

She dropped her hand, gulped her whiskey, and muttered, "Oh, my God."

"So, Claire, you were there this morning. Doesn't look so good for you, does it?"

"Oh, my God."

"So, why don't you tell me what condition he was in when you left the ranch?"

She stared at him for a moment. "He let go of my arm, actually threw it against my side, and watched me leave his study. I was carrying, and I think he knew that. He made for his desk, and I thought I saw a gun when he jerked open a desk drawer. When I got to the front hall, I heard him pick up his phone. I was curious, so I hung around for a few minutes. I heard him tell someone to come to the house, then I got the hell out of there. I didn't realize anyone else was there. He was certainly upright, and still breathing at that point. Terrified, I bolted off his front porch, jumped in my car, and hightailed it out of there."

"Anything else you noticed? Did you see anyone?"

"No. Well, after I got on the blacktop, heading back to highway 56, I noticed a pickup following me. A male driver, but I couldn't see who it was. He tailed me through Council Grove—I thought he'd surely stop there—and then on to the Turnpike. He gave up at that point."

"And again, you didn't see fit to call me?"

She winced but offered no reply.

"Claire…"

"Okay, I acted stupid. It's done. What else do you want me to say?"

"What time was all this?"

"Early. I got there a little after seven-fifteen. When I looked at my car clock again, as I turned onto the two-lane, it was almost eight."

Fletcher stood from his chair and moved to the side of her desk. He pulled a small, curved object from his inside pocket, glanced at her head, and held it up. "Need this to complete your set?"

She gasped, and reached for her unkempt hair.

He rounded the desk corner and stood to the side of her chair, slowly spinning it around. He touched her hair, noting its silky feel, then dropped his hand. "Stand up, Claire."

Without resisting, she did as ordered. "Fletcher, I can explain."

"I'm sure you can. And I hope it's the truth."

She gazed at him, a mere foot separating them. He handed her the missing tortoise comb. "I thought your hair looked a little messy. We found this on the rug in Carlisle's study. Thought it might belong to Erica Simons. I have to admit, when I arrived and saw the other one still in your hair, I felt sick."

"Fletcher, it dropped out, no doubt, when he grabbed my arm and spun me around."

"Of course."

"It doesn't mean I did anything. Frankly, in the heat of the moment, I didn't notice it was gone."

He stepped closer and without hesitating, wrapped his arms around her. She dropped her head onto his shoulder. He could feel her wilt in his arms. "Claire…"

After a pause, she softly answered, "What, Fletch?"

"Did you kill Langston Carlisle?"

She eased from his embrace, a blank look on her face.

51

Brock drove down the quiet, tree-lined street, Wolf riding shotgun, with his head stuck out the side window. It was calm and sunny that Friday afternoon. Scattered blooming dogwood and redbud trees dotted the manicured lawns. Tulips lined well-tended flowerbeds. He slowed when he saw the stately brick Georgian colonial ahead. A woman walking her Bichon made note of his approach and smiled. Checking out only his side of the street, Wolf didn't see the other dog. After they passed, Brock turned into the long driveway.

They had sent him away for the weekend. A little action might have proved fun, but he was glad they wanted him out of the way. An escort wasn't far behind and never out of sight. It was okay. He'd rather have surveillance for the time being than worry about getting clobbered somewhere, unexpectedly.

During the five-hour drive, straight through Topeka, he had considered numerous approaches he could use to explain the photographs, which were tucked in his small suitcase. The best opportunity was there, away from home and work to initiate the conversation with Meredith. Her parents would expect them to want time alone. And this discussion would likely engender a good bit of talk. To say he dreaded it was an understatement. But he'd resolved to be honest with her. Avoidance could only set the stage for disaster later on.

Getting out of his vehicle, his joints felt stiff. All the tension of the last few weeks and lack of intentional exercise was taking its toll. He feared the mountain of stress and worry had aged him. As he made his way up the landscaped front walk, he wondered what was going down back home. When would he hear something? Wolf dashed around the front lawn, raised his leg, and quickly rejoined him on the front steps. Brock stood on the porch, took a breath, and depressed the bell.

He heard footsteps approach. There was a pause before anyone opened the door. He looked up at the peep hole, wondering what that person might think. The door swung open, and a stunned woman stood there. A few moments passed before a broad smile spread across her face.

"Brock!"

He smiled back. "Hi."

"Let me look at you...we didn't know you were coming."

"Mom, who is it?" came another familiar voice. Meredith moved up behind her mother, paused only for an instant then flew across the threshold into Brock's arms. "Oh, my God...you're here!"

Wolf barked and danced around the front porch.

Her arms draped around his neck, Meredith stood on her toes and kissed her husband. Encircling her waist, he rocked back and forth. With one full-body tremble, he suddenly relaxed; his dread evaporated.

Her mother beamed and stepped back. "I'll see you two inside."

Brock and Meredith made no note of her words or her withdrawal. They held each other, swaying and laughing. "I can't believe you're here," she finally managed.

"Me either," he answered, planting another kiss on her neck.

A green sedan eased slowly by and turned at the next corner, noticed by neither of them.

Breaking apart, Meredith took his hand. "Come on in." Wolf darted past them into the front hall.

Once inside, the smell of dinner preparations welcomed him. Two cats skittered away to adjacent rooms, as Wolf bounded down the hall in pursuit. Before they could shut the front door, Brock heard a commotion from the back of the house, and another familiar shrieking voice. Feet pounded the wood floor. A small silhouette rounded the corner from the kitchen, caught sight of them, and made a bee line down the hall.

"Daddy, Daddy! You're here!"

"Yes, sweetie, I'm here."

Grabbing him around the legs, little Fayth implored, "Can we go home now, Daddy?"

He knelt down and scooped up his daughter, "Yes, honey we can…soon, very soon."

EPILOGUE

October 2016

The court reporter fiddled with her video camera, adjusting first the setup then the focus. Finally satisfied, she signaled her readiness, and the attorney cleared his throat and turned to Brock.

"Doctor, for the record, would you please state your full name, date of birth, and current address?"

"Home or practice?"

"Your practice address, please."

"Brock Andrew Stafford. August 1, 1978. Capital Memorial Medical Center, 1700 Southwest Seventh Street, Topeka, Kansas, 66606.

"Thank you. Please state where you completed your undergraduate degree, your medical degree, and the years in which you obtained those degrees."

"BS, Kansas State University in 2000. MD, 2004, University of Kansas School of Medicine."

"And, for the record, your residency training was in what field and from which institution?"

"Emergency medicine, Northwestern University Medical Center."

"That's in Chicago, Illinois, correct?"

"Yes."

"And you completed your residency in…?"

"2008."

"And you are board-certified?"

"Yes, in emergency medicine."

"When did you accomplish that?"

"November 2008."

"So, you passed boards the first time you took them?"

"Yes."

The defense attorney nodded, and again referred to his laptop and notes. Brock knew they had all that information, and more, at their fingertips. Claire, sitting to his left, had encouraged him to answer all their questions succinctly. No running on or offering additional information, particularly not any smart aleck remarks. He was happy to comply and make them work for filler.

The attorney glanced up from his screen and smiled briefly. "So, for the record, Dr. Stafford, have you obtained any further training such as a fellowship?"

"No. Subspecialty fellowships are generally not pursued in emergency medicine. Perhaps if one is in an academic position. But it's not common in emergency medicine practice in general."

"Okay. Would you give us a brief rundown now on continuing education activities you have completed in the past three years? Any courses you've attended, that sort of thing."

Brock answered, "I usually attend the American College of Emergency Physicians' annual meeting. I also take other courses from time to time which are pertinent to emergency medicine." He pulled three stapled papers from the leather portfolio lying in front of him and slid the document across the table to the attorney. "I've prepared a list."

The attorney quickly scanned the three typed sheets. "We'll enter these pages into the record." He passed the document down the table to his junior partner and a paralegal. "Thank you."

Brock nodded. Through the large windows of the conference room, just over the lawyer's shoulder, he could see the flaming maple trees outside. The afternoon sun hit them at just the right angle, setting their colors afire. Such a beautiful fall it was. A beautiful relief after a long, hot summer. A long, tense summer. Claire had arranged for him to give his deposition in this setting, at the law offices of Lewis, Bates, and Dunning in Kansas City, not at the other firm. It had actually come together a lot sooner than he had expected.

Several weeks before he'd given his deposition as a witness in the Nettley case. That one had been harder, and not because he was on the hot seat. Recounting what had happened to Boyd Nettley, and how he and Karen looked the morning of March first, rekindled anger and tension Brock hadn't expected. This one he rather enjoyed, having gotten used to the deposition routine, and because of who this man represented.

After rearranging various papers, including Brock's continuing education contribution, the defendant's attorney looked up and began.

"So now, Dr. Stafford, will you describe what happened the morning you met the unfortunate patient Mr. Nettley at the Capital Memorial ER, and why that stimulated your special interest in the Independent Practice Act?"

"Objection…prejudicial inference," Claire stated. "Please restate the question."

"So noted," the attorney responded. Gazing at Brock over his reading glasses, he rephrased, "Dr. Stafford, will you describe what happened the morning of March first at the Capital Memorial ER when you met Mr. Boyd Nettley?"

"I met Mr. Nettley and his wife Karen shortly after I came on duty at seven that morning. He was very ill…he had abdominal pain, fever, abnormal lab work and scans. He was not doing well."

No less than two hours later, after a brief break, they all reconvened around the long table.

"We're close to finishing up, Doctor. I expect we'll be done here in under an hour. I trust that you're okay with that."

"Of course," Brock answered.

Their earlier discussion had focused on Brock fleshing out his initial encounter with the Nettleys and the course of events that followed. When counsel had veered off into the morass of details associated with the Nettley suit, Claire had reined him in effectively, reminding him this was not testimony for the malpractice case. Before the break, the defendant's lawyer plunged into Brock's reason for researching the clinics and what he knew of the various players involved, including his client, Witter Scanlon. It appeared he wasn't done with that line of questioning yet. Brock wondered how they were going to wrap this up in about another hour.

"Dr. Stafford, you said you called Mr. Hughes at the State Board of Medical Arts in March, after you wrote him a letter and expressed your personal concerns about various patient outcomes, correct?"

"Yes, on March 24th I called him."

Studying Brock, the attorney added, "And you also left a message for your state representative, Yates Garwood."

"Is that a question? Yes, I did."

"And did you stay in touch with those gentlemen?"

"Not regularly, no."

"Would you, for the record, clarify your contact with

those individuals?"

"Representative Garwood returned my call on March 28th while I was at the ER, working. I never spoke again with Mr. Hughes." Brock hoped his recall for specific dates might enhance his credibility with this man, and cut short this line of questioning. But if necessary, he had studied all the pertinent dates and so noted those on a calendar, which he was half-hoping he'd have the opportunity to produce.

"All right, thank you. Following that, you became involved with counsel here, Ms. Randolph, due to the malpractice lawsuit she filed on behalf of the Nettleys."

Claire jumped in. "Objection. Form. Also, the tone of your statement, counselor, could imply an improper relationship between myself and the doctor. Please restate your observation, or better yet, please rephrase as a question."

"Very well." He paused, then asked, "You began working with Ms. Randolph, attorney for the Nettleys, after you had conversations with Representative Garwood, correct?"

"Yes. I met with Claire Randolph for the first time regarding the Nettley case on April 4th at her office."

"Would you please tell us when you had any contact—contact of any sort—with my client, Mr. Witter Scanlon?"

"I never did."

Witt's attorney stared at Brock, who returned his regard before he went on. "And, what about contact with other individuals? A Mr. Kemp Anderson, Mr. Langston Carlisle, Ms. Erica Simons, or Mr. Garwood's colleague Representative Dirk Benson?"

"I had no contact, in person or through other means, with any of those individuals."

"No contact whatsoever?"

"That's correct."

The lawyer shuffled papers, studied his computer screen then looked at Claire. "Doctor, when did you contact

Fletcher Steele at the KBI?"

"I didn't."

"So, you're telling us you ended up at a safe house in an unknown neighborhood in Topeka sometime in April, but you had no contact with Director Steele?"

"No. I believe I said *I* did not contact him."

The lawyer leveled a steady look at Brock, who didn't flinch under his gaze. After sufficient scrutiny, he glanced at his junior partner and paralegal, who, Brock noticed, managed nearly imperceptible nods.

Claire leaned forward and interrupted, "Counselor, we all know that I contacted KBI Director Fletcher Steele regarding the episodes of harassment my client Dr. Stafford experienced, specifically the automobile brake failure and the stalking of his five-year-old daughter in mid to late April. Following that, his family's ranch was torched. Director Steele sent Dr. Stafford's wife and young daughter to St. Louis and placed him in protective custody at a safe house. That was the first time they met or spoke. I believe you have all that in your records. And I fail to see where this line of questioning is leading. We certainly won't be done here in under an hour unless you get to the point."

"Very well." After a brief pause, during which he rearranged his pile of papers, the attorney looked at Brock and asked, "Dr. Stafford, did you ever go to the Comprehensive Care Clinic in Elston as a patient?"

Brock restrained himself from shifting in his seat, looked the lawyer in the eye, and answered, "Yes, as a matter of fact, I did. On April 20th."

"And what did you hope to accomplish by visiting that clinic as a patient?"

"Honestly, I hoped to get an inside look at how they operated...a look at what kind of care they delivered."

"And who did you see there?"

"A nurse practitioner, Rosalind Barnett. The nurse who'd first seen Boyd Nettley."

"Was that planned? Did you ask to see that particular nurse? Did you think you might entrap them by going there?"

"No. No. And no."

"Did you see or meet Erica Simons during your visit there?"

"No, I did not."

"So, exactly why did you go there?"

"By that time, I was very frustrated with the situation and frightened for my family. And I was curious about the clinic and how it was run. I subjected myself to a visit and examination to see how they conducted themselves as medical practitioners. We'd had four cases present to our hospital from there over the past year. Cases, in my opinion, which had been mishandled."

"Did Claire Randolph know you went to the clinic?"

"No."

"Not at all? Never?"

"Not in advance. I eventually told her about the visit while I was sequestered at the safe house."

"Did she approve of your visit there?" The attorney watched Claire as Brock answered.

"She never said that to me."

"Were the expenses you incurred while at the clinic reimbursed by anyone?"

"Not as of now." The attorney glanced at Claire.

Silence fell over the room. After studying his papers again, the attorney turned his attention to another topic, but before he began, Brock spoke up. Without Claire's blessing.

"And, there was another case from a clinic in Northridge, Kansas. A man who ended up being diagnosed with lung cancer. A cancer which had been missed, his symptoms and X-ray findings attributed to pneumonia. There was no follow-up planned for the abnormal X-ray. I spoke with the patient and his wife on two occasions. I learned that following the correct diagnosis, he received care at the Center for Diagnosis & Treatment-Ca in Des Moines. His treatment and all his wife's travel expenses were paid for by that small clinic in that small town of Northridge. That piqued my interest."

The attorney stared at Brock, did not respond to his unsolicited remarks, and asked, "Dr. Stafford, are you aware of any outcomes of the individuals I previously mentioned?"

"I'm not sure what you're asking. Can you please rephrase your question?"

"Yes. Are you aware of what has happened to any of the individuals I asked you about earlier: Mr. Kemp Anderson, Mr. Langston Carlisle, Ms. Erica Simons, or Rep. Dirk Benson?"

"Any adverse outcomes they may have suffered?" Brock asked. Not waiting for clarification, he went on, "I am aware Langston Carlisle was found dead. I'm aware Erica Simons initially disappeared, was later located in Texas alive and well. I understand Representative Benson resigned from his house seat. I know nothing about Mr. Kemp Anderson."

"How did you attain this knowledge?"

"Claire Randolph and Fletcher Steele updated me over the summer. And through open news sources."

"What knowledge did you attain about my client Mr. Witter Scanlon?"

"I was told only that he had resigned from his position at the CEF organization, and that his business Creative Business Solutions closed."

"Are you referring to the Citizens for Economic Freedom organization?"

"Yes."

"Doctor, do you know how Mr. Langston Carlisle died?"

"I heard he was shot. It was in the news."

"Do you have an opinion about who may have done that?"

"Objection. Counsel is asking the witness to speculate. And I would remind you, we are not here to discuss the murder of Mr. Langston Carlisle."

"So noted," the attorney answered, a sly smile curving his thin lips. After assuming a serious expression, Witt's attorney turned his attention to his laptop, wasted several minutes, then looked up and changed subjects.

"Dr. Stafford, are you familiar with the governor's newly-formed commission to study the issue of the advanced practice clinics and the use of extenders in healthcare settings?"

"Yes, I am."

"Are you a member of that commission?"

"I have been invited to join that group."

"So, have you or have you not met with them?"

"I have not yet met with the commission members."

"And why is that?"

"I could not re-arrange my work schedule to attend their first meeting in September. There's a second meeting next month which I plan to attend."

"But, since late last spring, many of those clinics have suspended operations, including Comprehensive Care Clinic in Elston, correct?"

"Some have, yes."

"Do you know why that is?"

"It is my understanding that the state board, in early June, made a decision to launch an investigation and require direct physician supervision or oversight for all the advanced practice clinics during the investigative period. If physician coverage was not available within a certain mile radius of a clinic, then yes, that particular clinic had to suspend operations. The legislature was not in session after May and could not address the issue through legislation, as the board had requested."

"Thank you. Your answer was quite thorough. Now, Doctor, are you familiar with the phrase 'scope creep'?"

Now there's a question. Was this a trap? Choosing his words carefully, Brock recovered, and said, "Yes, I've heard that used."

"What does that phrase mean to you?"

"Basically, you're referring to expanding the scope of practice for nonphysicians...the use of PAs or nurse practitioners in place of a physician, at times inappropriately, considering the potential severity of the clinical situations they may encounter."

"Thank you."

Brock added, "Which many feel is a problem given the significant difference in our education and training. And our experience."

Looking tired, the attorney asked, "Dr. Stafford, do you work with extenders?"

"Yes, I do."

"And do you wish to see them removed from your emergency room?"

"No. We work as a team in our ER. But I don't believe extenders should be considered doctor replacements, or assume responsibility for clinical situations which warrant a physician's evaluation. It isn't wise, in my opinion, for extenders to function completely independent of physician supervision or oversight. Their training doesn't go far enough for that, and too many things can go wrong, fast."

"As in the case of Mr. Boyd Nettley?"

"That's one example."

The attorney stared at Brock, then pivoted back to the commission's purpose. "Does the commission plan to limit their study to the advanced practice issue, or eventually address other issues concerning medical practice?"

"I'm aware of a plan to study the ongoing issue of physician shortages in the state."

"Doctor, is it your opinion that there are physician

shortages in this state?"

"Yes, particularly in certain rural areas and in certain specialties."

"And those would be?"

"Internal medicine, pediatrics, and emergency medicine. And family medicine is stretched too thin, considering obvious distances between clinics in rural areas."

"And how is emergency medicine impacted by these shortages?"

"Many smaller town ERs are staffed by extenders only, or family medicine doctors who fill in from time to time, or by hired locums."

"For clarification, you're referring to the term, *locum tenens*?"

"Yes, that's right."

"Now, Doctor, is it your opinion that physician shortages are related to the issue of nonphysicians' independent practice?"

"Yes, those two issues are closely related." Brock waited, expecting he would continue in that vein. But the lawyer did not, apparently not interested in belaboring the point, or weary of the long afternoon and him.

"Thank you, Doctor. I think those are all the questions I have for now."

Brock smiled. "You're welcome."

"Now, one more thing…have I given you a fair chance to answer my questions, and have we gotten along today?"

"Yes, I believe we have."

~ ~ ~

The elevator doors slid open. The only occupants, Brock and Claire silently emerged. As they made their way across the lobby, his cell phone vibrated. Realizing he'd left it muted, he fumbled through his sport coat and retrieved the device. A text from Meredith waited. Oh, crap—her appointment. Well, he had been a bit preoccupied since leaving Topeka that morning. But that was really no excuse for forgetting her afternoon. And what it meant to them. He and Claire pushed through the heavy glass doors. The crisp fall breeze swirled around them and ruffled the leaves overhead.

"Anything urgent?" Claire asked.

"Not sure," he replied.

Before he could explain further, Meredith pulled to the curb. Brock and Claire watched as his wife climbed out of the driver's seat and maneuvered around the rear of her SUV, wearing a wide smile and a loose red knit dress. She appeared to glow in the late afternoon sun, blending into the brilliant autumn landscape surrounding Corporate Woods' parking lot.

"Hi there," Brock said. He felt his face loosen and his shoulders release. It *was* very good to see her after his long day.

She returned his greeting as she drew near. An awkward silence developed before Meredith extended her hand. "Hello, Claire." She added, "I hope the afternoon went well."

"It did," Brock said.

"Very well. Your husband is an old hand at this, now."

Meredith smiled, and turning to Brock, said, "If you're done, I'll take you to dinner."

"I'm surprised to see *you* here in town. You had an appointment in Topeka this afternoon."

"I did, and I'm sorry you missed it."

"Oh?"

"Yes, and I'll fill you in over dinner."

"Okay, then." Suddenly tired, he knew he sounded flat and unenthusiastic. He turned to Claire, shook hands and took his leave.

"I'll be in touch, later," she advised him, as Brock and Meredith made their way to the SUV.

When they reached the car, Brock held open his wife's door and watched as Claire disappeared inside the building. It was time to re-direct.

Jumping into the driver's seat, he started the ignition and put the vehicle in reverse. Before releasing the brake pedal, he leaned over and gave Meredith a quick kiss on the cheek. "I'm glad you came. Do you have a restaurant in mind?" Not waiting for her answer, he added, "We'll drop by and get my car on our way home."

She smiled, leaned in, and whispered, "It's a boy."

Startled, Brock took a moment to process before exclaiming, "God, no kidding?" He grabbed her shoulders, pulled her close and smothered her mouth with a kiss, his foot slipping off the brake in the process. Releasing his grip on her, a wide grin stretched his face. This day had turned out very well, indeed. In fact, terrific!

"Brock, we're rolling! There's a car!"

Grinning, he stamped his foot on the brake just in time, slammed the gear shift into drive, and took off, declaring, "Oh, what the hell…let's get out of here!"

AUTHOR NOTE

My background is in internal medicine and before that, obstetric nursing. The landscape of healthcare is certainly changing; I believe we can all agree on that. When considering writing about such significant shifts, I chose to go the route of fiction, and suspense fit the bill.

In fact, it's all fiction. These characters and their maladies are not based on any specific individuals I've attended. If passages involving state investigators seem authentic, all the better. Any mistakes in those depictions are entirely mine.

My research carried me back to northeast Kansas, including the capital Topeka, and the beautiful flint hills of east central Kansas. The area is replete with numerous enduring native limestone structures which inspired several of my settings. Particularly in the tiny town of Alma. A special thanks to Ken and Joan Benjamin who paved my way to attend legislative sessions, to visit less accessible portions of the capitol, and together to travel area back roads. Very fun and informative!

Many thanks to my steadfast editor Laura Taylor, who encouraged me from the start to stick with it, and who patiently prodded me to hone my writing. Thanks also to Sharon Kizziah-Holmes for manuscript formatting, Jaycee DeLorenzo for cover design – and to both for their excellent advice – and to many others who provided valuable input and support.

And to all of you who read the book and arrived at this page – I truly appreciate you sharing your time.

I hope you enjoyed this tale. If you feel so inclined, please leave a review at Amazon.com.

You can keep an eye out for updates, new releases and fresh content at my website: jjrenek.com. While there, consider joining my quarterly newsletter group and stay in the loop.

Thanks!

JJ Renek

www.ingramcontent.com/pod-product-compliance
Lightning Source LLC
Chambersburg PA
CBHW071849220626
47052CB00002B/31